The Grim Reaper's Dance

Books by Judy Clemens

The Stella Crown Series
Till the Cows Come Home
Three Can Keep a Secret
To Thine Own Self Be True
The Day Will Come
Different Paths

The Grim Reaper Series
Embrace the Grim Reaper
The Grim Reaper's Dance

The Grim Reaper's Dance

A Grim Reaper Mystery

Judy Clemens

Poisoned Pen Press

*Poisoned
Pen
Press*

Copyright © 2010 by Judy Clemens

First Edition 2010

10 9 8 7 6 5 4 3 2 1

Library of Congress Catalog Card Number: 2009924206

ISBN: 9781590587317   Hardcover
      9781590587331   Trade Paperback

Poisoned Pen Press
6962 E. First Ave., Ste. 103
Scottsdale, AZ 85251
www.poisonedpenpress.com
info@poisonedpenpress.com

Printed in the United States of America

For Nancy Clemens, mother and friend

Acknowledgments

The world of trucking is not one with which I was familiar before writing this book. I would like to thank Dan Hunsberger, co-owner of Home Again, Inc., for his invaluable help in understanding what goes on in the business. Thanks also to Scott Schmucker for his stories about life on the road. If anything in the book does not follow the actual way the trucking world works, it is my fault. I claim artistic license, and I'm sticking to it.

Lee Jay Diller, owner of Northwest Recycling here in Ohio, was the inspiration for Davey Wainwright and his scrap yard. Thanks for all your help, Lee!

Jenny Baumgartner entertains my questions about hapkido and helps me figure out how Casey can defend herself (and beat people up). It is so fun to have a friend who knows this stuff, and who is willing to talk about it. As her husband said, "I can guarantee that nowhere else in the country are two women returning from grocery shopping and talking about nun chucks." Thanks also to Master Doug Custer, who encourages my interest and answers whatever questions I throw his way.

Thanks once again to Lorin Beidler, MD, for answering medical questions. I know Blue Lake's sleepy ER is not what he's used to, but when you live in the sticks things are a lot quieter than in the Big City.

My uncle, Randy Thomas, was generous with his farming wisdom, and took time out of his busy work day to tell me about Midwest crops and land ownership.

Barbara Peters and Annette Rogers are enthusiastic and constructive editors who make the process fun. Jessica, Marilyn, Nan, and Rob, you make publishing a pleasure. Monty, you were a blessing from the very beginning. May you find peace in your new place. Thanks to all at Poisoned Pen.

Thanks to Nancy Clemens for reading the first draft and making sure it made sense.

And always, thanks to Steve, Tristan, and Sophia for supporting my career.

Chapter One

"This here's my daughter Katie. She's thirteen and lives for marching band. Plays the flute. You wouldn't believe the way they work them kids. She's in better shape than I ever been." Evan the trucker laughed and patted his sizable gut, which almost touched the steering wheel of the semi.

Death gave out a snort, chin to chest, mouth open. The trucker's conversation obviously wasn't interesting enough to keep the Grim Reaper awake, and the lack of traffic on the sleepy highway gave no relief from the steady clicking of the tires on the pavement, or the view of flat Iowa and Kansas farmland. Casey wasn't having trouble staying awake, having slept the first seven hours of her escape from Clymer, Ohio, despite the throbbing in her arm from the injury in a knife fight only hours before. Her wrist hurt, she was bleeding from the gash in her shoulder, and so many terrible things had happened she should have, by all rights, been kept awake by mere horror. Instead, her body had shut down into a sleep so deep the trucker's pit stops hadn't even awakened her. Evan had finally poked her, saying he wanted to make sure she wasn't dead.

Death had gotten a real kick out of that.

"And this one?" Now, Casey pointed at the other girl in the photo hanging from the dashboard.

"Susanna. Just turned seven. First grade." He shook his head. "Can you believe how they got them little kids reading? Books and math and every other thing. It's crazy. All I remember from first grade is going up against Willie Yonkers to see which one of us could spit the farthest." He grinned, revealing two missing teeth. "He always won. And wouldn't you know, he's the one made it big today."

Casey's eyebrows rose. "Willie Yonkers spits for a living?"

Evan barked a laugh. "Wouldn't that be a good one. No, Willie's a businessman. Owns his own place. He's the boy in town who made it. It's a good job."

"Don't you have a good job?"

"Oh, sure, I love it. Wouldn't want to do nothin' else, most of the time, anyway." He gave a ghost of a smile, then patted the steering wheel. "These reefers are fun to drive." Refrigerated trucks, he meant. "But Willie…" He leaned over a bit toward Casey, stopping when a brush with Death's arm made him shiver. "Willie's got the whole shebang. Brand new house. New car every summer. Wads of cash he don't know what to do with. All for ordering other people around, sitting behind his desk in his fancy clothes. Lots of folks would kill for a job like that. Heck, they'd kill for any job at all." He sighed, leaning the other direction to set his elbow on the door. His sudden silence left space for the rain to fill as it pounded on the windshield and cab. The wipers worked overtime, back and forth, back and forth…

Casey glanced once more at the photograph where Evan's arm draped over the shoulders of a plump, pretty woman with frosted hair. Virginia, he'd called her. Ginny. His older daughter stood behind him, a hand on his shoulder, and the younger sat on his lap. "But," Casey said, "does Willie have a family?"

Evan laughed. "Sure does. A son in college who hates him, a wife that left him, and a daughter who's not exactly the kind I want my Katie hanging around, if you know what I mean."

She knew. "So you've actually got it much better than Willie, don't you, Evan?"

He grinned again. "I do, I know it. My girls are waiting for me about forty miles down the road. And this time? I'm staying for a good long while. I've been working my tail off and I need a break. You'll have to catch another ride from there, darlin'."

"Sure."

He sighed. "Still, it'd be nice to have the cash sometimes, to set my family up the way I'd like. I drive by Willie's house sometimes, just wishing…"

Death groaned, tilting toward Casey, and she scooted over, not wanting to feel the chill that always accompanied an accidental touch.

She looked out her window at the water that ran in sporadic rivulets down the glass. Cash wasn't just a luxury. You couldn't live without it. So shouldn't that, in turn, mean that if you had a lot of it you'd live well and long? With all her money, stashed away in the bank, she should live forever. She just wouldn't have the family to spend it on. Not since they'd been—

"Oh, *shit*." Evan stomped on the gas and spun the steering wheel to the right. Casey clutched the dashboard, panic rising in her throat. Two construction vehicles sat across the road in front of them. The cab of the semi skidded sideways on the wet pavement as the trailer pushed forward, not ready to stop on such sudden demand. Evan spun the steering wheel the other way, trying to reverse the skid, but there was no going back.

The semi hit the dump truck with a force that sent Casey hurtling against her seatbelt, breath knocked from her lungs, neck snapping sideways, head cracking against the window. Metal screamed as it tore, tires squealed, and blood splattered across Casey's arms and face.

The movement stopped almost as suddenly as it started, and Casey lay against the door, heart pounding, hands shaking. She blinked. "Reuben?" She struggled into an upright position. "Omar?" She wrenched her head around, neck already stiffening.

No, it was not her family. Not the accident she dreamed of every night—and sometimes during the day.

It was Evan Tague, the trucker.

Evan lay scrunched between sheets of metal. They used to be his door. Now they were sharp knives, cutting through him, shearing him almost in two as he gasped for breath, eyes wide.

"Evan!" Casey struggled out of her seatbelt, clambering over the seat to grab Evan's hand, which still clutched the steering wheel. Evan's mouth opened and shut with raspy, bubbling breaths. Rain pattered on the cab, dripping down onto Casey and Evan's bloodied face.

Wide awake now, Death hunched over Evan, intensely interested.

"Get away!" Casey hissed. "Get out!"

Death smiled sadly. "I'm sorry, love, but of all the times to be shooing me away, this isn't the best. He needs me."

"He doesn't need you. He doesn't *want* you. Evan! Evan, I'm here!" She clutched the trucker's hand and leaned toward the opening where his window used to be, past Death's form. "Help!" she screamed. "We need help!"

"It's too late," Death said. "No one can help him now."

"Virginia?" Evan whispered the name.

"No, Evan, it's…it's Casey."

"Ginny?" He reached up, as if he saw his wife's face instead of the specter of Death hovering above him.

Casey yanked the photo from the dashboard, wiping blood from its surface, and held it out, blocking Death's face. Evan didn't see it, focusing on Casey instead. His eyes went wide. Panicky. He took a quick, wet breath. "Back…trim. Insu…lation. Don't let…" He gasped. Swallowed. "Don't let them get…" He gurgled, and blood streamed out of his mouth.

"Help!" Casey screamed again. She pulled a padded jacket from a hook behind the seat and held it over Evan's abdomen, around a deadly piece of metal.

"Casey," Death said. "You have to let me take him."

"No! He has a family…"

Footsteps sounded behind her, and the cab sank as a man climbed in. He grabbed Casey and shoved her backward, toward the passenger door, where another man caught her and pulled her from the seat.

"Evan!" the first man said. "Goddammit, Evan, don't you *dare* die on me."

"Stop!" Casey said. "Wait! Evan!"

"We got it," the second man said, and dumped her on the wet ground at the feet of two more large men. She scrambled up, and one of them grabbed her around the waist. "Nothing you can do, anymore, sweetheart. We'll take care of him."

She shook herself from his grasp and stepped toward the truck. The man reached for her again, grabbing her elbow. "So where is it?" The rain made trails through his dirty blond hair and snaked down his face. His eyes were a startling green.

"Where is what?"

He pulled her closer. "You have it on you now? Is that the way it is?"

The other man stood still, his arms crossed over his chest as he watched Casey's face.

With his free hand the man holding Casey felt the back of her pants, moving to the front. When he went for her chest, Casey grabbed his wrist and twisted it inward, pushing his palm toward his arm and pointing his fingers to the sky. She rolled his arm forward, her hand on his elbow, and bent him toward the ground. Digging her finger into a pressure point on the back of his arm, she spoke into his ear. "I said, 'where is *what?*'"

"I called 911! They're coming!" A woman in a bright red suit ran toward Casey, tottering on high heels, holding an umbrella and waving a cell phone. She stopped at the sight of Casey with the man in an armlock. "It'll just be minutes," she finished weakly. "They're coming."

"Good." Casey pushed the man's wrist toward his arm, shoving him into the other guy, who caught him and let him go so suddenly he almost fell. Blondie regained his balance and glared at Casey, one side of his lip raised as he cradled his arm protectively.

The woman stepped between Casey and the men. "Come on, honey, you need to sit down."

"But—"

"Come on." She led Casey to the shoulder of the road and eased her onto a grassy patch, holding the umbrella over both of them. "You all right?" She bent her head to look at Casey's face. "You're not going into shock, are you?"

"I'm fine." Why were those men gathered at the door of the truck, looking around as if they were afraid of getting caught? And how did they know Evan's name?

Casey locked eyes with the frisker. He stared at her from under his mess of wet hair, as if trying to read something in her eyes. Or figure out a way to kill her.

"Who are they?" Casey said to herself.

The woman glanced up. "Just people who stopped to help, I guess. Like me. Oh, good, I hear sirens." She took a few steps away, waving frantically as an ambulance pulled to the side of the road. "Over here! Here!" She went a few more paces until one of the paramedics saw her and walked briskly their way, carrying a bag of equipment. He knelt beside Casey, the woman shielding them both from the rain with her umbrella.

"In the truck," Casey said. "You need to help him."

"We're on it, miss. We got him. Now, where are you cut?"

"I'm not. I'm fine. It's Evan…"

His face grew grave, and his lips compressed. "I need to check you out, okay? Hold still now."

Casey complied, except for swiveling her stiffening neck toward the cab of the truck. The men who had pulled her out were being evicted by the paramedics, who climbed up toward Evan, and the blood, and the photograph—

But no, Casey still held the photo, crumpled tightly in her hand. She unclenched her fingers to look down at the little family. Life would never be the same for them, after the phone call they were about to receive.

The group of men clustered by the back of the reefer, heads bent together. The one who'd grabbed Casey leaned back to look at her, and she held his gaze. He finally broke eye contact and she watched the others, trying to read their lips, but she'd really clocked her head on the window, and everything was going in and out of being blurry. She took a deep breath, trying to center herself, and was getting ready to leave the paramedic and move closer to the men when cops invaded the scene, cordoning off the area, telling whoever was listening that "there's nothing to see here."

How wrong that sounded.

Cars on the road were stopped now, blocked from forward progress by the accident, and drivers were leaving their vehicles to see what was going on. Some wanted to help, others just wanted to take cell phone pictures of the carnage. Casey turned her head as one man aimed his phone her way.

"You're pretty beat up," the paramedic said, "but there's nothing major at first glance. A few cuts and bruises. You'll need to go to the ER to get checked out, though. Make sure there's no internal bleeding." He lifted her sleeve away from the gash she'd received the night before.

"I'm fine." Casey pulled away from him. "I don't need to go to the hospital."

"Yes, you do. Larry!" The paramedic signaled one of his partners, and together they hauled Casey upright, grabbing under her arms, as the woman in red stepped back with her umbrella.

"I can walk," Casey said, batting their hands away.

"You going to be all right?" The woman in the red suit frowned. "You're looking sort of pale…"

Casey's eyes rolled back, and hands clutched her elbows.

"We've got her, ma'am," the paramedic said. "Thank you."

Casey wrenched her eyes open. "Thank you, for…"

"You're welcome, honey. You take care, you hear? Do you need me to call anybody?"

The paramedics were walking away with her. "No one to call. I'm alone. It's just me." She and Death, who hovered in the cab of the truck, waiting to whisk Evan away.

A police officer followed Casey into the ambulance and hunched at the rear. "Can I get a statement?"

The paramedic strapped Casey down. "Make it quick."

"Tell me what happened, ma'am?"

Casey closed her eyes, seeing the construction vehicles, Evan's panicked face, the metal embedded in Evan's side. "They were just…there. The dump truck and the other one. We came over the hill and the road was so slick and…" She swallowed. "It didn't take very long."

"How fast were you going?"

"Speed limit. He wasn't a leadfoot."

The cop nodded. "Been drinking?"

"No!"

The paramedic turned to grab the door handle. "You'll have to get more later, Officer. At the hospital."

"Wait!" Casey said. "The truck. Where will it go?"

The cop looked back at the mangled cab. "Won't be going anywhere for a while, but when it does…I don't know. Shop, maybe? Closest one's a few miles down the road. The way it's looking, though…it's probably headed for the junk yard."

"What about those men?"

"What men?"

"The ones talking at the back of the truck, when the paramedics got out of the cab."

The cop pointed his pen at the paramedic. "You know who she's talking about?"

He nodded. "Couple of guys were in the truck, administering CPR. Don't know who they were."

Casey tried to sit up, but was held down by the straps. She strained her neck as far as she could. The men weren't at the back of the truck anymore. She couldn't see them anywhere. "You have to find them. They know something."

"Nothing to know, ma'am. It was an accident."

"An accident involving vehicles parked across the road. Why were they there?"

He looked at her. "There's all kind of construction going on—"

"Where are the workers?"

He paused. "I don't know."

Casey's head swam, and she dropped it back onto the gurney.

"We gotta go," the paramedic said.

"No!" Casey said. "Wait!"

But the cop stepped back and closed the door. Casey raised her head high enough to see out the back window, just in time to see Death walking in the opposite direction, carrying Evan's spirit like a baby.

Chapter Two

"Name?"

"Casey Jones."

The young admissions clerk scribbled on her clipboard and cracked her gum. "ID?"

"Don't have any."

That made the girl look up. "You don't have any *ID*?"

Should Casey give her the whole story? How she'd left it hidden in a garage back in Ohio, hanging with the rest of her earthly belongings? Her wedding ring, Omar's baby cap, her *dobak*, her money... Should Casey tell the girl she was wanted for the murder of a Louisville thug? Or for questioning about the death of one of the Ohio town's citizens? Or by the psycho CEO of Pegasus, the car company that killed Casey's family?

"My wallet got stolen," Casey said. "I don't have anything."

"Well..." The girl chewed her gum harder, as if it helped her to think. "We need to have information. Address. Insurance. You know."

"Sure. Leave the paper with me, and I'll fill it out the best I can."

"You have a phone, at least? So you can call somebody?" The girl looked hopeful.

"No."

"Oh. Well." The clerk floundered in a tight half-circle, her feet shuffling on the tile floor.

"You do have phones here at the hospital?"

"Phones? Here? Oh, I see. Yeah, you can use one of those, I guess."

Casey took a deep, calming breath. "I'll fill out what I can, and then find a phone. Okay?"

The girl held out the clipboard, then took it back, then held it out again. "I'm really supposed to fill it out myself. From the ID."

Casey snagged the clipboard, yanking it from the clerk's hand. "I'll do it."

"Well—"

"So, what have we here?" A doctor in a white coat flapped through the dividing curtain, beaming at Casey from more beard and mustache than Casey thought should be allowed on a medical professional.

"Doctor Shinnob," he boomed. "At your service."

The clerk took the opportunity to scuttle away, casting a worried glance back toward Casey. Casey smiled wearily and held up the clipboard, nodding to the girl in what she hoped was a reassuring fashion.

A petite, dark-skinned nurse dressed in lavender scrubs with cats on them stood slightly behind the doctor. She scribbled on yet another chart. "Name?"

"Casey Jones."

"Birthdate?"

Casey made one up.

"Social security number?"

Casey rattled off nine non-sequential numbers.

"Done, are we, then, Felicia?" The doctor held out his hands.

The nurse frowned, crossing her arms over her paperwork and holding it against her chest.

"So, you were in a little accident, were you?" The doctor lifted Casey's chin and shone a flashlight in her eyes. "I'm sorry to hear about that."

"The driver—"

"Got the worst of it. Yes, I'm sorry about that, too. Did you know him well?"

"No, not all that well." She wasn't about to tell him she'd just met Evan that morning, when she'd desperately hitched a ride.

"I see." He flicked the light away, and then back. "How's your vision?"

"Blurry."

"What I thought. I'm afraid you have a concussion, my dear." He rubbed his fingers together beside her right ear. "Can you hear that?"

"Yes."

"And that?" Her left ear.

She nodded.

"Good, good. Now, breathe in and out deeply, mouth open, please." She obliged, and he nodded, pursing his lips as he listened to her back through his stethoscope. He moved the instrument to her chest, listening to her heart. "Good. Can you lie down now, please?" He pushed gently on her stomach. "Does that hurt when I do this? Or this? No? That's good, that's good." He smiled at the nurse, who gave him a stare right back. He leaned toward Casey. "Don't worry about Felicia. Trauma makes her grumpy."

"I'm not grumpy." Felicia's voice sounded brittle.

"Whatever you say, whatever you say." The doctor winked at Casey. "Now, you tell me if anything hurts." He felt her from top to bottom—her arms, her ribs, her legs. Nothing hurt, except for the cut on her arm. She tried not to show it, but he noticed anyway. "Tell me about this injury. That's not from the accident." He peered at her above the rims of his glasses.

"Got cut yesterday. I tried to fix it up."

"Didn't do a very good job of it, did you?" He clicked his tongue. "Felicia, how about some antiseptic wash?"

Between Dr. Shinnob and Felicia they cleaned out the cut and covered it with sterile gauze and an Ace bandage. Casey did her best not to scream at the pain.

"I can't stitch it," Dr. Shinnob said. "It's too swollen, and the tissues have already begun to heal themselves. I'm afraid you'll have a scar there, as a reminder of whatever you did."

Great. "Thank you. It will be fine."

He studied her face, then broke back into a big grin.

"There are some police officers in the waiting room who want to talk with you. Are you ready for them?"

Casey looked at Felicia. "Do I have to be?"

The nurse shook her head.

"You don't have to be ready at all," the doctor said. "They can't see you until I say they can, and I think I'll have them wait a little longer. Not that they aren't doing their best—I just don't want them disturbing you before you're up to it. There's plenty of time. Now, we'll be setting you up with a CT scan, to make sure there's nothing going on inside your head that we can't see."

"Internal bleeding? Wouldn't we know by now?"

He tilted his hand back and forth. "Maybe, maybe not. I like to be thorough, don't I, Felicia?"

The nurse rolled her eyes.

"She loves me," Shinnob said. "She just doesn't know how to show it." He took the clipboard from Felicia, scrawled a few things on it, and handed it back to her. "Felicia will take care of you now, Ms...Jones, was it? I'll see you again soon."

Casey and the nurse watched as the doctor strode out through the curtain, greeting someone else at high decibels. Felicia closed her eyes briefly, then turned to Casey. "I'm sorry, I just can't be as happy-go-lucky as he is."

Casey shrugged. "Who can?"

Felicia held up her chart. "So I need to know a few more things. You're not pregnant?"

Casey let out a surprised laugh. "No."

"Taking any medications?"

"Nope."

"Eaten anything in the last six hours?"

Casey had to think. "Drank some water. That's it."

Felicia nodded. "You hungry?"

"Yes."

"Best to wait till the test is done, then we'll get you something, all right?" She pulled out some syringes. "I need to get some blood samples. Check things out, especially since you have…well, since this isn't all your own blood. Usually they do this right away when you come in, but with all the excitement today about the driver, and all…"

"I really don't think bloodwork is necessary."

Felicia smiled gently. "Dr. Shinnob will decide that. For now, just grit your teeth and let me see a vein."

Casey reluctantly stuck out her arm.

Felicia took the blood and covered the needle site with a cotton ball and bandage. "I know this has been difficult, Ms. Jones. Feel free to lie down and rest while I get things set up, okay?" Her face had softened to a degree it hadn't while the doctor had been in the cubicle. "From what I can see you're going to be fine. The doctor just likes to make sure."

"After all," Casey said, "he is thorough."

Felicia laughed. "I'll be back. Don't go anywhere." She left through the part in the curtains.

Don't go anywhere. The exact instructions Casey couldn't follow. She glanced down at the chart the clerk had left with her, covered with blanks she couldn't fill. Not if she wanted to avoid jail.

She slipped off of the table, wincing at the pull on her shoulder, and looked down at her clothes. Yet again a bloody mess. She couldn't even turn the sweatshirt inside out, as the other side was stained with someone *else's* blood, from the day before. The fresh blood on her pants more than covered the faded blotches there. She laughed under her breath without a stitch of humor—she was a crime scene investigator's nightmare.

She filled the cup by her bed with water and drank it all, hoping it would help with her dizziness. It didn't.

She peeked out from the curtain. There were several closed-off areas, but mostly empty beds. From the lack of busy-ness, Casey assumed Evan's body had been taken elsewhere. Felicia was gone, and a couple of orderlies at the far end of the room were the only people Casey could see. A counter at the side of the room held a few snack essentials for those waiting—crackers and peanut butter the most attractive to Casey. Close to the counter was a door with an EXIT sign above it. Casey waited until the orderlies turned their backs, then left her area, scooping up several packs of crackers, some containers of peanut butter, and a small bag of Oreos. Not exactly a full meal, but it would have to do.

The exit door opened silently, and she slipped out into an empty corridor. No more exits were in sight, so she took a chance and turned right. Hearing someone coming, she ducked into a family bathroom until the footsteps passed. After several seconds she opened the door, scanning the hallway. No one. She went out, turned the corner, and found a large sign pointing her toward radiology, outpatient surgery, and the gift shop. She followed the path to the gift shop, hoping it would be close to the front door. It was. She walked briskly past the volunteers at the information desk and headed outside, where it had stopped raining, remaining overcast and muggy.

There were no taxis, of course, and even if there were she had no money to pay them. She headed toward the side of the hospital, wanting to get out of sight as soon as possible. The building sat in a residential area, so she was able to find a small side street within a minute, ducking around corners until the hospital was hidden behind houses and trees.

She kept walking, not sure where to go. Not sure where she even *was*. Kansas, somewhere. Another small town. She paused briefly to catch her breath and shake her head, hoping her vision would clear. She'd had concussions before. It would go away. Eventually. Until then, she'd just have to stay awake. And while she was awake, she might as well get something done. Like find out what those men at the accident site were looking for, and why Evan so desperately didn't want them to find it. She had to assume it was one and the same item they were talking about.

Looking up toward the main street she could see a gas station on the corner of the nearest intersection. Blue Lake Gas and Go. It looked like it had a garage attached, so someone there might be able to tell her where Evan's truck would have been taken.

She walked up and stopped in front of the dark garage. She'd forgotten. Sunday. Not even the gas station part was open, let alone the shop. She put her face up to the window and squinted, trying to read the clock on the wall. Almost eight. She sighed, leaning her forehead against the glass.

"Tough day, huh?"

Casey didn't even flinch at Death's presence. "Back so soon?"

"Doesn't take long. Evan says hi."

She rolled her head sideways on the window so she could see Death, who twanged a rubber band between teeth and fingers. "He didn't happen to tell you what he hid in his truck, or why those men are after it?"

Death spoke around the rubber band. "I didn't know I was supposed to ask him about *that*."

Casey pushed herself off the window, hesitating at the sight of a cop car idling at the traffic light. She walked around the corner of the garage. "Guess I ought to figure out somewhere to go."

"You could call Don. Or Ricky." Her lawyer. Her brother.

"I could."

"They'd send you money."

"On a Sunday? Where would they do that?"

Death twanged the rubber band. "You know, Casey, there are these things called computers—"

"Which would give up my location in a heartbeat. I can't do that to them. They'd want to help, and since they don't know about…about what happened in Clymer…they'd just get me locked up. And themselves in trouble." She shuddered. "Plus, it would put Pegasus back on my tail, and I *certainly* don't need that." The car company had made the faulty car that killed her family, and now they were afraid Casey would ruin them. They weren't about to stop looking for her.

"You've got to get money somewhere," Death said. "Or go to a homeless shelter."

Visions of the soup kitchen in Clymer flitted through Casey's mind. Home Sweet Home, where she'd met Eric VanDiepenbos and found out things that had almost gotten her killed.

"I think I'll take my chances somewhere else."

The cop car was gone, so she began walking, heading toward the outskirts of town. She crossed a railroad track, an abandoned factory, and a new and unfinished development, and in about a half hour she was traveling along fields of corn. Miles and miles of it standing tall and golden, just waiting for harvest.

Death had deserted her long before, having tired of the walking. Of the *boredom* of it. Casey had said so long, glad to be rid of the incessant rubber band twanging. Besides, she was furious that Death had taken Evan and didn't even seem sorry about it.

She walked several more miles, seeing only two vehicles the entire time, then angled into the cornfield, pushing across rows, the leaves scratchy, smacking her face. She found a place about a quarter mile in where a patch of grassy weeds had grown, brown now, like the corn, but soft, and mostly dry. She eased to the ground, her neck stiff, her shoulder throbbing, and lay flat on her back. She thought about pulling those crackers and cookies out of her pocket, but it seemed like too much effort. Instead, she closed her eyes, and willed herself to relax. A train whistle drifted across the fields, accompanying the clouds, and she gradually sank deeper into the weeds. She knew she shouldn't sleep, not with her concussion, and she didn't figure she would, not with the image of Evan begging her not to let *them* have it, whatever it was, but it couldn't hurt to close her eyes for a few minutes. She was so *tired…*

She fell asleep so quickly she didn't even notice when Death chopped an armful of grass and tucked it under her head, like a pillow.

Chapter Three

"You really shouldn't be so crabby with me," Death said. "It's not *all* my fault, you know. The farmers were out awfully early."

It was true. As soon as the sun had given even a hint of morning light the tractors were in the fields. Not Casey's field of residence, so she wasn't afraid of getting run over, but the harvesters were close enough she had no hope of getting back to sleep. But she wasn't blaming the farmers. "*You're* the one who woke me up a million times during the night."

Death nodded. "Every two hours. That's what they say about concussions."

"Or what? I'll *die*? Certainly wouldn't want *that* to happen." It was, in fact, what Casey had wanted ever since Death had taken her husband and baby, almost a year before. Death, however, had other ideas.

Death chucked Casey under the chin. "And who says you're not a morning person?"

Casey swished Death's hand away and stomped along the road, back into town. She made a breakfast of the hospital food as she walked, and while it wasn't exactly her normal fare, it at least got her stomach to stop cramping. She ran her fingers through her hair, re-tied it into a ponytail, and hoped she didn't look too much like she'd spent the night in a cornfield.

"You know," Death said, "you've looked better."

Casey, giving in to her baser nature, held up her middle finger.

Death kept quiet after that.

But really, where was she even going? Casey stopped suddenly, taking a deep breath. If she went back to town the most likely thing to happen would be that someone would notice her, the cops would find her, and she'd end up in jail for what had happened in Clymer. She should turn around. She should get as far as she could from this town, from the truck accident, and from anyone who could connect her with it.

But Evan's last request, his last *breath*, was to plead with her not to let them get it. Whatever *it* was. And whoever *they* were. Could she turn her back on a dying man's plea? A man who could no longer act for himself?

She stood at the side of the road, her thoughts in turmoil.

"So what's it going to be?" Death asked. "You know what they teach in school: Safety First."

Casey laughed without humor. "I am so, so far beyond safety. And I'm not sure I could…"

"What?"

"I don't think I could live with myself if I let them win."

"But you don't even know who *them* is."

"No. But Evan did. And he begged me to help."

Death turned and continued walking toward town.

"Where are you going?"

"Where you're headed. To find out who killed Evan, and to keep them from getting what they wanted."

Death knew her too well.

Blue Lake Gas and Go was open this time, and three men in dark blue coveralls stood in one of the bays, laughing. They stopped abruptly when Casey walked in, their expressions ranging from boredom to curiosity to shock.

Death chuckled. "Well, aren't they just the sweetest things?"

Casey took a step away from Death, who stood so close Casey could feel the dropping temperature. "They should know where the cops took the truck."

"They *should*."

"Um, can we help you?" the bored mechanic asked.

"I hope so. Where would a damaged semi be taken?"

He blinked, and took so long answering she thought she should repeat the question. Finally, he spoke. "I'd say Wainwrights' Scrap Metal. Sound right to you guys?"

The curious mechanic nodded. "I guess. How bad was it?" He looked at Casey's blood-splattered clothes.

"The truck wasn't running anymore. Cab wasn't even…wasn't even in one piece."

"Oh. That wreck out on the highway? Guy died?"

"That was the one."

"Yeah, I'd say Wainwrights', then. Metal recycling and junk yard. You think?" He looked at the shocked mechanic, who still stood with his mouth hanging open. He closed his mouth, swallowed, and nodded, only to return to his dope-like state.

"Okay." Casey gestured toward the road. "How do I get there?"

The bored man scratched his chin. "Few miles from here. Town doesn't have public transportation. At least not to speak of."

"I'll take her." Mr. Curious. "That is, if you guys can spare me."

Bored Guy rolled his eyes. "Take the rest of the day, if you want. Then I don't have to pay you."

"Hey, now. I'll be back soon. Don't want you trying to run this place on your own."

The bored guy showed some emotion at that, snapping the other with a greasy rag.

"Okay, um, Wendell." Casey could just read the name on the patch sewed onto the curious man's coveralls. "You ready?"

Wendell dodged away from the rag and grabbed a ring of keys off the wall. "Come on. I'll take you in my truck."

Like Casey wanted to get in another truck. The pick-up he indicated might not have been a semi, but it was enough to cause her to shudder. She hesitated by the passenger door while Wendell got in his side.

"Second thoughts?" Death sat on the hood, twanging that awful rubber band. Casey hoped it would break, and snap Death's fingers.

"Of course I have second thoughts."

"You know, someday you're going to have to get over it."

Casey inhaled deeply through her nostrils, telling herself it would do no good, trying to beat up Death. "In case you've forgotten, I was in another fatal accident *yesterday*."

"Of course I haven't forgotten. I just know how to compartmentalize my feelings."

Casey gritted her teeth and climbed into the truck. Death stayed on the hood.

"So, you leave something in the semi?" Wendell turned the key, and the truck roared to life.

"Yes."

"Figured you were in it when it got wrecked." He turned out of the lot and made a point of looking at her clothes. "You must be the one who got away. News said you walked out of the ER."

Casey jerked backward, her hand going to the door handle.

"Don't worry," Wendell said. "I figure you got your reasons for skipping out. I hate hospitals, myself. But are you sure you're okay?"

Casey looked at the man, trying to figure out whether he was driving her to the junk yard, or making a bee-line to the police station. "I'm fine. This isn't my blood."

"The driver's?"

"Yes."

He shook his head. "Poor guy. You know him?"

"Just a little." She pulled Evan's family photo from her pocket and held it out so Wendell could see. "That's him and his 'girls,' as he called them."

Wendell glanced at the picture. "They got a bad visit last night."

Casey nodded, her throat tight, and studied the photo a bit more before sliding it back into her pocket. A rush of anger welled up in her chest and she glared at Death, who now lay sideways across the hood of the truck, whistling, as if ushering someone to the other side had no more meaning than assisting them across the street. If only Casey had been able to help Evan, or even been at his side when he died, instead of getting wrenched away by those men who had pulled her out of the cab.

Casey thought back to that moment. Who *were* those men at the crash site? They obviously weren't cops, as they had disappeared as soon as the real law had arrived, and cops wouldn't manhandle her the way that guy had when he'd frisked her. The men were looking for something. Something Evan had.

"You know," Wendell said. "The police don't know why those construction vehicles were on the road like that."

"I'd assumed they weren't supposed to be."

"Yeah. They've been doing some work out on that stretch of highway, but the machines had been parked way to the side, since Sunday's a day off. Somebody moved them. Don't know why someone else hadn't seen 'em or crashed into 'em before you folks. That may be a quiet road, but it's not *that* quiet."

So they'd been watching. They'd known where Evan was traveling and had picked a place to waylay him. From the first man's attitude—*Goddammit, Evan, don't you dare die on me*—they hadn't wanted him to die. At least, not until they'd gotten their information, whatever it was. It just so happened it was raining, and a semi plus a slippery road didn't make for good stopping.

"You sure you're okay?"

Casey shuddered. "Yes, I'm all right."

Death regarded Casey with amusement, obviously hearing just fine through the windshield.

"How far yet?" Casey was ready to be out of the truck.

"Just up here. See that pile of metal on the other side of the corn field?"

She couldn't miss it. A stack of car parts, rusty barrels, broken railings, and appliances, reaching as high as a barn. Higher, maybe. Behind it sat more piles, and two crane-like machines, with magnetic pinchers. A metal fence surrounded the yard, enclosing the piles as well as two large pole barns and rows of junked vehicles.

Wendell pulled into the open gate, bypassed a truck scale, and pulled up next to a trailer with "Office" painted on the siding. "Here we are."

Death had disappeared from the hood, and Casey slid out of the passenger side. A little dog came running from beneath the trailer, yipping and prancing around Casey's feet. She looked down at it nervously, hoping it wouldn't choose to make her ankles its breakfast.

"Davey!" Wendell hollered toward the trailer, then stepped up to the door, poking his head in. "Davey? Oh, there you are." He backed off the cement step.

A man in yet another set of dark blue coveralls filled the doorway, a powdered donut in his hand. "Wendell! Awful early to see you today."

"Yeah, well, I brought you a visitor."

Davey turned his attention to Casey, not batting an eye at the state of her appearance. "You had breakfast? Got a dozen donuts here looking for a home."

"No, thank you, I—"

The dog barked louder, jumping, its nose reaching Casey's waist at the peak of its leap.

"Trixie!" Davey yelled. "Come on, girl! Leave the poor woman alone. She's not doing anything to you."

The dog dropped onto its rump, grinning happily at Casey, its tongue lolling out of its mouth.

"Got coffee, too," Davey said. "To go with the donuts. It's fresh. Come on up." He waved Casey and Wendell in, and disappeared into the trailer.

Wendell held out a hand for Casey to go first. She went up, relieved when Trixie stayed outside.

The trailer was neater than she'd expected. A few chairs, some desks, and a counter with one of those big red "Easy" buttons on it. She fought the urge to push it.

"Have a seat," Davey said, pointing to one of the vinyl-covered chairs. He handed her a steaming cup of coffee. "Milk? Sugar?"

She shook her head. "Thank you."

"My pleasure, my pleasure." He held out the box of donuts, but Casey declined.

"No, thank you. Really."

"You a health nut or somethin'? Got bagels. Granola bars. *Fruit.*" He said the last like it was a bad word.

Casey perked up. "Bananas?"

Davey rolled his eyes good-naturedly. "Should'a known you'd bring me a body Nazi, Wendell."

Wendell laughed. "She's here looking for that semi."

Davey paused, the bowl of fruit in his hand. "That one from yesterday?"

"That's the one."

Davey studied Casey more closely. "Sure is a popular vehicle."

Casey sat up. "Someone else has been looking for it?"

Davey held the bowl closer, and Casey yanked out a banana.

"Few people. Cops, of course. Wanted to see if it'd been messed with. Brakes, so forth."

"Had they?"

"Not that I could tell. But then, that truck was in bad shape. No telling what could've happened to it that we can't see anymore."

Casey gestured at him with the banana. "And someone else came?"

"Middle of the night. Set Trixie to barking something fierce. I came right out to see what was going on."

"You live here?"

He jerked his thumb toward the road. "Across the street. Close enough I hear when something's going on. Anyhow, I come over and Trixie's got three men cornered by the scrap picker. One of 'em looks like he might be going for a gun, so I grab a pipe and tuck it under my arm, like it might be a rifle." He gave a little smile. "Lighting's not so great out here at night, so I thought it could pass, easy."

"And what did they do?"

"Peed their pants, probably." He grinned wider. "But I wasn't close enough I could tell. I asked them what they thought they were doing, breaking into my property. The one smiles real nice, tells me they just want a look at the semi before it gets hauled away in the morning." He shook his head once, hard. "Like someone was gonna bother taking that thing out once it finally got in here. Not something you want to do twice." He took another bite of donut, powder sprinkling his shirt. "So I told them they could see just fine from where they were standing, and that they'd better get their eyefill, because if I saw them again I was calling the police."

"So did they leave?"

"After a bit. Seems they were finally convinced by Trixie's teeth and my pipe." He laughed. "They figured I could shoot them quicker than they could shoot me."

"And they haven't been back today?"

"Nope. And believe me, Trixie would know."

Casey found a new appreciation for the little dog.

She paused, wanting to word her question the right way. "Any chance you would let me take a look at the truck? Please?"

Davey ran his tongue over his teeth.

"She's been in it before," Wendell said.

Davey didn't take his gaze from her face.

"In the accident," Wendell said. "She was there."

Davey's eyes didn't waver. "You a friend of the driver's?"

"As much as you can be in one day."

"You hitchin'?"

"Yes."

He chewed on his lip, then rose from his chair. "Rachel!"

Casey jumped as a woman stuck her head out from a door at the end of the trailer. She was mostly hidden behind a massive file cabinet.

"Going out for a minute."

The woman nodded and disappeared back behind the cabinet.

"Come on." Davey led them out the door and across the yard, Trixie dancing around their feet, panting joyously. "That's a good girl." He tossed her the remainder of his donut.

They rounded the corner of the first pole barn and Casey stopped abruptly, bending over, trying to catch her breath. The sight of the semi was like getting kicked in the chest.

It took the men a moment to realize she wasn't with them. Wendell came back. "You all right?"

She filled her cheeks with air and let it out slowly. "I will be in a minute."

Trixie ran over and snuffled up in Casey's face, her wet nose cold against Casey's. Casey ruffled the fur on the dog's head. "Okay."

The truck lay broken and battered, slumping sideways, two of its front tires flat, its remaining windows creased with spider-web cracks. Casey was relieved to see the refrigerated trailer still attached. She'd been afraid it had been hauled away separately.

"Is the load still in there?" Casey asked.

Davey shook his head. "Company came and took it all away. Meats and stuff. Probably have to trash it all, but I guess they wanted to salvage what they could. It was still pretty cold in there, even by the time they got the rig here."

"Cab's not looking any too safe," Wendell said.

Casey smiled grimly. "I don't need the cab."

Davey and Wendell glanced at each other.

"Well, then," Davey said. "What is it you need?"

"A crowbar."

Davey smiled. "I think I just might have one of those."

In fact, he had about a dozen, and Casey picked the most heavy duty. Wendell and Davey each chose one, too.

"What are we looking for?" Wendell stood at the back of the truck, holding his crowbar over his shoulder.

Casey eyed the trim, still remarkably intact. "I'm not sure. But Evan said whatever it is was in the back trim, in the insulation, and that I shouldn't let them have it." At least that's what she'd inferred. She had been, admittedly, rather shaken up at the time.

"Well, then," Davey said. "Let's have at it. Unless you want to look around a bit first."

A good idea. If whatever Evan was hiding was something he'd want access to, he'd have to make himself a way to get at it. But after twenty minutes of fruitless searching, they hadn't found anything.

Davey stepped back. "Looks like we need the crowbars, after all."

With the screeching and wrenching of metal, the three of them tore away at the trim. It was harder than Casey had expected, and sweat soon ran down her scalp and between her shoulder blades and breasts. She stepped back, wiping her eyes, and felt something squish beneath her foot. Great. The banana, which she'd completely forgotten about.

Wendell and Davey were each pulling on a section of trim, their muscles straining with the effort. Casey took a breath and pulled back a new section, sliding out the insulation.

And she saw it.

She hollered for the other two to stop, and they hopped down from the back bumper to gather around her. Carefully she peeled back several more inches of trim and eased the insulation out from around the corner of a manila envelope. Soon she could get the entire thing out, and the three of them stood looking at it.

"What do you think's in it?" Wendell said.

"It feels like papers."

"Open it up," Davey said. "Let's have a look."

She eased her finger under the envelope's flap and wiggled it across, not wanting to rip anything, since this envelope's contents were, in all likelihood, what Evan had died for.

"Come on," Wendell said. "Let's see it."

Casey lifted the flap, and looked inside.

Chapter Four

"What is it?" Wendell leaned over to peer into the envelope.

"Lots of things." Casey was surprised how much Evan had stuffed in, and she tilted the envelope so the men could see just how many papers were there.

"Come on," Davey said. "Let's go back to the office so you don't lose anything. And you can get another banana." He looked at the ground, where Casey's fruit had met its fate.

Trixie accompanied them back to the office, and Casey reached down to pet her. "Good girl."

Trixie turned in a circle, chasing her tail.

Inside the trailer office, Davey cleared one of the desks with a sweep of his arm and pulled up two extra chairs before grabbing the donuts and the few pieces of fruit and plunking them on the surface. Casey peeled the last banana and took a bite before emptying the envelope onto the desk. Papers, photos, and forms slid out into a messy pile.

"Wow," Wendell said.

Davey picked up a photo. "This is them."

"Them who?"

"The guys who were here last night. I mean, not all of them, but a couple." He handed the photo to Casey. She wasn't surprised when the picture's subjects looked familiar. The whole group of them had been at the crash, she thought, but a few in particular stood out.

"That guy messed with me." She pointed to the guy with dirty blond hair and green eyes, the one who had frisked her. "And that one." The man who had climbed into the cab and shoved her out, all the while yelling at Evan not to die.

Casey swallowed down a bad taste in her mouth. Davey got up, filled a cup at the water cooler in the corner, and set it down in front of her. She drank it all, then ate the rest of the banana in two big bites.

"So," she said as she chewed. "What's the rest of this stuff?"

"More pictures," Wendell said. "Looks like truckers, along with these guys again. Truck stops. Highway signs. All with dates written on the back. Like Evan was making a photo journal or something."

He was right. The photos—mostly Polaroids, which was interesting, since Casey hadn't been sure Polaroids still existed—could be organized chronologically, with locations and names. A lot of the people were repeated, but several faces appeared only once.

"These papers," Davey said, holding them out at arm's length and squinting. "Some of 'em are truck manifests. Where the truck had been, where it was going, mileage, load, fuel stops, all that stuff."

Casey took a bite of an almost-ripe apple and scanned one of the pages. "Do they say what exactly the trucks were hauling?"

Davey shuffled through the pages. "All sorts of things. Grain, office supplies, hardware, frozen broccoli. I don't see a pattern, right off. I'd need some time with this stuff in order to figure anything out. I'm not an expert on trucking."

"This is just notes." Wendell held up a small, spiral-bound notebook. "Names, companies, questions. Like Evan was trying to figure something out by writing it all down."

Trixie barked outside, the sound harsher than her happy conversational yipping. The barks ended with a loud whine, and then silence. Davey looked out the window, and Casey could see immediately that something was wrong. She scooped the papers, photos and last pieces of fruit into a wastebasket at the side of the desk and grabbed it, heading toward the door where

Rachel had appeared earlier. Rachel, who sat at a table with an adding machine, looked up as Casey entered, and Casey put a finger to her lips.

Casey closed the door almost completely, still able to peer out the crack, just around the file cabinet, but from knee level, where no one would think to look.

Davey stood, plunking cups of coffee down on the desk where they'd been working, one in front of Wendell, and one at his spot. He was just sitting back down with a donut when a man came in the door—a man Casey recognized from the crash site and from the photos in the wastebasket—the man who had climbed up into the cab and yelled at Evan not to die.

"Help you?" Davey said, his voice an attempt at casual. Casey hoped the man couldn't hear the underlying nervousness.

"Hope you can," the man said. "I believe you met some of my friends last night, and you didn't show them any of our famous Midwestern hospitality."

Davey took a bite of donut and chewed it. "Don't recall as I'm supposed to be charming to folks who trespass in the wee hours of the morning."

The man smiled. "The middle of the night—just when people might need your help the most."

Casey glanced around the small room where she found herself. There were two small windows, and a larger one probably meant as an emergency exit. She studied it, hoping it could be opened without noise.

"You have something I want here in your junk yard," the man said. "A semi, would've come in yesterday, late afternoon."

"Sounds familiar," Davey said. "What's your business with it?"

"Don't think I need to tell you that, do I?"

Rachel had gotten up from her chair to join Casey, and she pinched two buttons together on the right-hand side of the window. The pane slid quietly sideways, to reveal a screen. With another pinch the screen lifted up and out, squealing. Casey froze.

"If there's something in it you're looking for, I could tell you if we found it or not," Davey said. "We've been through it pretty good."

"And?"

"Didn't find much. Nothing unusual, anyhow."

Casey let out her breath. The man hadn't heard the screen. She stuck her head out the window, hoping he didn't have an accomplice standing just outside. No one there. If he had a partner, he was probably out front.

"I don't think you'd find what I'm looking for," the man said. "It was probably hidden."

"Well, then, I don't guess you were meant to find it, were you?" Davey took a loud a sip of coffee.

"I think I was," the man said. "And you're going to help me."

Davey and Wendell both exclaimed, and Casey dashed back to the crack in the door. The man was pointing a gun across the counter, directly at Davey's face.

Casey mouthed a thank you at Rachel, who was punching 911 into her phone, and eased the wastebasket liner, along with the papers and photos, from the trashcan. She tied the top with a loop and held it, climbing onto a chair to ease out of the open window, right leg first. She swung her left leg out, then hung onto the window frame, dropping quietly to the ground. She held her breath, listening. No movement outside. Not even Trixie, who lay motionless in the driveway.

On her hands and knees, Casey crawled to the back of the trailer, and saw no one there. A stack of crates sat at the front corner of the trailer, so she couldn't see around to the front. She lay on her stomach and looked underneath. Two sets of feet. She sat on her heels. The man inside had a gun, so she had to assume these two did, as well. The first man would be bringing Davey and Wendell outside soon, and she wanted to get these others out of the way before she dealt with him.

Quietly, she slid the bag of papers as far underneath the trailer as she could, then looked around for something to use as a weapon. Bricks. Rocks. A shop broom. She grabbed the broom and twisted the head until she freed the stick. She stood and balanced it in her hands. Heavier than the Bo she used in hapkido, but about the same length.

Taking a deep breath and centering herself, she stood with her left side against the crates, her back against the trailer. She held the broomstick against her right side, her right arm extended along underneath it, resting the stick on her fingers, the back of her left hand flat against her right shoulder, the stick balanced on her palm.

She scraped her foot along the ground, the gravel loud in the quiet afternoon.

One of the men out front said something, and she heard footsteps. He came around the corner, turning toward her when he cleared the crates. Casey swung the stick upward, striking him in the groin. He bent over with a grunt, and she stepped forward, sweeping the stick over her head to strike him on the back of the neck. He sprawled at her feet, unconscious.

The second man ran around the corner, gun extended. Casey rocked back, pivoting on her left foot and swinging the stick upward. It hit the man's wrist, knocking his arm back, but he held onto the gun. Pulling the stick forward, Casey hit the bony back of his wrist, and the gun flew about ten feet away. The man lunged toward it, and Casey leapt after him, striking the side of his knee with the point of the stick.

He screamed and fell to the ground, clutching his now-useless knee. Casey jumped forward, flicking the gun away with her staff, and swung the stick around under the man's chin, lifting his face toward hers. "Who *are* you guys?"

He groaned, his eyes bright with pain.

The door to the trailer slapped open and Wendell walked down the steps, his face white. Davey came next, followed by the man with the gun, who held the pistol against his thigh. When he saw Casey he dropped the casual pose and wrapped his arm around Davey's neck, holding the gun at his temple.

Casey looked quickly for the gun on the ground, but she'd knocked it too far away for her to reach. The man on the ground gave a strangled half-laugh, half-groan, and Casey swung the stick from under his chin and knocked the side of his head, putting him out of his immediate misery, laying him flat out on the ground. She faced the last man, the stick balanced in her hands.

"You again?" the man said, a mocking smile on his face. "Dix will be glad to hear you're still around."

"Dix?"

"My friend you met at the accident yesterday. You embarrassed him in front of the guys."

"You can tell him I'm not sorry."

The man laughed. "Oh, I'll tell him. Now, honey, why don't you just put down that little stick of yours."

Casey gripped the staff tighter.

"Put it *down*." The man emphasized the last word by shoving the gun harder against Davey's head. Davey winced, and Wendell went even paler.

Casey clenched her jaw, then slowly lowered the stick to the ground. She rose, her hands palms-out at her shoulders. "Let the men go."

"And do what with them? Let them go back inside and call the cops? I don't think so."

The sound of a siren split the air.

Casey kept her hands up. "Guess they won't have to call now, will they?"

The man looked wildly at his fallen comrades, then dropped his gun hand and ran around the trailer. Casey ran the other way, jumping over her first victim and keeping out of the gunman's sightlines so she wouldn't be a target if he still wanted to shoot somebody.

But he wasn't looking for her anymore. He jumped into a dark blue Explorer and flew out of the driveway, tires spinning on the gravel as he sped in the opposite direction as the sirens.

"Let's go after him!" Wendell was behind her, his color more than fully back.

"The cops will get him." Casey returned to the side of the trailer and dropped to her knees, pulling the bag out from under the trailer. "But I don't want them to get me, too."

"Where are you going? I'll drive you."

Davey came around the side of the trailer, Trixie limp in his arms. Where Wendell was now beet red, Davey had gone almost completely white.

"You guys will be in a lot of trouble because of me," Casey said, indicating the two unconscious men. "I'm sorry."

"I'm not." Davey's voice shook. "They deserved what you gave them."

Casey looked at Trixie. "Is she alive?"

Davey clutched her to his chest. "She's breathing."

"I want to *do* something." Wendell's voice grew loud.

Casey held up the bag. "You already have."

The sirens came closer, and Rachel stuck her head out of the open window. "I see cruisers."

"I'm sorry," Casey said again, and ran toward the far end of the lot, where she climbed a stack of crushed cars, dropped over the fence, and sprinted as fast as she could through the cornfield.

Chapter Five

"You know," Death said, "you really have to stop doing things like this."

Casey groaned and held her stomach. The banana and not-quite-ripe apple weren't sitting too well after her two-mile run through the corn. She lay now in a thicket of trees which had yet to be cut down to make more farmland, probably because a creek ran through it, gurgling and spitting over rocks.

"You kill somebody, you run," Death said. "You get in an accident, you run. You beat up some guys, you run. You're getting predictable."

Casey groaned again and rolled over, holding her arm over her ear to block out Death's yammering.

"You should at least do something no one expects," Death said, "like giving yourself up to the police, or heading home."

Casey took her arm away from her face. "Are you *serious*?"

Death grinned. "Not really. I just wanted to see if I could get you to do something other than moan and writhe around."

Casey put her arm back up to her head. "Can you just shut up? For a few minutes, at least?"

"If you say the magic word."

"Fine. Can you just shut *the hell* up?"

Death sighed. "That's *two* words. But okay. I'll stop talking."

Casey relaxed against the ground. Silence. Blissful silence.

A shrill chord rent the air, and Casey shot up. Death was blowing into a harmonica.

"What are you *doing*?" Casey shrieked.

"Playing a song," Death said. "To help you sleep."

Casey wrenched the harmonica from Death's hands and threw it into the creek, where it immediately sank under the water.

"Well," Death said. "*That* wasn't very nice."

"I'm not a very nice person."

"I guess not."

Casey fell back onto the ground and watched as Death went sloshing into the creek, feeling around the creek's rocky bed and pulling the harmonica from its watery resting place.

Death shook water from the instrument and traipsed back to the dry ground. "You know, Wendell and Davey are probably your only hope for figuring out that information."

Casey closed her eyes. "I can't exactly go back to the junk yard at this moment, can I?"

"No, but maybe later."

"Yeah, after the cops have cleared away the bad guys, questioned Davey and Wendell for hours, and put someone at the yard to watch the truck, that would be a *great* time for me to go back to talk to the guys. Thanks so much for the advice."

"No need to be sarcastic. I'm only trying to help."

"Yeah, well, maybe it would be more help if you would just *leave me alone.*"

Death didn't reply.

Casey peeked out from under her eyelids, then perched on her elbows. Death was gone. She collapsed back onto the ground and cursed to herself. What had she gotten herself into this time? Could *nothing* be straightforward? Could she not hitch a ride with a normal truck driver who was driving a normal truck and didn't have squads of bad guys chasing him and setting up accidents to kill him? Was that too much to ask? That she could just have one day where nothing out of the ordinary happened?

She lay there for a few moments, thinking. If her previous assumptions were correct, the men weren't trying to actually *kill* Evan—at least not until they'd gotten what they were after. They most likely wanted to stop the truck, question Evan, and take whatever information he had gathered. Which Casey now had. She glanced at the bag, lying on the ground beside her, and clenched her hand around the handles, crinkling the plastic. She had gotten Davey and Wendell in trouble for sure. What were they going to tell the cops about those two men lying senseless in the yard, one of them with a destroyed knee? And what was *with* her, hurting someone like that again? She had to comfort herself with the idea that the men were attacking her and that she hadn't killed them—even though she would have liked to, after they'd hurt Trixie like that.

She rolled onto her stomach, resting her face on her forearm. It would serve her right if Davey and Wendell told the police about her. She had stumbled into their lives, bringing questions and secrets and men with guns. They should tell the cops everything, sending them on a quest to find her and haul her in. She was a killer and a thief, taking what wasn't hers, messing up people's lives, making even more of a hash of her own…

Oh, God, she was tired.

Her brain went fuzzy for a moment, and sleep pushed its way into her consciousness. She *wanted* to sleep. *Needed* to sleep. But not there, where the next farmer to drive his John Deere out to harvest corn would see her.

She forced herself to her hands and knees, then into a squat. Her arm throbbed where her wrist had been almost crushed the day before—two days before now, wasn't it?—and her shoulder wound had opened up again, adding her own bright red blood to Evan's, which had darkened on her clothes into a crusty black. She shook her head, took a deep breath, and stood, blinking as she gained her equilibrium. She had to find somewhere to go where she could rest and look over the contents of the bag more carefully.

Sticking to the creek bed and cornfields, Casey made her way further from Davey's business and the town, heading into miles and miles of golden corn. The sun gained in its height, heating up the day, and Casey knelt more than once to scoop water from the stream. At one point a herd of cows watched her, each raising its head as she walked by, returning to grazing once it realized she was neither threat nor server of food.

She startled a lone antelope when she stepped out of a cornfield and onto an empty road. The animal stood half-in and half-out of the stalks on the opposite side of the gravel, staring at her wide-eyed, long neck stretched as it determined the danger. Casey waited, watching the trembling legs of the animal, wondering why it had been separated from its herd. A breeze wafted through the corn, rattling the dry leaves, and the antelope spun, leaping into the field and out of sight.

Casey moved into the middle of the road, bag dangling at her side, sweat running down the side of her face. A bird flew overhead, screeching, and Casey followed its path with her eyes as it flitted away, disappearing into the clear blue sky. Which way should she go?

"How about this way?" Death appeared in front of her, arm pointed to the west.

"Why?"

"I did a little scouting last night when I wasn't waking you up and suffering your abusive language. I found a place."

Having no reason not to, Casey turned west and followed. After a while the cornfields ended, and a wave of soybeans began, shimmering under the glaring light. In the distance, in the middle of the field, crouched an old shed, sides weather-beaten, red paint flaking off to reveal graying lumber. The tin roof reflected the sun's rays, and the large sliding door hung crooked on its track, revealing the black of the interior. Again Casey looked up and down the road. She had neither seen nor heard any vehicles for miles, which meant there had been nothing and no one to see her.

"So what's so great about that place?"

"It's perfect," Death said. "You'll see."

Casey looked around, her hands on her hips.

"You're not going to get a better offer, you know. No money, no ID, no decent clothes—"

"All *right.*" Casey put her hands over her ears. "Fine. Just... stop talking."

Death ran a finger across closed lips and gave a little bow, gesturing for Casey to continue. She walked past and arrived at the end of a long lane leading toward the shed. She examined the ground. The dirt was hard and gave no indication of recent activity. But then, it had rained only a day before. She looked around again, then headed down the lane.

The shed was larger than she had first thought, big enough to house a tractor or two, although there was nothing there at the moment. A few rusty and unidentifiable implements and tools hung from nails, along with some burlap sacks and a dusty oil lamp. Several five-gallon buckets were lined up against the wall, and a broom leaned crookedly on a wall slat. This broom probably wouldn't make such a good weapon, its handle cracked almost in half. But it still had its straw tines, and she could see tracks in the dirt floor where it had been used to sweep.

Outside the shed were more rusty implements, large but outdated tractor attachments. Tall grass partially hid them, winding around the curves of the metal. On the far side of the shed an old pump stood beside the wall. Casey couldn't tell just by looking if it was still usable, so she grabbed the handle and pulled up. It stuck at first, but she felt something give, and with a little more work she got the handle to its upright position, perpendicular to the pump itself.

Nothing happened.

"Nice," Casey said.

Death held up a finger. "Wait for it."

A quiet gurgle sounded from the depths of the pipes, and a trickle of water dripped from the spigot. The water was brown with rust, but after a minute or so ran clear. Casey splashed her face and drank her fill. She was going to push the handle back down, but hesitated, looking at her shirt. She spun her finger in the air. "Do you mind?"

Death laughed. "Like I haven't seen—"

Casey frowned.

"Okay, okay. You don't have to be so *touchy*." Death turned around.

Casey pulled off the sweatshirt and held it under the water, rubbing the fabric against itself. She knew the bloodstains wouldn't come out entirely, but at least she could get the nastiest crust off. She scrubbed as long as her hands could take the cold, then wrung out as much water as possible. She laid the shirt over one of the implements on the far side of the shed, figuring the hot sun would dry it in minutes.

Leaving Death outside, Casey checked out the inside of the shed. The shade was a relief, and she was surprised at the amount of open space. It had been a couple of days since she'd exercised, and she knew she would be able to concentrate on things much better if she could get in a good session. The area was enough for her needs. She pushed the buckets to the corners of the room, clearing even more space, and found a spot to begin, centering herself and her body.

"I'm leaving," Death said, peeking in the door. "You're too boring."

"Good. This time don't come back."

Casey's muscles were sore from sleeping on the ground, and in the truck before that. She began slowly, taking the time to stretch and perform some jumping jacks and sit-ups. Her bad shoulder complained at the fingertip push-ups, but overall her body seemed happy to be moving in the ways it was used to. When she was ready for the actual *kata,* the hapkido patterns she went through every day, she chose weapons forms, having been reminded that morning how useful it was to have her body ready for the Bo.

A half-hour later she'd had enough, considering that besides her lack of sleep she hadn't had a decent meal in days. Sweat poured off of her body, and with another glance outside to make sure she was still alone, she removed her bra, running it under the water from the pump. She took off her shoes and rinsed her socks and pants, hanging them to dry in the sun, taking the chance to even wash and wring out her underwear.

Her underclothes dried in almost no time, so she put them on and got herself settled in the shed to go over the information she'd found in Evan's truck. She piled the burlap sacks to create a semi-soft place to sit, and spread the bag's contents in front of her on yet another sack.

Picking out the photos, she laid them in chronological order. The earliest ones showed mostly the men Casey had seen, but soon other faces began to appear, along with trucks. One picture showed the blond guy and the man who'd gotten away from Davey's seated across a table from an older couple in a diner. Casey would guess they were in their upper sixties. The photo had been taken through the front window, and caught Gun Man leaning over, his finger in the couple's faces, as if he were making a strong point. Blond Guy sat back, arms crossed, smirking. The man's and woman's expressions told different stories. The man's mouth was open, his eyes wide, as if what he was being told surprised or frightened him. The woman didn't look afraid. She looked *pissed*. Her eyes were narrow slits, and her lips were tight, her chin thrust out in what had to be defiance. Too bad Evan hadn't been able to get audio.

Other photos weren't as clear, and displayed a varying group of people. The woman at the table was the only female, the rest of the truckers being men ranging from young to what could have been considered past retirement age. Blond Guy—Dix, Gun Man had said—and Gun Man were present in most of the photos, with a supporting cast of others from the crash site, including the two Casey had laid out at Davey's. In all of the situations the men were talking, often violating the truckers' personal space. In one they stood at the open back of a semi trailer, Gun Man looking up at the load of boxes. In another, Dix was handing a trucker a small package. No chance of telling what it contained. Casey still couldn't see a pattern, but hoped that would come with studying the rest of the notes.

Leaving the photos spread out in front of her, Casey picked up the stack of truck manifests. These seemed freshly copied and were held together by a large black clip. They listed drivers and their trucks, along with the trucks' contents, mileage, fuel stops, and the dates they traveled. Casey could see nothing linking the loads or mentioning a trucking company. As Davey had pointed out, the shipments included a wide range of items, from food to computers to lumber. There didn't seem to be any consistent inventory.

Finally, she picked up Evan's spiral-bound notebook, in which he'd scribbled things, many of which were just about illegible. With patience and the return of her headache, Casey was able to work her way through them. For the most part, the notes were a companion to the other information—adding a list of names. Dix, aka Owen Dixon, featured prominently in Evan's notes, just behind Gun Man, also known as Randy Westing. The two others at Davey's were named as well, along with the rest of what Evan was calling The Team. A real *team* of winners, from everything Casey could see.

One page of the notebook featured names Casey figured were the truckers'. She was wrong. None of the names matched the names on the manifests. The names in the book, however, were the ones that matched the photos, if she could trust the squiggly writing on their backs. So she had two different groups of people: the people in the photos and notebook, and the people in the manifests. The notebook held more than just names, however. The last page was filled with personal information. Personal as pertaining to the other truckers, not to Evan himself. Casey read over part of the list, which named the people in the photos.

JOHN SIMONES: UK 2008
MICK AND WENDY HALVESTON: 04-09
SANDY GREENE: DV
PAT PARNELL: Carl Billings, SF
HANK NANCE: Jan, Mar, Jul

Casey couldn't make sense of Evan's shorthand notes. The one obviously indicated months—but what about them? The months beside Hank Nance didn't match up with the photos Evan had—the photos came from much later. And the SF by Carl Billings' name—what was that supposed to mean? Death would probably suggest it meant Safety First.

Casey's eyes drooped, and her headache had worsened. She piled the papers and slid them back into the plastic bag, deciding she wouldn't be able to retain any new information even if she found it. After checking outside again for signs of life—well, *human* life—and seeing there weren't any, she put on her now-dry jeans and sweatshirt. Back inside, she rolled up the bag in a burlap sack to use as a pillow, and lay down on her makeshift mattress.

It didn't take more than a few minutes for her body to give up the fight to stay awake.

Chapter Six

She woke with a start. It was dark. So dark she couldn't see the other end of the shed. Noises came from outside—the sound of tires on gravel. Not heavy tires, like a tractor, but something lighter. The sounds stopped briefly, then resumed, accompanied by footsteps.

"Here they come!" Death's breath hissed in her ear.

Casey eased silently to her feet, her brain instantly clear of fuzziness. "Here comes who?" Her muscles tingled and her breath deepened, her senses on hyper alert. Her eyes adjusted quickly to the darkness, and she watched the outline of two bicycles and their riders enter the shed. The people kicked the stands to prop up the bikes, not speaking, or even whispering. Casey waited, hands loose at her sides, balanced on the balls of her feet.

Death watched, quiet now, but so close Casey could feel the chill.

The taller of the two shadows turned toward Casey and jumped back, grabbing toward the other.

"Who are you?" The taller one's voice—a man's, Casey thought—was husky, and quiet.

"Nobody," Casey said.

Death chuckled.

"What do you want?" The second figure. Female, this time.

"I was just sleeping. I didn't take anything."

The taller one hesitated, but the female stepped forward, her eyes narrowed in the darkness. "There's nothing here to take."

More sounds came from the outside, and three additional people came in the door, halting when they saw the postures of the first two.

"What's wrong?" Another female voice.

The tall one gestured toward Casey. "We have a guest."

All three new people turned to Casey, one of them flicking on a flashlight and shining it in her face. "What do you want?"

They were very concerned with that.

Casey held up a hand to shield her eyes. "A place to sleep. That's all."

The one with the flashlight ran the light up and down Casey's body, taking in the burlap bed at her feet. Death struck a pose as the flashlight came near, but the light went straight through, illuminating only the wall of the shed.

"What's your name?" The first female again—a teenager, if Casey was seeing correctly.

"Casey."

"Casey what?"

Casey hesitated. "Jones." With a pang she thought of Eric, from back in Clymer, Ohio. She'd told him Smith, and he'd immediately equated it with Jones, yet another anonymous name. She should probably just go ahead and use Doe.

This girl seemed to believe Jones as much as Eric had believed Smith. "Terry, close the door."

One of the last three—a guy this time—pulled the sliding door, and with a grunt shut off the only exit to the outside.

Casey remembered the broom with the cracked handle, as well as the iron implements hanging behind her. Plenty of weapons, but one against five? Only if she took them by surprise. And she didn't exactly like the idea of beating up teenagers.

"Sheryl, can you light us up, please?" the first girl said.

The second girl handed her flashlight to another person and lit a match, holding it up to the oil lamp Casey had seen earlier. It cast a glow over the center of the shed, leaving the corners shadowed.

The teenagers looked like any group of kids. The girls were both slim, within an inch or two of Casey's height. The second one, who had lit the lamp, was fair, freckled, and pretty; the other, who seemed to be the leader of the group, had dark hair, her skin pale in the light. While she wasn't a traditional beauty, she was striking, and Casey could feel her charisma and focus. Casey wondered if the girl's hair was naturally dark, or if it had had help from a bottle. Her fingernails, painted black, had Casey leaning toward the direction of cosmetics.

The boys were about as different from each other as they could be. The first was tall, thick, and handsome, his mouth partway open as he stared. His elevator didn't look to be stopping at all the floors. The second boy was shorter—as short as the girls, light-haired, and thin—and cute as a hormonal button. More with-it, definitely, than the tall boy. The third one was still growing into his face, his ears and nose larger than what might be required, and his body hung softer and rounder than the others.

Death wandered toward the lamp and stopped at its base, blowing at the flame. It flickered, but didn't go out.

"This is our place," the tall guy said.

Casey held out her hands in a placating gesture. "I'll go. I'm not trying to step on anyone's toes. I just needed a place to sleep."

"Wait." The first girl came closer, studying Casey's clothes. "You don't look so good."

Death laughed. "Told you so."

"Where are you from?"

Casey held her non-threatening stance. "I'm just traveling through. I can leave."

"No. Hold on." The girl nodded to the guy holding the flashlight—Terry, had the girl called him? "You bring the usual?"

"Sure. Everybody's favorite."

Oh, great. A teenage drinking party. Or something worse. Casey let her hands drop. "Look. I'll just go, okay?"

"No. Stay." The girl gave a little smile. "I'm Bailey. Bailey Jones."

Casey checked a laugh. "Nice to meet you, Bailey. Are we related?"

"Probably, if we go back far enough. That's Johnny." She pointed at the tall one. "Sheryl, Martin, and Terry." She indicated the pudgy one. "Terry's got the goods. Martin?"

Martin slid a bulging backpack from his shoulders and pulled out two little speakers. He set them on one of the wall's wooden slats and attached them to an iPod. Music filled the room; some singer-songwriter Casey didn't recognize. Death immediately pulled out a guitar and began strumming, crooning along with the music, following a tune Casey had never heard.

From his still-fat pack Martin retrieved a blanket, which he spread out on the dirt floor. Terry, also carrying a bag, set it down and pulled out a stack of napkins, paper cups, and plates, setting them all in the middle of the blanket.

Casey wondered when teenagers had gotten so finicky about getting drunk.

"Pick a spot," Bailey said.

When Casey hesitated Bailey took a seat herself, followed by all three guys. Only Sheryl still stood, watching Casey from beside the oil lamp.

"So sit," Death said, strumming a chord. "At least *pretend* to be social."

Casey found a place on the edge of the blanket and sat butterfly style, ready to jump up at a moment's provocation. She could feel Sheryl watching her, and kept the girl in her sightlines.

"What did you bring tonight?" Bailey leaned toward Terry.

Terry smiled and reached into his bag. When he brought his hand back out, it was holding a Tupperware container, one of the kind big enough to hold a pie.

Casey glanced at Death, who had stopped playing long enough to stand over Terry, sniffing. "Looks promising."

Terry set the container down, looking around at the others. *"Voilà!"* He peeled off the lid, and there sat…

"Cinnamon rolls?"

Terry glanced at Casey, his eyes pained. "What's wrong with cinnamon rolls?"

"Nothing. I mean, cinnamon rolls are great, but…just not what I was expecting."

"Oh. You were probably expecting this." He reached back into his bag and pulled out a half-gallon jug of milk.

Casey laughed. "Nope. Can't say I was expecting that, either."

Bailey grinned. "Terry's folks own the bakery in town, so Terry's always bringing us day-olds. What was it last night?"

Johnny moaned. "Blueberry muffins. They were *amazing*."

"Yeah," Martin said. "I missed those. Bummer."

"Wait a minute." Casey rubbed her forehead. "Do your parents know you're here?"

The kids looked at her in shock. All except Sheryl, who still watched from the lamp, her face a blank.

"Our parents don't even know we're *gone*," Terry said. "As far as they know, we're in bed."

Casey automatically looked at her wrist, where she used to wear a watch. "What time is it?"

"About two." Bailey shrugged. "Our parents are way dead asleep. Now, Terry, how about passing out those rolls?"

Casey wasn't going to say no, and her roll was gone in four quick bites, her milk in a few swallows. When she finished she found five pairs of eyes riveted on her face. Six, if you counted Death's.

"What?" she said.

"Want another one?" Terry held out the Tupperware. "You look…um…a little hungry?"

"Sorry. I guess… I'd love another one."

She ate another two, and finished off the milk. By the time the rolls were gone, the kids were digging in their packs and handing her more food. A granola bar, a bruised peach, a Snickers, and even a pack of gum.

"I'm okay," she said. "Really. You don't have to—"

"I know who you are." Sheryl. Her voice was hard. "You're the one who was in that truck accident. You ran away from the cops."

Death winced, strumming an atonal chord. "Uh-oh."

"I didn't run from the cops," Casey said. "I left the hospital. Nothing illegal about that."

"Yeah, except they've been asking for you to come in to the station."

Casey looked at Death, who shrugged.

"I didn't know that. What else are they saying?"

Sheryl turned to her friends. "She's wanted for questioning about the accident. The trucker *died*. She was with him. It was probably her fault."

"They're saying that?" Casey was shocked.

"No." Bailey shot Sheryl a look. "That's Sheryl's interpretation. They're just saying they want to ask you questions so they can *determine* what happened. They're not blaming you. Right, Martin?"

He nodded.

"They're also saying if anybody sees her they're supposed to turn her in." Sheryl reached into her pocket and pulled out her phone. "Anybody want to do the honors?"

"Sheryl," Bailey said. "Cut it out. Put the phone away."

"We're supposed to—"

"And since when do we do everything we're supposed to? Come *on*."

Sheryl glared at Bailey, her thumb over her phone.

"Come on, Sher." Terry this time, his voice gentler than Bailey's. "Give the lady a break."

"Why?"

"Because if you call you give up our place here. And because it would drive your parents crazy."

Sheryl stared at him a long time before sticking her phone back in her pocket. "For *now*."

Casey let out her breath. She had to get out of the area, and fast. She could take the bag of information with her, and figure it out on the road.

"You're still wearing the same clothes, aren't you?" Bailey indicated Casey's shirt.

"I didn't have any others."

"And couldn't buy any?"

"I don't have any money."

"Don't have— Why not?"

"Because she's a fugitive," Sheryl said. "Her stuff's probably still in the truck."

Casey ignored her. "It's a long story. Look, I'll just be going."

She stood, but Bailey grabbed her pants leg. "Don't go. Please."

"Thanks for the food. Really, I appreciate it. But I can't be found here. I didn't have anything to do with the accident. It wasn't my fault. And I don't want you folks getting in trouble because of me."

"We won't. And I believe you about the accident. We all believe you. Don't we?" She widened her eyes at her friends, all of whom nodded vigorously. Except, again, for Sheryl.

"If it wasn't your fault," Sheryl said, "why can't you talk to the cops? She's running from something." This last was to the other teens.

"So what?" Martin said. "Isn't everybody? Aren't you?"

"I am not running from the *cops*."

"Sheryl…" Bailey sounded irritated.

"Don't *Sheryl* me. You… She…" Sheryl shoved the sliding door open and barged out.

Bailey sighed. "Terry—"

"I'm on it." He jumped up and followed Sheryl out the door.

"I'm sorry," Casey said. "I didn't mean to cause trouble."

Bailey waved a hand. "Not your fault. Sheryl doesn't exactly like strangers, or any adults, really."

"Yeah," Johnny said. "Especially after last week, when—."

The others looked at him sharply and he jerked back, as if they'd slapped him. "Sorry. I didn't mean to say anything."

"Stay here." Bailey wouldn't let go of Casey's pants. "Nobody will find you."

"But Sheryl—"

"—will be fine. We'll take care of her. Believe me, the *last* thing Sheryl wants is to call the cops."

"We'll bring you stuff," Martin said. "Clothes and food and a sleeping bag. Stay as long as you want."

"But won't someone find me?"

"No one ever comes out here except us," Bailey said. "I should know. We own this shed and all twelve hundred acres around it."

"But—"

"You're safe here. Even when these fields get harvested no one bothers with the shed."

Casey glanced over at Death, who was humming along with the present song, eyes closed. Big help there. She really didn't *want* to leave the area. She wanted to stay close, within range of Evan's truck, close to where she knew Owen Dixon and Randy Westing—Blond Guy and Gun Man—were. Unless they'd already run off.

"You are hiding, aren't you?" Terry and Sheryl were back inside, Terry inquisitive, Sheryl lurking behind him.

Casey considered Terry, and his question. "I am."

"Why?" Terry didn't look angry, or scared. Just…curious.

Casey looked at Death again, and this time got a little shrug, like what did she have to lose? And really…not much. But these kids? They did, whoever they were. Knowing too much could only get them in trouble.

"I just need some time," Casey said. "I was in a…a bad situation."

Sheryl shook her hair out of her face. "Killing somebody would do that."

"*Sheryl*," Bailey said, her voice sharp. "She didn't kill anybody."

Sheryl stared at the far corner of the shed.

"I promise," Casey said, looking right at Sheryl. "I didn't kill the truck driver. I just need a place to stay. Just for a little while. If what Bailey says is true, no one will even know I'm here."

"It is true," Bailey said. "But you know, there are…places you can go. No one will know where you are. *He* won't know where you are."

He? "Um," Casey said. "Who won't?"

"You know," Bailey said. "Whoever it is that you're running from. Your boyfriend? Husband?"

"No," Casey said, "that's not it, I—"

"We can't get mixed up with this," Sheryl said. "With *her*. Whoever she really is."

Terry nodded. "Sheryl's right."

"No, she's not," Martin said. "Sheryl means *she* can't get mixed up in it."

"*Martin!*" Terry looked shocked.

"What? Just because Sheryl's—" He stopped, glancing at Casey. "Look, it doesn't mean the rest of us can't do anything. Sheryl can stay out of it."

Sheryl gasped. "That's not fair!"

"We'll keep you safe," Bailey said to Casey. "I promise. You can stay here as long as you want."

Casey gave a short laugh under her breath. It was Bailey's own little group of night owls Bailey should be protecting. Casey didn't exactly have a good record of late. She should tell Bailey to get the hell away from her while she and her friends still had a chance to survive unscathed.

"Thanks," she said instead. "I would love to stay."

Chapter Seven

"Cute kids." The guitar was gone, but Death still hummed the last tune from Martin's iPod.

"Cute and confusing," Casey said. "Who ever heard of kids who sneak out to eat baked goods?"

Death laughed. "I like it."

"So do I. I like *them*." She rolled up from her burlap bed and began her morning stretches. From the height of the sun it was at least mid-morning. The kids had left somewhere around five, after hours of talking—among themselves, since Casey wouldn't answer any more of their questions—and dancing to Martin's iPod, and it had taken Casey ages to get to sleep after that. She was surprised she'd been able to sleep at all; at least Death hadn't felt it necessary to wake her every two hours, like the night before. "You knew they were going to come."

Death grinned. "They were here night before last, eating those blueberry muffins they talked about. I would have taken one if I could have, but that would've been breaking the rules."

"What rules? You have rules?"

Death shrugged. "They change on a regular basis. That night I didn't want to scare the kiddies. Anyhow, this group could be helpful. They're smart, well, except for the tall one, and they're well-connected. I mean, that Goth girl's family owns all this." Death gestured to the shed.

"Yeah," Casey said. "Real helpful."

"Just you wait. You'll see."

Casey stretched her arms to the ceiling, hearing her joints crack.

"So." Death jumped up beside her. "What's on the agenda for today other than your boring *kata*?"

Casey took a deep breath. "Other things you'll find equally dull. You might as well go back to wherever you go when you're not bothering me. Don't you have some people to go transport on your little boat?"

"I don't have a boat. And if I did, it wouldn't be little."

"So all of those stories about you rowing dead people across the river Styx?"

"Complete bunk. I hate water." Death gave a shudder. "Bad experience when I was young."

Casey dropped her hands. "*You* were *young*?"

"What? Do I look that bad?"

Casey laughed and began her sit-ups.

"You know," Death said. "You really aren't very nice to me."

Casey counted under her breath.

"You treat me like I *wanted* to take your husband and son."

Twelve. Thirteen. Fourteen.

"The accident wasn't my fault, remember. I just came when I was called."

Twenty. Twenty-One. Twenty-Two.

"Fine. Ignore me. I'll be back when you're ready to be friendly."

Casey squeezed her eyes shut. When she counted to two hundred, she opened them. Death was gone.

Casey went through a set of hapkido forms and took a long drink from the pump. She could hear tractors in the distance, but couldn't see anything other than clouds of dust billowing into the sky. After washing her face she went back into the shed to consider how she might be able to get in contact with either Wendell or Davey. She'd have to be careful. As she'd said to Death, getting in touch with those guys so soon after they'd been involved with the police wasn't ideal, but Casey needed to know what had happened. Had they turned her in? Had they

gotten in trouble? Were the guys she'd knocked out—or Gun
Man—in custody?

While Casey considered her options, she took out Evan's
photos and studied them, memorizing faces. If she ran across
any of the people, she wanted to know it. She could put names
to these faces, with Evan's notes, but wouldn't recognize the
drivers on the manifests.

The sound of a vehicle coming up the lane broke into her
thoughts, and she shoved the photos back into the bag, rolled
up her makeshift bed, and stashed them both in one of the five-
gallon buckets. She darted to the corner closest to the opening
of the door and eased into it, waiting.

Gravel popped under the tires of the vehicle as it slowed and
then stopped. A door opened and shut, and Casey balanced
herself, her weight on her back foot.

"Hello?" Bailey stuck her head in the door, her dark hair and
pale skin even more disconcerting in the daylight. Her lips were
painted as black as her hair, and her eyes stood out between
thick liner.

"Oh." Casey relaxed and stepped out from the corner.
"Bailey."

"Hey." Bailey looked around at the shed, toward the space
where Casey had been sleeping. "Where's your stuff?"

"I didn't know who was coming."

"So you cleaned it up." Bailey assessed her. "You don't take
any chances, do you?"

"I try not to."

"Dad let me drive the car *to school* today. He and Mom are
both at work. I thought you might want a shower. And maybe
some real food."

"Bailey, you don't have to—"

"Come on. If you're going to be sticking around you might
as well not stink." She grinned. "My sister's at college, and she
left some clothes. Mom won't notice if they're gone."

"Just like they don't miss you at night?"

Bailey laughed. "Exactly."

"And doesn't anybody miss you during the day? Like your teachers?"

Bailey shrugged. "I called in. Said I was my mom, and that *my daughter* wasn't feeling well today."

"Bailey, you shouldn't—"

"Hey. My choice. Don't give me a lecture."

Casey shut up and retrieved her bag from the bucket, following Bailey to a blue Honda Accord. "Won't you draw attention to the shed by driving back here?"

"Nah. I checked the fields before I turned in the lane. No one's within a couple miles."

Casey walked around to the passenger door and hesitated. Just being in the vicinity of another car made her heart race. She closed her eyes, concentrating on her breathing.

"You all right?" Bailey looked at her over the top of the car.

"It's just, the accident, you know, it makes me—"

"Freak out? Sure, I get it. I thought about bringing bikes, but there's no way to ride one and pull another one, so—"

"It's fine. I'll get in in a minute." Casey gritted her teeth, and opened the door.

Bailey kept up the chatter the whole way into town, and had the radio turned to a top forty station so loudly she had to raise her voice. "You like pancakes? I make good pancakes. Sausage, too. Or we have that bacon that's already cooked and you just have to warm it up. Or I could make eggs. Or cereal. We've got lots of that. How about toast? You could have cinnamon toast. Unless you want lunch? It is about lunchtime, actually, so we could have that. You want to stop at McDonalds? Or Taco Bell? Or maybe you'd rather have something from the house? I can make mac and cheese, or we have leftovers from last night. Lasagna. Or a sandwich. We have all the stuff to make sandwiches. Even that Amish Baby Swiss cheese."

Casey's stomach rumbled, whether from excitement or apprehension, she wasn't sure. The long list of food was rather overwhelming, as was the volume at which it was delivered.

Bailey suddenly stopped talking and pulled a cell phone out of her pocket. She slid it open and began punching keys at a rate faster than Casey could keep track of. Casey prayed silently that nothing would pull out in front of them, and that Bailey could keep at least one eye on the road.

Bailey closed her phone and set it on the seat beside her. "Martin. Wondered if I'd picked you up yet."

"He knows?"

"Sure. They all do. Martin and Johnny wanted to come, but I thought that would look weird, if we were all gone."

"Sheryl probably thought you shouldn't come."

"Yeah, well, she's got her reasons."

Bailey's phone buzzed again, and she snatched it up, laughing. "Martin says he looks forward to seeing how well you clean up."

Casey hoped she lived long enough to do it. Weren't there laws about this sort of thing? That you needed to actually pay attention to the road while driving?

Besides fearing for her life, Casey kept her eye out for traffic, thinking that in her present state she would be a source of interest, even if people didn't recognize her. They might also wonder why a school-age girl wasn't actually *in* school, but there was nothing she could do about that. She pulled down the sun visor to get at the mirror behind it, and blanched at the sight of her hair and face. The fact that Death was now in the back seat didn't faze her. The fact that the *rest* of the seat was filled with bagpipes was a little more disturbing.

"You keep asking to die," Death said. "What better chance do you have than with a teenage girl who texts while she drives?"

Casey blew her bangs off her forehead and ran her fingers through the rest of her hair, wincing at Death's blast on the bagpipes, which sounded like a dying whale.

Bailey glanced over, then reached into the back seat, putting her hand right through Death's leg and scrabbling around where the bagpipes lay. Casey clutched the dashboard as the car swerved dangerously toward the side of the road.

"Here." Bailey tossed a baseball cap into Casey's lap. "You can wear this till you get inside." She looked at her fingers, clenching them into a fist and blowing on them.

Rather than a ball team, the cap advertised a seed company. "You wear this often?"

Bailey wrinkled her nose. "It's Dad's. He has tons of them. Guys from the different places give him free stuff all the time, so we've got more crap than we know what to do with. Hats, pens, tablets, money clips—like who uses *those*—even T-shirts. Not that I wear them."

Casey pushed back her hair and put on the hat. Not great, but at least a little improvement.

"*Niiiiice*," Death said, giving Casey a thumbs up in the mirror. Casey flipped up the visor.

"That's our place," Bailey said, turning a corner. "White farmhouse down there." She pointed to a homestead about a quarter of a mile ahead.

"And all of this is your land?"

"A lot of it. We own over a thousand acres, and work about nine thousand more."

"That's a lot of land. It must take forever to farm it all."

"It's what Dad does. And with the new farm equipment nowadays it doesn't take all that long. Now, you might want to get down. We've got some guys who work for us, and unless you want to get me in trouble you'd better stay out of sight."

"Won't you be in trouble if they see you, anyway?"

"They'll probably just think it's my dad, coming home for lunch. They don't always know where he is. Stop worrying."

Casey hunched over in the seat, scooting down low into the leg area of the passenger seat and ducking her head as far as she could.

"This is fun." Death sat in the passenger seat, feet up on the dashboard, above Casey. "Think we could do this more often?"

Bailey pulled into the long driveway, driving faster than Casey liked, bumping Casey's head up into Death's legs. She was thankful she was wearing a hat. Bailey lurched to a stop, opened the electric garage door, and pulled in. "Stay down."

The garage door made its slow descent, ending with a quiet clunk.

"Okay," Bailey said. "You can get up now."

Death had already moved, so Casey unfolded from her position and climbed out of the car. She bent over, hands toward the floor, stretching her back.

"You okay?" Bailey stopped halfway to the door to the house.

Casey straightened and forced a smile. "I'm fine." She grabbed her bag of information and followed Bailey into the house, stopping just inside the door. This place was not just a "farmhouse," as Bailey had said. It was a state-of-the-art home, beginning with the kitchen into which they'd come. Stainless steel appliances shone in the brightly lit room—skylights and windows were everywhere—and the floor looked like original tile work, as did the counter top. Rows of expensive pots hung from hooks above a cooking island, and the tops of the custom cabinets were lined with cut glass bowls.

"Wow," Death said. "So much for the idea that farmers are back-woods."

Bailey dropped her purse onto the glass kitchen table. "Shower first, or food?"

No contest.

Death watched as Casey stashed her bag under a pile of towels in the bathroom's sink cabinet. "I'll guard your stuff."

"Oh, great. And how will you respond if Bailey comes in and looks around? Chill her to death?"

"No." Death's voice held exaggerated patience. "I'll tell you."

"Oh." Casey slid off the ball cap and waited.

"What?"

"Can you at least turn around?"

With rolling eyes Death spun toward the wall. "You are so sensitive these days. Are you having body-image issues?"

Casey pulled off her bloody sweatshirt. "I'm not— Never mind. How about you just *pretend* to respect my privacy?"

"Whatever. Maybe I'll just go see what your little friend is doing, instead."

"Fine."

"*Fine.*"

Casey watched Death walk through the closed bathroom door before she stepped into the shower. She stood under the steaming water for a long time, shampooing her hair twice and scrubbing her body roughly with the washcloth. The cut on her shoulder looked a little better than the day before, even with it re-opening after Davey's. The cleaning at the hospital had done wonders.

By the time she was done, her skin felt raw, and after patting it dry she slathered it with the scented body lotion on the counter. She rooted through the cupboard and found a large Band-Aid for her shoulder, and even some of that sticky wrap-around gauze. Finally, she pulled on Bailey's sister's clothes, which fit remarkably well, except for the length in the jeans; she was obviously taller than Casey, so Casey simply rolled up the hems.

"Feel better?" Bailey asked when Casey rejoined her in the kitchen.

"Much. Thank you." Casey put her bag of papers under her chair.

Death was nowhere to be seen.

Bailey stuck a grape in her mouth. "No problem. Heather's clothes fit you all right, huh? Hope you don't mind pink. That's pretty much all she owns."

Pink wasn't, in fact, one of Casey favorites, but she wasn't about to complain. "What can I do with these?" She held out her old clothes.

Bailey wrinkled her nose. "Burning barrel. Here." She rummaged under the sink and held out a grocery bag, into which Casey stuffed the clothes. "I'll take them out while you're eating."

"It sure smells good in here."

Bailey brightened. "Spaghetti. Sounded good to me, so I hope you like it."

It took a few minutes for Bailey to finish cooking, so Casey picked up the newspaper, which sat on the counter. Nothing on the front page about the accident or Wainwrights' Scrap Metal, but page three held a little of both. *Investigators Unsure of Accident's Cause*, one article said, and explained that it was a mystery as to why the construction vehicles were on the road. It described Casey's appearance and reiterated that she was wanted for questioning, as were a group of men who had been at the accident site.

Yeah, well, good luck finding them, Casey thought. *Or me.*

But there was more.

"It was so strange," Bethany Briggs said to reporters at the crash site. "I stopped to help, and the woman had a man in a headlock. She let go when I arrived, and pushed him out of the way. I don't know what she was doing, but I guess she was in shock. I mean, why else would she be wrestling with someone right after being in an accident?"

Casey rubbed a hand across her eyes. She'd forgotten about her Good Samaritan in the bright red suit, and hoped she wasn't going to become a problem. There wasn't anything more from Ms. Briggs in the piece; just the usual stuff about law enforcement keeping the public up-to-date.

She looked at the next article.

Junk Yard Trespassers Surprised

When David Wainwright, owner of Wainwright Scrap Metal and Recycling, heard his dog barking, he didn't think much of it until he saw the men on his property. "They just showed up," he said. "I don't know what they were doing there."

Wainwright and Wendell Harmon, a mechanic visiting the office, looked outside in time to see the two men confronted by a third, who immediately attacked the other two.

"He just went crazy," Harmon said. "We couldn't hear anything they were saying, and we weren't about to go outside. Instead, we called 911."

Wainwright, Harmon, and Rachel Ins-
keep, the scrap yard's secretary, watched
from safety as the third man incapaci-
tated the other two.

"As soon as we heard sirens," Harmon
said, "the man took off."

The two men, whose names are yet to
be released, were taken to the local
hospital, where they remain under a
physician's care. Police are waiting to
question them further.

Casey set down the paper. The men and Rachel had completely covered for her.

"*Ta da!*" Bailey set a steaming bowl of pasta on the table,
dumped a bag of salad into a bowl, sliced some bread, and set
out the grapes. While Casey filled her plate, Bailey took the bag
of clothes outside. Casey dove into the food, pushing aside her
anxiety. Bailey soon came back and ate her share, as well.

When they were done, Bailey put away the leftovers while
Casey placed the dirty dishes in the high-efficiency dishwasher.
Bailey wiped the table and threw the dishrag into the sink.

"Ask for a tour." Death's breath was cold in Casey's ear. "You'll
find something interesting.

Casey raised her eyebrows and mouthed, *what is it?*

"Ask," Death said.

"So," Casey said. "Any chance I could get a tour?"

Bailey shrugged. "Sure."

She took Casey through the sunroom, the den, the living
room, the rec room, the master bedroom and bath—which
were large enough to comfortably serve an entire family—and
the entertainment room, which housed an enormous flat-screen
TV and surround sound. In each room Casey looked to Death,
who hung back with crossed arms, head shaking "no." Finally,
they stood in front of a closed wooden door, and Death's face
became more animated.

"Dad's office," Bailey said, and swung open the door.

Casey gasped. All of those corner offices shown in movies or talked about in business circles, had nothing on this place. Bookshelves lined what walls weren't taken up by floor-to-ceiling windows looking out on miles of golden grain. Thick carpet lay under Casey's stockinged feet, and colorful artwork dotted the room—paintings, sculptures, even a quilt over the back of an antique sofa. A fireplace with dark red brick sat cold and clean along the far side of the room, with two comfortable—and beautiful—chairs in front of it.

"Does your father spend a lot of time in here?"

"Not most of the year. During the winter he'll use it, but the rest of the time he's too busy. He doesn't believe in hiring other people to do work he can do himself."

Casey wandered to a table that displayed an array of photographs and thought of Evan's family picture, which she'd transferred from her old clothes to the pocket of the jeans she was now wearing. On the table were pictures of Bailey's family throughout the years—as evidenced by Bailey's changing form and style, as well as her sister's—photos of dogs, and one of Bailey's father with another man, standing beside a tractor.

"My grandpa," Bailey said. "Dad took over the farm from him. He died a few years ago."

Casey didn't hear the sadness she would acquaint with losing a grandparent, and Bailey's face showed nothing. "You weren't close to him?"

Bailey shrugged. "He worked all the time. I didn't see him much. Kinda like Mom and Dad."

"Who's this?" Casey pointed to a photo of Bailey's dad with a group of men, sitting around a table at a restaurant.

"Dad's friends. Other farmers. Dad's known them forever. That picture was taken ages ago, like, five years."

Casey took a closer look, then sent a shocked glance toward Death, who sat smugly with a hip hitched up on the big desk. Sitting just two chairs away from Bailey's dad in the photo was one of the men from Evan's pack of pictures.

Chapter Eight

Casey did her best not to react to the image. She wracked her brain, trying to remember which of Evan's pictures the guy was in. He wasn't from the group of men at the car crash, she was pretty sure of that. He was one of the people photographed talking to Owen Dixon and Randy Westing. Casey itched to retrieve her bag from the kitchen.

"So," she said, keeping her voice casual. "Are all of these men grain farmers, like your dad?"

"Sure, mostly. Some of them have beef cattle, too, but it's mostly crops, as far as I know. So, what do you want to do now? I don't suppose you'd want to, like, watch a movie or something?"

"No, thanks, I... Any chance I could use a computer?"

Bailey knocked herself on the forehead. "Of course. Duh. You probably have people to e-mail."

"I just want to look up a few things."

Bailey glanced at her father's desk. "Not in here. Dad's pretty... his computer's the one thing he doesn't want us messing with."

Which of course made Casey want to mess with it.

Bailey led Casey back up to her room—with a pit stop in the kitchen, where Casey retrieved her bag—and pulled a laptop from a bookbag. She cleared off a spot on her desk and set the computer on it. "We've got wireless, so you can go on-line from anywhere in the house, but you might as well just sit here."

"Thanks, Bailey."

"Sure." Bailey dropped onto her bed, where she lay on her stomach and kicked her feet.

Casey hesitated. She couldn't exactly do her research with the girl sitting three feet away, so she took a little time to look around the room. Posters of rock stars competed with Edward Cullen and the other vampires from the Twilight series, and a full array of glow-in-the-dark stars adorned the ceiling. The bedspread and curtains had been hand-sewn out of black velvet, and the walls were a textured gray. The furniture, including the desk and headboard, had been painted black with globs of shining glitter, and the carpet was full-out gray and black shag. Casey had to give it to the girl—despite the dark color scheme and the immense amount of *stuff*, the room felt…comfortable.

Bailey pulled her phone from her pocket and rolled over on her back. Her fingers flew over the keypad. Casey angled the laptop away from the girl and punched in Davey—*David*—Wainwright's name, finding his home address and phone number, as well as the scrapyard's.

"Scratch paper?" she asked Bailey.

Bailey stretched to pull out a drawer on the desk. "There. Take all you want."

Casey raised her eyebrows at the stack of paper.

"I make lots of mistakes," Bailey said.

Casey grabbed a page and scribbled Davey's information. Wendell's numbers were easy to find, as well, and she wrote them down.

Bailey sat up. "Find something?"

Casey clicked out of that site, back to the search engine, and covered the paper with her hand. "Nothing much."

"You don't want me to see. All right. I get it." Her lower lip stuck out, and she looked around the room. "Well, I'm gonna go watch a movie, then. I might as well enjoy my day off. Get me if you need anything, all right?" She left the room, and Casey took a breath of relief.

"Good job," Death said from the bed. "Now you've ticked off your only friend."

"Not my *only* friend."

"The only one with a car."

Casey turned to the computer and typed in a name. Death pulled out the rubber band and began twanging.

Randy Westing. The search came up with nothing relevant—a musician with a slightly different last name, a film reviewer who obviously wasn't Casey's guy, plus about a million other hits that separated the two names, giving lots of *Randys* and *Westings.*

Owen Dixon. Casey laughed to herself. Lots of information for a *Sir* Owen Dixon, from Australia, popped up. Even *more* obviously not her man.

So these guys either had false names or they'd miraculously avoided appearing on the Internet. Or they just hadn't done anything interesting enough that anybody had noticed.

Casey opened her bag and pulled out Evan's notebook, paging to the place where he'd listed the truckers' names. She punched in the first.

John Simones. Casey sighed. Hundreds of thousands of hits, with more John Simones than she'd bargained for, as well as multiple listings for men named John Simone and John Simons. She went back to the search box and added Evan's note: *UK 2008.* This didn't help one bit.

She went through the rest of the names, including the ones on the manifests, but didn't hit on anything until she came to the name Mick Halveston—the male half of the couple seated across from Westing and Dixon at the diner. Halfway through the listed sites was an article about a truck accident in Missouri. Seems Mick had passed out while driving and run his truck up the side of an embankment, overturning and smashing a passenger car containing a family of five. The children and mother had died at the scene, the father at the hospital later that day.

"I remember that one," Death said over Casey's shoulder. "Not a fun job at all."

"What happened?"

"You don't want to know the details."

"No, I mean to the trucker. Why did he pass out?"

Death shrugged. "He didn't die, so I don't know. Want me to ask?" Death pointed toward the ceiling.

"Would you get an answer?"

"Probably not. I'd be told it wasn't in my *need to know* file."

Casey closed her eyes, frustration building in her chest. Of all the things to get mixed up in, did she *have* to find something involving the death of children in a vehicular accident?

"What's wrong?" Bailey stood in the doorway.

Casey jerked her head up and clicked out of the screen with the article. "Nothing. I'm fine."

Bailey's mouth pinched. "You don't look fine."

"Still tired, I guess."

Bailey obviously didn't believe her, but let it go. "I brought you a drink. Lemonade."

"Thank you." Casey took the glass and stopped Bailey on her way back out the door. "Those men in that photo with your dad, the other farmers? Do you know their names?"

"Most of them, why?"

"I thought I recognized one."

Bailey hesitated. "I thought you weren't from around here."

"I'm not."

Bailey studied her some more before turning and walking out of the room. Casey followed. Death stayed on the bed, twanging.

When they got to the photo, Bailey picked it up. "Which guy?"

Casey pointed at the familiar one.

"Oh. That's Pat Parnell. I've known him forever. He's from somewhere around Wichita. My dad's roommate in college. For a year anyway, and then he dropped out. Are you from out east?"

Casey shook her head. "Is he just a farmer?"

Bailey bristled. "That's not enough?"

"I don't mean that. I mean, does he have another job, that I might know him from?"

"Oh." She shrugged. "I don't know. I could ask Dad."

"No. He'd wonder why you were asking."

"Maybe. But I can lie pretty well."

Casey already knew that. "Okay, if you could find out, that would be great."

Bailey brightened. "Anything else?"

"Actually, yes. Can I use your phone? Unless you want me to use the landline."

"We don't have a landline." Bailey reached into her pocket. "Use it all you want. I've got unlimited minutes. Calls or texting."

Casey took the phone and went back to Bailey's room, where she shut the door. She punched in Davey's work number, waving at Death to stop with the rubber band. Death sighed heavily and twisted the band around a finger.

"Wainwright's Scrap Yard."

"Davey?"

"You got him."

"It's…Casey."

He let out a whoosh of air. "Oh, thank God. You're all right?"

"I'm fine. Are they still there?"

"No, they're at the hospital."

"The cops, I mean, not the men."

"Oh." He laughed. "I guess that would be strange if they were still lying there. No, the cops are gone. Followed the guys to the ER."

"Have you heard anything?"

"Just that they're awake now, and they're going to be all right. Except for the guy's knee. He's going to have to have some major work on that."

Casey winced. She wished—

"I can't really file any charges," Davey said, "since they *attacked each other*, so I'm pretty much out of the loop."

"Yeah, as for that police report…"

"No problem."

Casey rubbed her forehead. "I'm sorry about yesterday, about bringing that on you."

"Wasn't your fault."

"If it hadn't been for me—"

"They would've come anyway. It wasn't you they were after, remember."

Of course they were. They thought she knew about Evan's stash. But they didn't know she'd be at the scrap yard. They didn't know *where* she was. At *that* moment, yesterday, they'd been after the truck.

"In fact," Davey said, "if you hadn't been here, who knows what woulda happened, so I should be thanking you."

"How's Trixie?"

"She'll be okay. She got some broken ribs, so she's on pain-killers, lying here in the office."

"I'm glad she'll be all right."

The phone hissed in her ear.

"Well," Casey said, "I just wanted to thank you for telling the cops what you did. I appreciate that you didn't pull me into it."

"Glad to do it." He paused. "I do need to tell you, though…"

"What?"

"I'm getting rid of the truck. Don't want those guys coming back."

"Good. Make a big production of it, so they know it's gone."

"Don't worry."

She would, anyway. "Well, thanks again, Davey."

"Wait."

Casey waited.

"What about the papers and stuff? I want to help."

"Davey…"

"I can take care of myself. What can I do?"

Casey looked at Evan's manifests and photos. "Well, I need somebody that knows trucks and can help me…us…figure out what these papers mean."

He paused. "I got someone… Let me call him, and see if he's free."

"Davey, it's got to be somebody you trust."

He laughed. "He's my son-in-law, so I've trusted him with more than papers."

"Okay. You going to call me back?"

"Yup. This number? Where are you, anyway?"

"I'm safe. Thanks, Davey." She hung up.

"So, who's the guy in the photo?" Death picked up the rubber band again, and Casey snatched it away.

"Will you *stop* already?"

Death pouted. "The guy?"

"Old college friend of Bailey's dad." She dug through her notes, finding the photo of Pat Parnell. It was the picture where Blond Guy—Owen Dixon—was handing the trucker a package. But was Pat Parnell a trucker? Bailey seemed to think he was a farmer. Casey supposed he could be both.

The computer went into screensaver mode, with photos of Bailey and her friends moving in a slide show on the screen. Casey watched several slides of the kids she'd met the night before then sat up, her finger hovering over the keyboard.

"Uh-oh," Death said. "What are you doing?"

"There would be newspaper articles."

"Yeah, you already saw them. Davey and Wendell covered for you big time."

"Not about *that*. About…two days ago."

"Oh, boy. Huh-uh. Don't go there."

"But there's got to be something saying what's happening in Clymer." Her finger dropped, and the slide show evaporated. Casey clicked in the search engine box and wrote "Clymer, Ohio," and the date.

"This is a mistake," Death said.

Factory Closed for Good After Conspiracy Uncovered the headline screamed. Also in the "hit" list were, Curtains for Local Theater After Death of Cast Member, and Woman Wanted In Connection With Murders.

"That would be you," Death said helpfully.

The phone vibrated on the bed, where Casey had set it. The number displayed was Davey's. She answered, comforted that while he had this number, he at least wouldn't have Bailey's name displayed on his phone, since she wouldn't be in his contact list.

"Supper," Davey said. "Six-o'clock."

"Davey—"

"Where should I pick you up?"

"Where are we eating?"

"My daughter's place. She won't mind an extra mouth or two. She's already got five kids."

"No, Davey."

"No?" He sounded hurt.

"I won't go to your daughter's house. I'm not putting her or your grandchildren in danger." Plus that would be six more people who could identify Casey should cops—or anyone else—come calling. "Someplace else, Davey. Someplace we won't be seen by a lot of people."

"Well, I guess we could just meet at Tom's work."

"*People*, Davey."

"If we meet late enough, no one will be there. Or not many, anyway, and Tom has his own entrance. You won't have to see anybody but him."

"Okay. What's the business called?"

"Southwest Trucking. Tom's a co-owner."

"Great. Can we go later in the evening, to be sure people are gone?"

He hesitated. "After supper, then, I guess. Seven-thirty? That way Tom could still get home to help with bedtime."

"Sounds good. I'll meet you there."

"Can't I—"

"See you at seven-thirty, Davey. Thanks." She hung up and the phone buzzed, showing her a text message that had come while she was talking. Sheryl Crovitch. Great. The girl who wanted Casey to take a hike.

> *I cant blv u tuk hr 2 ur hous*
> *r u TRYNG 2 get in trble?*

Casey clenched her teeth. Bailey had said she'd told the whole group. Could they *possibly* keep it a secret?

The door flew open. "Casey, we have to go." Bailey's cool composure was gone, replaced by a manic look. "My dad's home, and if he catches me here I am *so* dead."

Chapter Nine

The last thing Casey wanted to do was get Bailey in even deeper trouble, but even more she didn't want Casey's dad to see *her.* "Suggestions?"

Bailey grabbed Casey's wrist and dragged her toward the door. "Dad drove the grain truck out to the barn and went in there. If we can get to the garage and out the lane while he's unloading we might escape."

"Bailey, he's sure to see—"

"It's our only chance."

Casey got free from Bailey's grasp long enough to shove her papers into the bag, put on her shoes, and delete the Clymer search from the computer before following the girl through the house, taking her place in the passenger legwell while Bailey started the car and prepared to back out.

"Bailey!" Casey said.

Bailey turned frightened eyes on her.

"The garage door."

"Oh." Bailey punched the button and the door slid up. *"Please don't let him see us, please don't let him see us."*

"But won't he *hear* us?"

Bailey shook her head sharply. "Not while the auger's going. You can't hear anything with that on."

As soon as they'd cleared the door Bailey was pushing the button again, and driving carefully down the lane. "I can make something up. I'm good at that, right? It's not like this would be the first time. I forgot some homework. I needed money. *I felt sick at school.* That would be a good one. It would go along with what my mom said when she called the school this morning."

"She didn't call the school."

"Well, *technically…*"

The car spun around a corner, and picked up speed.

"Okay," Bailey said. "You can get up now."

Casey climbed into the seat and strapped herself in.

"So now what?" Bailey glanced at the dashboard clock, her posture already relaxing, the farther they got from her home. "School will be out in an hour and a half and I'll need to go home. Without you. Where would you like to go until then? Back to the shed? It's so boring there."

Casey considered. Downtown was too small. If she went to the library or Wendell's gas station, she was sure to be noticed. Even if they didn't equate her with the woman from the accident she would be recognized as somebody new, and it would inevitably get back to the wrong people.

What she *really* wanted to do was impossible. Those two men she'd beat up were just lying there in the hospital, with all kinds of answers she'd like to hear. But even if there weren't cops waiting outside the doors, there would be nurses and doctors and nutritionists, and who knew who else. Besides, the men were bound to freak out if she showed up, and rip out their IVs and whatever other contraptions they were hooked up to. Not that the guy with the bad knee would be going anywhere.

"I guess the shed is it for now. I have an appointment this evening, so I'll just wait for that."

"An appointment? With who?"

Casey shook her head. "Nobody you need to know about."

Bailey opened her mouth, then shut it with a huff, glaring out the windshield.

Casey sighed. "If you could find out from your dad about his friend Pat and whether he has another job, that would be really helpful."

Bailey relaxed a bit. "I'll try. Except if he saw us just now I will be so grounded."

"Thank you."

They were quiet for a couple miles, and Bailey's phone buzzed in Casey's hand, where she still clenched it. She held it up. "Want me to answer?"

"What does it say?"

Casey grimaced. "I forgot to tell you Sheryl texted just before we left your house."

"Oh, great. Did you read it?"

"She was yelling at you for taking me to your house and wondering if you wanted to get in trouble."

"And this one?"

Casey glanced down. "It's from Martin."

I got thm Wil brng 2 shed 2nite

Casey looked up. "Got what?"

"Surprise for you."

"More cinnamon rolls?"

"That would be Terry, not Martin."

"Oh. Right."

"There's this girl that likes Martin, which is so annoying because she only started being interested this year, once he started growing his hair out and got control of his acne, while I've been around all this—" She stopped and glanced at Casey. "Not that *I* like Martin or anything. I mean, he's a nice guy, and he has his charms, and –

"Bailey. I liked Martin, too."

Bailey stopped talking and gave a little giggle. "Sorry. Anyway, this girl, her *mom* works for the police department. Their receptionist."

Casey tried to see where this was heading. "And?"

"And…Martin got copies of the report from your accident."

"What?" How had he known who she was? And why would this police department have access to an accident that had taken place almost two years earlier? Casey hadn't said anything about Reuben or Omar, or… "How did he know about it?"

Bailey blinked. "Um, you *told* us? It was in the paper? The trucker *died*."

Casey closed her eyes, trying to catch her breath and come back to the present time, and this accident. "Right. I'm…I'm sorry…I…" She shook her head. "What I meant was, how did Martin get the reports?"

Bailey grinned. "I told you, the lady's daughter's hot for Martin."

"But won't the girl—"

"Pay for it? Probably, at least a little. You want me to tell Martin to forget it?"

Casey clenched her teeth. "No."

"Fine, then. Let me write back."

"How 'bout you just tell me what to say?"

Bailey shrugged. "Whatever. Just tell him that's great. And thanks."

Casey keyed in the message and sent it off, and took the opportunity, while Bailey thought she was still texting, to delete the records of her call to Davey and his call back to her, getting his number off Bailey's phone. By the time she'd finished, Martin had sent a reply.

Hi KC hope u r ok c u 2nite

Casey sighed. "He knew it was me."

"Of course. You probably spelled everything wrong."

Casey laughed, and Bailey smiled, her teeth brilliant white between her dark lips. Casey stared at her, at her black-lined eyes, dark fingernails, and dyed hair. So different from the earlier family pictures on her father's office table. In fact, Casey didn't think she'd even recognize her if she took off all of her artificial coloring.

Bailey glanced at her. "What?"

"I think I do have something you can help me with. Any chance you'd lend me a few bucks?"

Chapter Ten

It took Bailey longer in the Family Dollar than Casey had foreseen. They'd driven to the next town, Bailey conscious of the fact that she was supposed to be in school and the clerk at the local pharmacy would be sure to tell *somebody* they'd seen her there. Bailey assured Casey that no one in this neighboring store would have the slightest idea who she was. Casey, having to take the girl's word for it, scrounged around in the back seat to find another ball cap, and pulled it low over her face as she sank down in her seat, keeping her eyes averted whenever she heard or saw movement outside the car. Casey had instructed Bailey to park in the far corner of the lot, hoping no one would come close enough they would get noticed.

Bailey finally exited the store. A man going toward the store did a double take, and Casey sucked in a breath. She unlocked the driver's door and Bailey slid in, thrusting the bag at Casey. "See what you think."

"You see that man?" He was just disappearing into the store.

"Yeah, I guess."

"You know him?"

"Don't think so. Why?"

"He sure noticed you."

"I'm telling you, Casey, no one in this town knows me. *Maybe* he just thought I was *pretty*."

Casey couldn't tell if this was a challenge or a plea for affirmation. "Of course he did." *Or* he wasn't used to seeing Gothish girls at their small town store. "I was just worried about you being recognized."

Bailey pulled the car out of the parking lot. "So, how did I do?"

Casey peered into the bag. "I don't think I had this many things on the list."

"Of course you didn't. But you obviously don't know the first thing about make-up."

She had, at one point. She could actually clean up pretty well. Reuben had always liked those nights when she would put on something other than her *dobak* or the yoga pants that were so comfortable for playing on the floor with Omar. Not that Omar could play much, at his age. He was at the point, though, that Casey spent a lot of time on the carpet, trying to convince him it was time to roll from his tummy to his back. But every once in a while the comfy clothes would come off, the dress and heels would go on, and Omar would have an overnight with Grandma. Casey could still see Reuben's eyes as he took her in, him looking handsome in his suit, his Mexican heritage showing in his dark skin and glossy black hair. He would take her in his arms, telling her they only had to play nice with his colleagues for a few hours and then they could come back home, and he would be happy to take her back out of that dress and heels…

Casey looked out the passenger window at the passing buildings, not wanting Bailey to see whatever was showing in her face. Those days with Reuben were long, *long* gone.

"Sorry," Bailey said. "I didn't mean anything by it. I'm sure you look pretty when you try."

Casey gave a little laugh. "Thanks. I think."

Bailey whapped herself on the forehead. "I'll shut up now."

Casey let herself be brought back to the car, and to the bag of make-up on her lap. She pulled out the hair color. "So, you think I can do this myself?"

Bailey wrinkled her nose. "I guess. It won't look professional."

"Good enough to fool a man?"

"Probably. But a woman would notice in a second."

"I guess I'll just have to chance it." Casey pulled out the other things, one by one. Lipstick, foundation… "Reading glasses?"

"Yeah, you didn't mention those, but they'll add years to your looks. You'll look ancient."

"Great. So when you see the transformation you'll run screaming."

"You know it."

Casey found the receipt in the bag and blanched at the total. Bailey had really outdone herself. "I'll pay you back."

"Oh, I'm not worried. This is the most exciting thing that's happened since Terry's dad discovered a recipe for chocolate bagels."

"Chocolate… But, Bailey, *two* sets of scrubs?"

"I couldn't decide, since you won't tell me what you're doing." She looked at Casey accusingly. "So I had to think…cats, or plain blue. On the one hand, the cats are cute, but maybe not the look you're going for, if you're not going to be around kids. On the other hand, the plain blue might make you look like some sort of surgical assistant, and I wasn't sure you wanted that. So, you know, if you'd give me more *information*, I wouldn't have had to buy more than one. So I'm *sorry*."

"No, *I'm* sorry. I'm asking a lot of you."

Bailey sulked for a few more seconds before breaking into a grin. "Like I really care, one way or the other. I'm having fun. Usually that just happens at night with the other kids. They're going to totally want to hear all about this."

"Yeah, Bailey, about tonight…"

"And really, don't worry about Sheryl. She's okay, normally."

"I hope so. Otherwise I don't know how you deal with her."

"She's had a hard time lately. Her dad lost his job a month ago, because he has Parkinson's and the company was afraid it would affect his work."

"Can they do that?"

"They did. And Sheryl's family doesn't have the money to hire a lawyer."

"So they're stressed."

"Not only that, but her folks announced last week that they're *moving*."

"And Sheryl doesn't want to move?"

Bailey gave her an astonished look. "Are you serious? Sheryl grew up here, with the rest of us. She's a junior. She doesn't want to go anywhere *now*."

"Where are they going?"

"Kansas City. That's where her mom is from, and they're going to live with her grandparents until her folks figure out what to do."

Casey felt sorry for Sheryl. Her parents, too. She knew what it felt like to be separated from all you hold dear. She hadn't seen her mom or brother in close to a year now, and she hated it. The house she'd shared with Reuben and Omar was on the market, and she hadn't stepped foot in her *dojang* in forever. Before, with only Pegasus after her, at least she could go home without landing in jail. Now…

"I invited Sher to come live with us, but her parents didn't think that was a good idea. I don't know why not."

Casey smiled. "Because they'd *miss* her."

"Oh. I hadn't thought of that. Huh. But anyway there's this private school they said they might send her to—there are scholarships, you know—but the only way they'll even apply is if she stops getting in trouble." She sighed. "Ever since they told Sheryl last month, she's been doing stupid things. Cheated on a test, snuck out at night—"

"But don't you *all* sneak out at night?"

"—stole some lipstick from the drugstore. She's a mess. So that's why she doesn't want to call the cops on you—she's been seeing them way to much these days."

They were nearing the shed, and Bailey held up her hand. "Anything around?"

"Nothing but corn and soybeans. And dust."

"Like I said, you know, about the excitement?"

Bailey stopped the car beside the shed and Casey opened the passenger door. "You coming in?"

"Wish I could, but that trip to the store ate up all my time for the school day. I have to get home."

"And if your dad saw you driving away earlier?"

"I've got all kinds of stories."

"Good, I hope he believes you." Casey opened her mouth to say something else, then shook her head. So now she was advocating kids lying to their parents. Some role model she was. Hitting up kids for money, using their phones and erasing messages, beating up strangers, then preparing to harass them as they lay in their hospital beds…

"You sure you won't let me help?" Bailey looked at her pleadingly. "I'm afraid of what you're going to do."

"I'll be fine. I'm going to safe places." At least, they were safe for everyone else, unless she took it into her head to maim them.

"I didn't mean that," Bailey said. "I meant with the hair color."

"Oh." Casey smiled. "I do think I'll survive that."

"Yeah, but I'm not sure your hair will."

Casey got out of the car and leaned back in, clutching her bags. "Thanks for everything, Bailey. If I don't see you, I'll send you the money to pay you back."

Bailey lunged across the seat, grabbing for Casey's arm, but was jerked back by her seat belt. "What do you mean if you don't see me? You're coming back to the shed tonight. I'm going to get that info for you about Pat."

Casey turned to look out at the fields. "That's what I wanted to tell you. I'll see how things go, okay?"

"You *promised.*"

"I did?" She did?

"You said you would let me see how you look. And I said I wouldn't run screaming. Remember?"

Was that a promise?

"I'll try, Bailey, okay? It's the most I can say."

Bailey's lips pinched together. "Fine. That's the last I'll be helping *you.*"

She gunned the engine and looked back over the seat. Casey jumped out from the door and slammed it shut, watching as

Bailey speed-reversed down the lane to the road, where she skidded into the gravel, sending up a plume of dust.

"Way to go," Death said, standing beside her and coughing as the dust blew their way. "You sure know how to make friends and influence people. It's a talent you have."

Casey glared at Death and went into the shed, where someone else was waiting for her.

Chapter Eleven

"Terry?" It was the pudgy one.

He got up from the five-gallon bucket, where he'd been sitting. His bike leaned against the wall in the corner, with his overloaded backpack on the floor beside it. He cleared his throat. "Is she gone?"

"You heard the gravel flying."

"What's she mad about this time?"

"She's mad a lot?"

"All the time. But she gets over it quick." He stuck his hands in his pockets, then took them out again. His eyes flicked to the right and left, not looking directly at Casey, and not seeing Death lounging against the doorway.

"What is it, Terry?"

"Nothing. I just…"

Casey overturned a bucket and sat on it. "How did you get here so quickly? Didn't school just let out?"

"I've got study hall last period. They don't care if we stay or not. At least, they don't say anything."

"And you decided to come see me. By yourself?"

Terry shuffled his feet, then sat down across from her. "I didn't want the others to know I was coming." He glanced up, meeting her eyes briefly.

Casey waited.

"It's…Sheryl."

Ah. Yet another kid worried about Sheryl. "What about her? Other than the fact that she doesn't like me?"

"It's not *you*."

"Could've fooled me. She was ready to turn me in last night."

"Not really. It was a show."

"For what?" Or for *whom*?

"She just…it's any adults. She doesn't trust them."

"And you do?"

He made a face. "My parents are…well…lame, I guess, but they're not bad."

"And hers are?"

"I didn't say it was her parents."

"You didn't have to. You went right from 'adults' to 'parents.' Sheryl's folks must be the problem."

Terry closed his eyes. "I didn't mean… Look, it would be a lot better for Sheryl if you would just…leave. Okay? She doesn't need anything else right now. She's having a hard time."

"Oh, *spare* me." Death made a gagging motion. "This poor sap is so far gone I want to puke. Pathetic."

Casey studied the boy's face. Death was right. Casey didn't figure the whole being in love thing was reciprocated, from what she'd seen the night before, but Sheryl did seem to at least be the kid's friend. "Terry, I don't want to make things worse for anybody, believe me. But I've got a few things to do before I take off. Sheryl doesn't need to come anywhere near me. She can pretend I don't exist, okay? And I'll be gone before she knows it."

Terry put his elbows on his knees and clasped his hands together. "What can I do?"

"To help me?"

"No. To get you to leave. Is it money you want? Other clothes?" He looked at her pink shirt.

"I told you. I have things to do."

"We can stop you." His look of determination turned his baby face into something different. Older.

Casey looked straight into his eyes. "Look, Terry. The quicker I get my business done, the quicker I'll go. Getting in my way is only going to make things harder. Just…let me do what I need to, and I'll leave you—and Sheryl—alone, forever. Ask Bailey. I told her the same thing."

"Which is why she was mad."

"How do you know that?"

"Because she likes you. She's not going to want you to leave."

"Then Bailey is going to be disappointed."

Something in Terry's face changed. He *liked* the idea of Bailey not getting what she wanted. And of Casey leaving.

Casey stood. "I think you should go now."

"But…I want to help."

"Sure. Great."

"Really. If helping you will make you go away, then that's what I'll do." His face reverted to its usual softness. "Just don't tell Sheryl, okay? Or Bailey."

Casey looked at Death, who had pulled out a new rubber band and was twanging it. "I won't tell. And I'll let you know if I think of something."

Terry had to accept this. He got his bike and wheeled it to the door. "I guess I'll see you tonight."

"What are you bringing?"

He shrugged. "It might just be store-bought cookies this time. I have to go home and take a nap."

"I wondered when you guys slept."

"I tell my folks school wears me out. They believe me."

Or they pretended to and worried secretly about what their son was doing that they didn't know about.

Casey followed him outside. "See you then."

"You won't say anything about—"

"You were never here."

Casey and Death watched as Terry rode away, heading back toward town.

"That boy's in for a lot of heartache," Death said. The rubber band was silent now.

"They all are," Casey said. "It's part of growing up. The sad part is, it will probably never go away."

Chapter Twelve

"I don't know," Death said, head cocked. "I think I liked you better as a brunette."

Casey peered into the little mirror Bailey had bought. Her hair now matched the black velvet curtains in Bailey's room. It couldn't be any darker. Underneath it, her face looked like ivory. Or like she spent her days in a coffin. "It's not permanent. I hope."

"Try the lipstick."

Casey pulled out the tube. "At least she found me a real color for this. Not black, like she wears."

"It's cute on her."

"Yeah, you would think so." She colored her lips, and rubbed them together. "Not too bad."

Death considered it. "A little light for you, but it goes with the pink shirt."

"I'm not going to be *wearing* the pink shirt."

"Right. Blue scrubs. Very attractive."

Casey clenched her jaw. "I'm not *trying* to be attractive. I'm trying to be *different.*"

"You know they're going to recognize you anyway."

"Thanks for the optimism."

"Hey, think about who you're talking to."

Casey looked at the rest of the cosmetics in the bag. "To be continued."

"Aw, you're not going to finish?"

She wiped the lipstick off with a tissue—also provided by Bailey, who obviously spent a lot of time with make-up. "Davey and his son-in-law don't need to see the new me. The less people who do, the better."

"They're going to see the hair."

Casey grabbed the cap she'd put on in Bailey's car and jammed it on her head, shoving all of her hair up into it. "Better?"

"Some. You've still got the little stringy ones at your neck."

"They're not going to be thinking about my hair. They're men."

"True."

Casey grabbed the bag with Evan's papers. "So, are you coming?"

"You're walking?"

"How else am I going to get there?"

Death huffed. "You should've asked Bailey for a bike."

"Yeah, in-between running from her dad and skipping school and taking me to the store, she has lots of time for that."

"I'm just saying…"

Casey made sure there were no people or tractors in sight and slipped out of the shed, starting down the lane.

"You know where you're going?" Death skipped past her, then walked backwards in front of her.

"I called Southwest Trucking and got directions while Bailey was in the Family Dollar.

"So they know we're coming?"

"No, they know some guy named Bob from a paper company is coming."

"Oh." Death stopped, perplexed. "But how did you know a guy named Bob was going?"

Casey angled around Death and kept walking. "He's not! I mean, I made him up. What is *wrong* with you? Are you going senile?"

Death caught up with her. "I don't think so. But it has been ages since I've taken a vacation."

Casey gasped and clasped her hands together. "Well, then, don't you think now would be the perfect time? Go! Vacate!"

Death made a face. "You are so weird."

When they got to the road, Casey turned east. "I'm wondering. Do I show Davey's son-in-law everything?"

"If you want complete answers I would think you'd have to."

"Yeah. I just don't want to—"

"—get him in trouble? Casey, darling, you have got to stop worrying about that, or you're never going to get anywhere in life."

"I'm just trying to—"

"—be thoughtful?" Death gave a raspberry. "Do you think these people have no brains of their own? They want to help, and you're making it awfully difficult."

"I just—"

"You *just*, you *just*, you *just*… You're as pathetic as that fat boy."

"Am not."

"Are t—"

"Stop." Casey held up her hand. "I'm not playing that game with you. Now shut up and let me think."

Thinking didn't help. Instead of coming up with a solution, she was fighting off the image of Evan in his last moments, the sickening feeling of jackknifing, and the realization that she was penniless in the middle of a state where she had no connections that hadn't been made within the last twenty-four hours.

They'd walked almost a mile further when Death pulled out a mandolin and started singing.

> *How many roads can Casey walk down*
> *before she knows she's alive?*
> *How many kids can offer a ride*
> *Before she remembers how to drive?*
> *How many truckers will die in her arms*
> *Before she's forever—*

"Aah!" Casey wrenched the mandolin from Death, a. disintegrated in her hands. "You are so...so..."

"Talented?"

"You call that talent? Terrible rhymes and bad rhythm? Wha was going to be the last word, anyhow? Before I'm forever what? Five?"

Death sulked. "I hadn't gotten there yet."

Casey gave a scream of frustration before setting off in a jog.

"Well, if you're going to be *that* way about it," Death called after her, "maybe I *won't* come along!"

Casey was a mile down the road before she stopped and bent over, her hands on her knees. She had to keep going. She couldn't stop now. She was going to be late for her appointment.

But the sun was warm on her back, the sky was a clear blue, and all she could hear was an airplane, so high in the sky it couldn't possibly see her.

She stayed, chest heaving, and allowed her tears to fall onto the dusty road.

Chapter Thirteen

Davey was waiting for her in his pickup at the front of the parking lot, his head resting against the back of the driver's seat. Talk radio leaked from the cab, and Casey wondered which annoying host he was listening to, and if he agreed with anything that was being said.

The parking lot was well-lit, and Davey's truck was the only vehicle in sight. The closest neighboring business was on the other side of a chain link fence, with a parking lot that was just as deserted. On the other side of the building sat a thick grove of trees. Casey waited, listening, but could hear nothing other than Davey's radio, distant traffic, and the quiet hum of the building's air conditioner.

She walked in the gate and up to Davey's truck, tapping on the driver's side window. He jumped and put a hand to his chest.

"Sorry," Casey said as he climbed down from the cab. "Didn't mean to scare you."

"S'okay." He looked her up and down. "You're looking better, I gotta say. You do something to your hair?"

Casey looked around, but Death was not there to smirk. "Just washed up. You ready?"

"Sure. Tom's entrance is over here. He's expecting us."

An old but clean white Silverado was parked in the spot next to Tom's door, on the same side as the grove of trees. Davey knocked, and the door was opened by a man about Casey's age. He wore wrinkled khakis and a light-blue button-down shirt with the collar open, and his hair had lost whatever neat part it might've once had. His brown loafers were scuffed, but serviceable, and his glasses sat slightly crooked on his Roman nose. He shook Casey's hand. "Tom Haab. Nice to meet you."

Casey liked his handshake, and immediately felt more confident about talking with him. "Casey Jones. Thanks for coming out again after supper."

"Glad to help. Better make it quick, though. Davey's daughter needs help with the kids at bedtime."

Davey grunted.

Tom led Casey to an empty table. "So what do we have?"

She pulled the papers from her bag and set them down in chronological order. "I've also got a journal that Evan—the trucker who died—was keeping, and this stack of papers. Can you take a look and see if any of this makes sense to you?"

Tom pulled up a chair and scanned the top papers. "These are truck manifests from a company called Class A Trucking. You can see the logo here." He pointed to one of the photos, where Casey could just make out the edge of something that looked like a tire on the cab's door. "It matches some of the paperwork."

Of course. Casey hadn't thought twice about the "Class A" on the papers, because she figured it was a rating of the trucks, or the load, or something. And the sketch of the tire was so generic-looking she'd thought it was standard on this kind of form. Exactly why she needed an expert.

"But some of these manifests are different. They don't have a company logo. These trucks are driven by independent operators." He squinted at the photos, holding some of them next to each other. "But look—this is the same truck, only on this photo it's got the Class A logo, and this one it doesn't. Must be a magnet, or a vinyl patch."

"Why would they do that?"

He shook his head. "Don't know. But it doesn't make much sense. Either you're an indie, or you drive for a company. But see, some of these manifests have Class A listed, and some don't. It's strange."

"Do you know Class A Trucking?"

"Heard of them. They're relatively new, starting in the last couple of years. I don't deal with them directly, because they're in the same business as me, but I've known some folks who have."

"And what is your job, exactly?"

"I'm a broker."

"Which means..."

"I assign drivers to take loads from here to there."

"How, exactly?"

"Okay." He leaned his chair back on two legs. "Say there's a company in, oh, Colorado, all right? They have a truckload of frozen broccoli that needs to get to Texas by Friday. The guy there knows me, so he calls and asks if I've got anybody who can pick it up. I check my truckers, find somebody who's going to be in that area on Wednesday, and assign them to pick it up."

"So you're not driving trucks yourself?"

He laughed. "Heck, no. I could, I've got my CDL—"

"Commercial Driver's License," Davey said.

"—but I don't drive unless I absolutely have to. I'm in the business of giving *other* truckers work. I like to stay home."

"So the truckers work for Southwest Trucking?"

"Not exclusively. They're mostly independent contractors. A few work almost entirely for me, but they'll take the odd job here and there from another broker when it works."

"And you pay them per trip?"

"Yup. Let's say you're a trucker, and I contact you to pick up the load in Colorado. I'll calculate how much fuel it's going to take to drive that load all the way to Texas. Around a thousand dollars, maybe."

"Wow."

"I know. Anyhow, we've also got to calculate payment for the truckers. So we'll say the whole trip is two thousand. The truckers have a grand for fuel, which leaves the other thousand.

I'll take ten percent. So I get a hundred dollars, and the truckers get nine. Make sense?"

"I guess. Doesn't seem like anybody makes much."

"It's not a big money maker. But it's a huge risk for me."

"How so?"

He dropped his chair legs to the ground. "I'm like a bank. I pay the truckers their money up front so they can buy the fuel and make their mortgage or their insurance payment, or whatever, then I wait to get paid by the company in Colorado. Sometimes it takes a month or so for the money to come in."

"So how do you stay afloat? Make a living?"

"Lots of trucks." He grinned. "There's one and a half million on the road at any given time. A portion are doing jobs for me."

"How many?"

"Well, we have access to lots of independent contractors—folks with their own rigs. Sixty to seventy of them, maybe. And a few trucking companies. They'll have thirty to forty drivers we can use. Not all at the same time, of course, but whenever we've got work."

"You said they work for other brokers, too."

"Sure. We have to share drivers sometimes."

"So you're competing with other brokers?"

"I guess. But competing for truckers isn't the problem. It's the customers that could be the sticky part."

"How do you work that out?"

He shrugged. "Sort of an unspoken agreement. You stay away from my customers, I'll stay away from yours."

"And your customers—how do you get them? Advertising? Connections?" Casey waved her hand over Evan's photos. "These trucks are carrying all kinds of stuff—not any one particular thing."

"Customers come from word of mouth, mostly. I just had a guy call me today, said his buddy used Southwest Trucking, and recommended us. It's all about trust, really. A guy in Idaho calls me, I can't exactly see his eyes and shake his hand. Sometimes we use a signed contract, but most of the time..." He held out his hands. "We take people at their word that we'll do the job and they'll pay us."

"Seems…old-fashioned."

He grinned. "You don't trust people?"

Casey looked away. "So what do these pictures show? What do you see?"

"If you don't trust people, how come you're here with Davey? You didn't know him before yesterday. And you met me fifteen minutes ago."

"I know. I guess sometimes you just…" She took a deep breath through her nose and let it out.

Davey tapped one of the photos. "So what do you see, Tom?"

Tom hesitated, but turned to his father-in-law. "Can't tell you right off. Nothing here looks wrong, except maybe this one picture showing this guy handing a package to the other guy. Nothing illegal about that, though, unless whatever's in the package is illegal."

Casey looked at the photo, with Owen Dixon handing Hank Nance an envelope. "What could they be doing?"

"That's crooked?" Tom gave a short laugh. "Any number of things. I haven't heard anything about these folks, so I don't have anything to go on."

"Examples?"

"Smuggling. Stolen goods. Drugs. Illegal Immigrants. Who knows? Unless you can get something on these guys there's no telling *what* they're doing."

Casey went quiet, staring down at the photos. "Do you know any of these truckers?"

Tom scanned their faces. "With all of those one and a half million trucks it would be…wait. This guy." He pointed at the one Bailey's dad had roomed with. "He looks familiar."

"Pat Parnell. He's from around here. Wichita."

"Well, that's probably it, then. More than likely I've dealt with him at some point, but not recently. Just a sec." He went to his desk and typed something into his computer. "Yup. Did some jobs for me several years ago, but dropped off my radar after that."

"What about this guy?" She showed him another one of the pictures. "Name's Mick Halveston. Had a bad accident a while back. Killed a family when his truck flipped under an overpass."

Tom winced. "I remember that. Never worked with him, though. I knew a broker that did."

"He say anything about him?"

"Just that he was glad Halveston wasn't driving for him when the accident happened."

"And the rest of these?"

He punched in Hank Nance, John Simones, and Sandy Greene. Greene had driven for Tom several years ago, but he'd never dealt with either of the other two.

"What about the names on these manifests? We don't have photos of these guys. Any of them sound familiar?"

He glanced over them, but shook his head. "Don't know any. Now, that doesn't mean they've never driven for me, because I can't remember everybody, but I really don't think so." He keyed in their names, just in case, but none of them showed up in his driver history.

"Another question." Casey tapped the paper. "Can you think of any reason a trucker would drive under a different name?"

He grinned. "Legally?"

"Let's say not."

"Then there would be lots of reasons."

"Like?"

"If under your real name your license was suspended, you have a medical condition that prevents you from driving, you've had a DUI, you're wanted by the cops…what kind of thing are you looking for?"

"Reasons these guys," she tapped the photos, "would actually be these guys." She tapped the stack of manifests.

"Any of those things I mentioned." He shrugged. "Fake IDs are easy to get. You can buy a license over the Internet these days."

"Really?"

"Might not be the greatest fakes, but they'd get past most people."

Casey wondered how much they cost. A fake license could solve her own problems. She'd no longer have to worry about the cops or Pegasus or even her brother tracking her down. How could she get one without anyone knowing where the money from her account ended up?

Tom was still talking. "Wish I could help more."

She shook herself. "Maybe you can. Do you have a database on your computer where you could look up any trucker you want?"

"Nope. There is such a thing, but you have to purchase it."

"You know anybody who has one?"

"I could ask around."

"That would be great. But…can you do it without giving too many details?"

"I can try." He studied her face. "You look scared, Casey. What do *you* think is going on?"

Casey shook her head. "I don't know. But it's something bad. Something worth killing for. And I really don't want you to get in these guys' sightlines."

He swallowed, and glanced at Davey. "Thanks a lot, Dad."

Davey shrugged. "When you know something's the right thing to do, Tom, you gotta do it. You know that."

Tom nodded, and stood up, extending his hand once again to Casey. "Here's to doing the right thing."

Casey clasped his hand, praying with all her might she hadn't just brought Tom Haab an early visit from Death.

Chapter Fourteen

"So where were you?" Casey looked at Death in the hospital bathroom's mirror. She'd allowed Davey to take her as far as the edge of town, then insisted on being dropped at a quiet intersection. She'd ducked quickly down a side street and zig-zagged through the neighborhood, making sure he didn't follow. The last thing she needed was for the guys in the hospital to see him. The one—Craig Mifflin, according to Evan's photos—had been unconscious when Davey had come out of the trailer with Randy Westing's gun at his head, but the second guy—Bruce Willoughby—could probably ID Davey, unless he'd been in such pain from his knee he didn't remember anything.

Casey finished lining her eyes and put on the mascara, topping it off with a dusting of eye shadow.

"Those high school boys aren't going to know what to do with themselves tonight when they show up at the shed," Death said. "You're turning *hot*."

"Teenage boys don't have eyes for old ladies like me."

Death snorted. "And I have wings and shoot arrows at lovers. Come *on*, Casey. Do you not remember what boys that age are like?"

"I guess not." She stepped back, trying to view herself in the slanted, handicapped-accessible mirror. She'd locked herself into the one-person bathroom after ducking onto the cardiac wing. The floor was dark and quiet, the patients bedded down for the night.

"And I was wrong about the scrubs," Death said. "They're more attractive than I thought they'd be, in a professional, woman-in-charge sort of way. Except you really should take off your other clothes instead of wearing the scrubs over them."

"And put them where?"

"I don't know. Nurse's locker?"

Casey considered it, but shook her head. "Too much opportunity for seeing other nurses who would know I don't belong." She put on the lipstick and blotted her lips with a paper towel. "So, anyway, where were you? I thought you wanted to be there when I was questioning the trucking guy."

"I did, and was planning on meeting you there, but I was called away. Business."

"What happened to the whole Santa Claus comparison you gave me last week? That you can be in multiple places at once?"

Death made a face. "Do you really want to know? I was trying to spare you."

"Oh. Okay, forget it."

"Suicide bomber in Iraq, military action in Afghanistan, and an earthquake in Peru. All at the same time. Very messy."

"I said forget it!"

Someone knocked on the door. "Everything okay in there?"

Casey glared at Death. "Fine, thank you!"

"You're not on the phone, are you? You know you can't use them on this floor."

"No phone. Just talking to myself."

Death gave a little giggle, but quickly smothered it.

The person stopped talking, and Casey hoped she'd gone away. Casey slid the reading glasses on, and Death's nose wrinkled. "Well, *that* kills the hotness factor."

It did. It also added several years to her appearance, as Bailey had predicted. An added benefit was the hiding of her eyes. She really did look different. She hoped it was enough to get her into the hospital room and close enough for her questioning.

She gave Death another silencing glance and reached for the door, putting the make-up in the bag with Evan's photos. She peeked out. The closest person was a woman in pink scrubs, who sat behind the counter at the nurse's station. Casey went the other direction, toward the elevator.

"So where are these guys?" Death asked.

"I asked at the visitors' desk when I got here. Craig Mifflin's already been released. Bruce Willoughby is still here to get his knee worked on. Orthopedics."

"Let's go get him."

Orthopedics, illogically, was on the third floor. Casey would've thought people who needed help walking should be on the first.

They were almost to the elevator when a familiar person came out of a room, coat flapping. "Nurse, can you please make sure the patient in 113B gets a new gown? We made a little mess."

"Yes, Doctor." Casey nodded her head deferentially, as she imagined a nurse might do, and kept walking. Of all the people to run into, did she *have* to find Dr. Shinnob? She glanced back, and he was watching her with a confused expression, as if he wasn't sure what to think. Great.

She scooted into the next room and stood up against the wall, peering back out into the hallway through the door's little window. Dr. Shinnob still looked her way. He was taking a step. Casey gritted her teeth. What was she going to do?

Dr. Shinnob stopped, and the woman in the pink scrubs came up to him with a chart. He took it, gave one more look Casey's way, then followed the nurse in the other direction. Casey heaved a sigh of relief and leaned against the wall, her heart pounding. Her disguise obviously wasn't enough.

"Um, Casey," Death said.

She looked up. A man lay in the hospital bed, sunk deep into his pillows. He was alone. And he was watching her, smiling.

"Hello, sweetheart. Did you come to take me away?"

Casey glanced at Death, who gave a subtle shake of the head. "No, sir," Casey said. "Just checking in."

"Come sit with me a minute." The man patted the bed beside him.

"I don't really have time—"

His smile faded. "Of course. You're all so busy."

Casey's stomach fell. "I've got a minute or two."

"No, you don't," Death said. "That doctor's going to come in here and find out you're a fraud."

Casey went to stand beside the bed. "What would you like to talk about?"

The man lifted his skinny arm, his hand feeling for hers. She clasped his fingers.

"I don't want to talk," he said, his voice weak. "You talk. Tell me something happy."

Death groaned.

Something *happy*? The poor man had asked precisely the wrong person. "I don't know what—"

"Anything," the man said. "You have to have *something* to say, a young, pretty girl like you."

Casey tried to clear her mind of everything that had happened during the past day, the past week, the past *year*. When had she ever been happy? Or young? Or even pretty? What did that feel like?

"My wedding day," she said aloud.

The man smiled again. "Yes."

She thought back. "We weren't sure if it was going to rain. The clouds were heavy and gray, with just a hint of blue sky in-between, and the air was chilly, with a light breeze. But they always say rain on your wedding day is lucky, right? So we didn't care. We got married in a little church, with just a small group of family and friends. My mom and brother, a few cousins, the guys from my *dojang*." She glanced at the man, who didn't seem to notice she'd just said something unusual. "I wore my mother's wedding dress, an ivory sheath, with just a bit of lace, and he wore a new gray suit, with a red sash. He's Mexican," she explained.

The man nodded.

"There was lots of singing, and good food planned for the reception—homemade soup in bread bowls, and my mother's famous German Chocolate cake. But during the ceremony, just after Reuben slid the ring on my finger and the minister declared us husband and wife, a bolt of lightening lit up the sky outside the windows, and thunder rolled over, shaking the floor. The rain came so suddenly, pounding the roof, running down the windows. Reuben kissed me, and I laughed, happy we would be together forever." Her voice cracked, and she came back to the hospital room.

"Forever," the old man said. "That's a long time."

Casey looked at her finger, and thought about the rings, hanging with the rest of her things in a garage in Clymer, Ohio. "Yes."

"My Joyce is already gone. But I'll be joining her soon." His voice wavered, and a spark of fear entered his eyes.

Death swooped over the man, sniffing, peering into the man's eyes. "Maybe. Maybe not. I haven't heard anything yet."

"It will be all right," Casey said to the man. "You don't need to be afraid. Death is…" She glanced at her companion. "Death isn't always as terrible as you think."

The man looked at her. "You've dealt with it?"

"More than I like. It's with me constantly."

"Yes," the man said. "I believe you. I can see it in your face."

Casey smiled gently. "I'm sorry, but I really need to be going. Can I get you anything?"

"A drink of water would be nice."

Casey picked up the blue hospital cup from the bedside table and tilted the straw toward the man's mouth, supporting his shoulders while he drank.

He took several swallows before sinking back into the pillows. "Thank you, dear."

"You're welcome." She set the cup down and patted his hand. "Do you have anyone to come visit?"

"My children and grandchildren come in and out, but no one stays. Everyone's busy, has places to go. It's all right."

Casey's face went hot. "Aren't there at least volunteers who will sit with you?"

"No. The candystripers want to spend their time in the pediatrics ward. I can't blame them. No one—especially a teen-aged volunteer—wants to spend time with old people. We're boring. And crabby."

Casey gently squeezed his hand. "I think you're nice."

He smiled. "You're nice, too. Now go on. Go do whatever it is you have to do. Even if you don't really work for the hospital."

She gasped.

"You're afraid of something, honey, even if it's not death, like me. I hope you can conquer it."

She bit her lip, not sure what to say.

"Now go on, get moving. Save the world. Run away. Whatever it is you're doing."

"I'm sorry," Casey said. "I wish—"

He flapped his hand toward the door. "Go."

Casey set his hand down and escaped, leaving the man and Dr. Shinnob behind.

Chapter Fifteen

The orthopedic floor was still and dark. No one rushed around, pushing carts and checking vitals. Casey could hear the hum of machines, but other than that it was as if the floor were deserted. She had opted for the stairway, figuring the elevator would open right at a desk, and she was glad she'd thought of it. A young man in green scrubs—of *course* not blue—stood at the counter with his back to her, examining an x-ray on a lighted screen.

From the numbers Casey could see by the room doors, Bruce Willoughby's would be down the hall. Casey would have to go past the man at the desk.

"Here's where the costume comes into play," Death whispered.

"Or I just wait till he goes to the bathroom."

"By that time, someone else will be there."

True.

A rolling desk with a computer sat just down the hallway—the kind used by nurses when making their rounds. Casey figured the staff didn't need to worry about patients on the ortho wing running off with it. Casey began pushing it down the hall, checking the room numbers. As she went past the desk the man glanced up, and Casey nodded, much as she had nodded to Dr. Shinnob only minutes before. The man nodded back, and returned to the x-ray he was examining on the lighted screen.

Nods were coming in very handy.

"Here," Death said, pointing into a room. "Your guy."

Casey stopped outside the door. "I wonder why there's no cop stationed here?"

"Not exactly a flight risk," Death said. "Plus, the only thing he did—that the cops know about—was get beat up at Davey's junk yard. By the time they got to him, he had no gun or anything."

Casey peered in the door's window, hoping Bruce would be asleep. No such luck. He had his hand on a remote, and his face was lit up by the television.

Death held up a finger. "Lights, camera—"

Casey slid her bag onto the shelf of the rolling desk and backed into the room, pulling the computer behind her, right up to the bed.

"Again?" Bruce whined. "How many times do I have to pee in a cup?"

"No peeing," Casey said, and she turned around.

"Then what?" Bruce kept his eyes on the TV. "Blood pressure? Temperature? Sponge bath?" He leered at that one.

Casey pinched the top of his shoulder on a pressure point, and his eyes went wide. She relaxed her grip enough he could turn to look at her. It took him a few moments, but recognition hit him like a brick. "*You?*"

"Yes, Bruce. It's me."

He fumbled for the nurse button on his bed, and Casey grabbed his arm. "If you so much as think about pushing that button, I'm going to do this." She tightened her fingers, and he dropped his hand.

"Good," Casey said. "We understand each other. Now, you are going to answer some questions."

He shook his head, as much as he could with his nerve pinched.

"No?" Casey laid her hand on his destroyed knee, and he whimpered. She wasn't really going to do anything to his poor leg, but the threat should be enough. "I think the people in this hospital—as well as the cops—would be very interested to know how you and your buddies came to the scrap yard with guns and threatened the owner."

He opened his mouth, but she continued. "There are *witnesses*, Bruce. Now, what's your name?"

"You seem to…know it." He panted in-between words.

"Just a test. Tell me."

"Bruce. Willoughby."

"Good. And the name of your boss?"

He shook his head.

"I already know that, too. After seeing him at the scrap yard I looked him up."

Bruce's forehead smoothed. "*Him*? That's Randy. Randy Westing."

So he wasn't Bruce's boss. Just an underling, of some sort. "And the other guy? Craig?"

Bruce sneered. "Dumbass." He looked her up and down, trying to look tough. "Knocked out by a girl without a fight."

Casey twisted his shoulder. "At least he's *walking*."

Bruce had no response for that. Not that he could've responded at that moment, anyway.

"So," Casey said. "Where is Randy camped out? Where is he waiting for you?"

"Don't know. He called. Said he'd…be in touch."

Casey nodded. "And what was it you were looking for at the scrap yard and at the accident? You wanted something in Evan's truck."

Bruce's eyes flicked away, and then back. "Something Randy wanted. I don't know what."

Casey shook her head and leaned ever so slightly on his knee. "You disappoint me, Bruce. I was expecting more."

He closed his eyes and turned his head away. "I can't…tell you what…I don't know."

Casey glanced up at Death, who shrugged. "Maybe he's just stupid."

Casey thought there was a good possibility of that.

"So who are all the others, Bruce?"

"Others? What…others?"

"The guys with you at the crash site? And why are they bothering the truckers?"

"Bother— Look, lady, you need to...get your facts...straight."

"So straighten me out."

Something flashed on the television screen, and his face went deathly pale before reverting to the blue. "We ain't *bothering* any truckers. The only trucker involved was Evan, and he ain't *bothered* anymore." He smiled wickedly.

Casey restrained herself from snapping his knee. "And how did you know Evan? Did he drive for Class A Trucking?"

Bruce blinked. "How do you know about that?"

"Evan. How else?"

His mouth dropped. "So you *did* find his stuff?"

Casey kept her hand on his knee and bent down to retrieve her bag from the computer desk. She dangled it just out of his reach. "It's all in here. Maybe you can help me decipher it."

She picked up her other hand and held it just above his knee. He nodded. "I ain't going anywhere."

Keeping a close eye on him, she reached into the bag and pulled out the first thing she found—a photo of Westing and Dixon sitting across from the Halvestons, the trucker couple.

"That's Randy," Bruce said. "And Dix."

"And who are the other people?"

His eyelids fluttered. "Don't know."

Casey licked her lips, watching him steadily. She set down the photo and pulled out another one. "How about him?" Pat Parnell.

A look of disgust flitted across his face. "Don't know."

"Um-hmm."

She pulled out another photo, and another. "I suppose you don't know any of these people, either."

"No, ma'am, not by name. Just Randy and Dix and Craig."

"And a few others of your group."

He hesitated, then nodded.

"Okay. I suppose you have no idea why these people are in the photos with your friends. Or with *you*, for that matter." She held up one of him with Hank Nance.

Bruce swallowed. "I suppose they could be…truckers?"

Casey gasped and clapped her hands twice, slow. "Good answer, Bruce. Now, try again. Why are you guys bothering the truckers?"

He shook his head.

"Are the truckers driving with fake licenses?"

He bit his lips together.

"And who is your boss?"

He lifted his chin. "Look, lady, I don't know who you are. You show up in Evan's truck, and we don't know why, or what you're doing there. Well, I ain't telling you anything more. And you can't *make* me." He clenched his jaw and stared at the ceiling.

Death's forehead furrowed. "He's not going to answer you. He's made up his mind and he *ain't* changing it."

"Okay, Bruce." Casey patted his thigh. "Here's what we're going to do. Hey. Look at me."

He did.

"You're going to get in touch with your buddies—"

"—I don't know how—"

"—and you are going to tell them I have what they're looking for—" she dangled the bag where he could see it "—and that I want to deal."

"But—"

She placed a finger just above his mouth, not touching him. "I am going to call you tomorrow. If you're in surgery I'll call back. You are going to tell me where and when to meet them *and…*" She held up a finger to keep him from talking. "You are going to give me a number where they can be reached."

"And if they don't call me before then?"

She leaned close, whispering. "Then I'll be back."

He whimpered. "Lady, who *are* you?"

"You shouldn't be worried about me. You should be worried about *that*." She pointed at Death.

Bruce looked where Casey was pointing. "The television?"

Casey opened her mouth, then shut it again. "Remember what I said about the nurse's button. Don't even breathe on it until I've been gone several minutes."

He shook his head. "I won't. I promise."

"Good." She held up the bag. "Until tomorrow then. I'll be talking to you."

Casey exited the room, leaving the rolling computer desk beside Bruce's bed. As the door eased shut, she glanced back. Bruce was turned toward the TV, but she would've bet none of it was registering.

Chapter Sixteen

"Wow, you were like Clint Eastwood in there," Death said. "Or maybe even the Terminator."

Casey jogged down the hospital steps and into the night air, taking a deep breath. She walked briskly down the sidewalk and into the residential section, leaving the bright ER sign behind her.

Death skipped ahead and stopped, studying her as she walked past. "But you look much more like Uma Thurman. Now *she's* a *badass*."

"I wish you wouldn't use words like that."

"Uma Thurman?"

Casey stopped, getting herself acclimated. "That way." She retraced a few steps and turned a corner.

"We going back to the shed?"

"*I* am."

"Well, if *that's* the way you're going to be." Death pouted, and disappeared in a poof of smoke, a choir sounding in the night, like the last few measures of a choral symphony. Or like angels.

No, not angels.

It took Casey about forty-five minutes to make her way back. By the time she arrived the shed was already full of kids, and John Mayer was playing on Martin's iPod. Bailey and Martin were dancing to "Daughters."

"See! I *told* you she'd be back." Bailey bounced away from Martin. "She promised."

Sheryl lay on the floor, picking at a chocolate cake in the middle of the blanket. "Well, whoop-de-doo." Terry sat beside her, carefully not looking at Casey.

"I was right." Martin grinned at Casey. "You cleaned up pretty good."

"I'll take the credit for that." Bailey walked around Casey, examining her. "You didn't even destroy your hair. But you haven't slept on it or washed it yet. *Then* we'll see." She stopped in front of her. "So, did it work? Could you do whatever it was you wanted?"

"Well enough. I take it you didn't get caught this afternoon?"

"No problem. Dad was gone when I got back, and by the time Mom got home I was all set up doing my homework—my teachers sent my stuff home with Sheryl. So, you still have all the make-up?"

Casey held up the now-bulging bag. She had removed the scrubs when she was a safe distance from the hospital. If Bruce was brave—or stupid—enough to tell somebody at the hospital about her visit, she didn't want to be too obvious on the streets. "Can I keep them for a day or two? Just in case?"

Bailey waved her hand. "Keep them forever. Not exactly my style, you know. So sit. We've been waiting for you before we cut Terry's cake."

"You didn't have to."

"Bailey insisted." Terry held up a knife. "But now that you're here…"

Casey lowered herself to the blanket, wondering where Death had gone. She expected to hear that annoying rubber band twanging any second. She also wondered what had happened to the store-bought cookies. Terry must've skipped his nap and made a trip to the bakery, after all.

"Here." Bailey set another bag beside Casey. "Food. And more clothes."

Casey stomach rumbled in response. "Thank you. You guys are all really— Hey, where's Johnny?"

"Football." Bailey rolled her eyes. "His dad makes him play. He doesn't seem to realize that one more good knock to the head and Johnny's history."

"Really? Why? Too many concussions?"

"No," Sheryl said. "Because he's already dumb as rocks. Where can he go from there?"

"Sheryl…" Terry said, but it was half-hearted.

"Oh, Terry, don't be such a sap. You know it's true."

Terry looked away, obviously uncomfortable.

Bailey wrinkled her nose at Casey. "We all love Johnny, you know? He's a great guy, just—"

"—stupid." Sheryl said.

A heavy silence fell, with only Sheryl willing to lift her eyes.

"Anyway," Bailey finally said, "Johnny's dad's this bigwig doctor at the hospital."

Casey blinked. "Not Dr. Shinnob?"

"*Shinnob?*" Bailey laughed. "Hardly. Dr. *Cross*. That's Johnny's last name. And Dr. Cross seems to realize Johnny's never going to be doctor material, so he figures he'd better do something, like play football. You'd think the big doctor, of all people, would realize what that could do to Johnny's head, but…" She shrugged. "Oh, well."

"So, Martin," Casey said, feeling sorry for Johnny. "Bailey says you have something for me. Oh, thank you." She took the piece of cake Terry offered.

"I do." Martin waggled his eyebrows. "What you gonna give me for it?"

"*Martin!*"

"Just joking, Bail, don't have a shit fit. Here." He dug in his bag and pulled out a manila file. "One accident report, fresh from the cop shop."

"Thanks." Casey wiped her fingers on a napkin and took the folder. "Anything you noticed?"

"What? You think I read it?"

"Yes."

He grinned. "You're right. I did. And you know what bugs me? Those machines on the road. They weren't supposed to be there."

It seemed obvious. Casey had thought the same thing. They had mentioned it in the newspaper articles. Why had no answers been found?

"It wasn't a surprise the construction vehicles were around," Martin said. "They've been clogging up that road for weeks. But when the road crew left on Saturday they were parked way over to the side. Nowhere near the actual driving area. And there were still tons of caution signs around."

Casey hadn't seen any of those. "So someone moved them on purpose."

"Well, duh," Sheryl said.

Bailey smacked Sheryl's shoe.

"Another thing," Martin said, scooting forward on the bucket. "The cops gave someone a speeding ticket on that stretch of road *five minutes earlier*."

"Five minutes?"

"So the machines were beside the road then. Not on it." Martin's face was grim. "Whoever moved those machines did it just before you and the trucker came that way. Why would they do that?"

Casey's stomach twisted. She'd known it. It couldn't have been any other way. But to have confirmation that the machines were moved on purpose was almost too much to take.

"Casey?" Bailey looked up at her. "You knew that, didn't you?"

Casey nodded, and let out a huff of air. "What else does the report say?"

Martin gestured to the file in her hand. "It's all there."

"But what else stuck out to you?"

"No witnesses." Bailey spoke up this time.

Casey laughed. "You read it, too?"

"Of course."

"Did anyone *not* read it?"

Sheryl and Terry shrugged. They'd read it, too.

"Anyway," Bailey said, "there was *no one* who saw what happened. At least, no one who will come forward."

"But you know what they did find?" Martin said. "Just before the accident? Somebody stopped the traffic going east, on the other side of the highway. So nobody was coming the opposite direction to see anything, anyway."

"The police didn't check out the traffic problem?"

"They tried. But by the time they got there, whoever had stopped the cars was gone, and traffic was moving again. They couldn't find the people from the first stopped cars, who had seen what had stopped them to begin with. They were long gone."

"And," Bailey said, "the same thing happened on the western side. When the ambulances and stuff were coming to the accident from the other way, they had to get through a bunch of cars who'd been held up."

"And nobody saw what caused that, either?"

Martin shook his head. "I talked to one of the cops who was called to the scene, and he said there were construction signs all over the highway, saying there was stopped traffic, and then orange barrels across the road."

So that's where the warning signs had gone.

"But there were no people. The cops just left the barrels there while they worked on the crash and got...well...took you to the hospital."

Casey couldn't believe it. She didn't think these guys were that organized. "They planned every aspect of this."

"Who did?"

Casey wasn't sure who'd asked, but all four pairs of eyes were on her. "I don't know yet."

"But you know something," Bailey said. "Don't you?"

Casey knew some very important things, the main one being that the papers in her bag were worth killing for. No. The men hadn't *meant* to kill Evan. At least not right then. But Randy Westing, Bruce Willoughby, and the other guy had brought guns to Davey's scrapyard, and didn't seem nervous about using them. She rubbed her temples. What was in those papers that was so damaging? Could it be simply that the drivers were operating under false names? Tom hadn't seen anything blatantly illegal in the photos. Just that weird business of the logos being on, and then off, the trucks.

Casey looked around at the teenagers. Kids who were allying themselves with her. Forget herself—she was going to get *them* killed.

"You know, guys," she said. "I'm exhausted. It's been a long couple of days."

Bailey's lip stuck out. "Are you kicking us out?"

"She can't kick us out," Sheryl said. "It's your shed."

"And we're not done with the cake." Terry waved his fork over the half-eaten dessert.

Martin shut off the music. "Come on, guys. We said we'd help her out."

"And we are." Bailey grabbed Casey's sleeve, and Casey steeled herself not to react. "Come on, Casey. What else can we do?"

Casey closed her eyes and tried to relax her shoulders. "You're already giving me a place to stay, feeding me, clothing me, and getting me police reports. You've done a lot."

"And I can see what else we should do," Martin said. "Leave her alone."

"But—"

"Let's go, Bail," Sheryl said. "We can see when we're not wanted."

"Oh, guys," Casey said. "It's not that. Not at all. I like…you guys are great."

"Then what do you *need?*" Bailey pleaded.

What did she need? She needed these sweet, exasperating kids to be safe. Oh, yeah, there was something else. "Pat Parnell. Did you ask your dad if he has a second job?"

"Didn't have to. Asked Mom. And I didn't know it, but he doesn't farm anymore. Hasn't for awhile. He took up another job. Driving trucks."

Bingo.

"But he doesn't anymore."

"How come?"

"Don't know. Mom wouldn't say. In fact, when I asked about him, she got all weird."

"Weird? In what way?"

"Just got all...like she was creeped out. Or disgusted. Who knows with her. She gets freaked out if you even mention the word bellybutton."

Casey considered this new information. "I need to talk to him."

"Pat?"

"Can you get me his number?"

"Sure. Easy."

"*Without* your dad knowing."

"You forget," Bailey said with a smirk, "I do all sorts of things without my dad knowing. And anyway, this is simple." She pulled out her phone and dialed 411. She listened, said Pat's name and city, and waited. And frowned.

She slid her phone shut. "Unlisted." Her face cleared. "So I'll go home and get it. Dad would have his cell number."

"And I'll get it from you how?"

Bailey looked at Terry. "Ter, give Casey your phone."

"*What?*"

"No," Casey said. "I don't want—"

"Come on," Bailey said. "You hardly use it, anyway. You haven't sent me a text for at least three days."

"Bailey," Casey said. "Terry doesn't need to—"

"She's right." Terry handed Casey his phone. "Go ahead."

"Terry!" Sheryl was on her feet now. "Don't give her your *phone.*"

"The sooner she finds out what she wants to know, the sooner she's gone!" Terry said, his voice loud and harsh in the enclosed space.

That shut them all up.

"I'm sorry," Casey said. "I'm making things difficult for—"

"No," Bailey said. "You're making things exciting around here. For once. Don't listen to *him.*" She glared at Terry.

"Come on, guys. A few songs before we hit the road. I need the pick-me-up."

Martin programmed a few lively songs to play, and he and Bailey danced around the room, Sheryl and Terry watching from the sidelines. Several times Bailey tried to get them to join, but Sheryl simply sulked, and Terry was watching her for cues.

Finally Bailey dropped onto a bucket, wiping her forehead. "Okay, come on guys. Casey needs her sleep. And I need to go get this number."

"Thank you for the phone, Terry," Casey said.

He busied himself covering the cake and shoving trash into his bag. Sheryl sulked in the corner. Martin packed away his iPod and accessories. Everybody strapped their things onto their bikes and wheeled them outside.

"So I'll be in touch," Bailey said.

"Thanks so much. For everything."

Bailey led the group down the lane, Terry's bike wobbling with his heavy load.

Martin hung behind. "Don't worry about Terry. You're not the reason he's so crabby."

"Sheryl?"

Martin laughed. "So you see it, too?" He straddled his bike. "All I can say is, good luck with that. If she never sees him, it'll destroy him. But if she ever takes him up on it? She'll eat him alive." He hopped on the bike and pedaled down the lane, waving over his head.

Speaking of eating…

Casey went into the shed and devoured everything the kids had brought.

Chapter Seventeen

The Bugs Bunny theme blared, and Casey sat straight up. It was still dark. Terry's phone wasn't hard to find—it lit up her entire side of the shed. Casey grabbed it and pushed buttons until it quieted. She closed her eyes and took a deep breath, letting herself wake up.

"Annoying tune," Death said, from the darkness of a far corner. "Kids these days."

"Yeah, well, it's a tune I remember very well from my childhood. I'm surprised Terry even knows who Bugs Bunny *is*."

"Some things remain constant," Death said.

Casey read the phone's screen, which held Pat Parnell's cell phone number and address, and a demand that Casey let Bailey know she got it. Bailey Rossford. Her full name appeared on the screen. Casey pecked out a short reply and turned off the phone before lying back down.

"Want a lullaby?" Death asked.

Casey rolled over without answering, and went to sleep with Death singing *Away in a Manger*, accompanied by an autoharp.

Casey woke up alone and surprisingly rested. Her stomach growled, having been reminded the night before what it felt like full. Casey wished she hadn't been quite so greedy, eating everything all at once. She turned on Terry's phone to check the time. After nine. The kids should all be in school. At least, she hoped none of them had skipped.

Bugs Bunny began playing again, and Casey found the button to mute it. Bailey and Martin had each texted her. Martin once, saying good morning and that she should contact him if she needed to, and Bailey nine times, wondering where Casey was and why she hadn't texted back.

Casey let her head fall onto her arms. She just didn't have the energy for modern technology. Or kids.

After a round of hapkido forms, stripped to her underwear, Casey checked the field for farmers and rinsed off at the pump, pulling on the set of clothes Bailey had brought the night before. What would she do *without* those kids? And why wasn't she running from them as fast as she could?

"Because you need them," Death said.

Casey jumped. "Would you *stop* that?"

"Without the kids you'd be screwed. No money, no clothes, no way to be in touch with people." Death's chin tilted toward Terry's phone. "You thought about who else you could call on that phone?"

Of course she had. Her brother, Ricky. Her lawyer. Eric.

"If I call any of them I might as well just call Pegasus and the cops and tell them where I am. You know Ricky's phone is being watched, especially now that—" She shook her head. "You know my real name came out in Clymer."

"I would assume so. But maybe Ricky got a new phone."

"Which I wouldn't have the number for."

Death acknowledged the problems. "So we're pretty much in a deep, dark hole."

"Thank you *so much* for your helpful observations."

"I aim to please."

Casey sat down to tie her shoes.

"So," Death said. "What first?"

"First, I give our friend Bruce Willoughby a call." She dialed the hospital and asked for his room. The phone rang and rang until Casey finally hung up. She re-dialed, and when the receptionist answered, she asked if Mr. Willoughby had been released—although she couldn't imagine it. The receptionist assured her Mr. Willoughby was still booked into his room.

"Must be in surgery, or getting tested," Casey told Death. "I'll try later. Now for Mr. Pat Parnell." She picked up the phone and dialed the number, listening as the phone requested she listen to the music while her party was being reached. A song from *Oklahoma!* blared in her ear and she held the phone several inches away.

"What are you going to say?" Death asked. "'You don't know me, but I'm about to ask you a whole lot of personal questions?'"

"'Lo." A gruff voice answered.

"Hello," Casey said. "Mr. Parnell? I'm a friend of Bailey's, and—"

"Bailey Rossford? Danny's little girl?"

"That's right. Although she's not so little anymore."

"You got that right. Anyhow, what is it?"

"I was wondering if we might be able to get together to talk."

"About what?" His voice chilled a few degrees.

"About…trucks."

"Trucks?"

"And driving them."

"Listen, lady, I don't know what—"

"You know what happened this past Sunday, in Blue Lake."

Casey could hear him breathing.

"I don't want the same thing to happen to you."

"I don't know why you would think that. I have nothing to do with what happened. Besides, I'm not driving again till Friday."

"Mr. Parnell. I have pictures."

His breath hitched. "Pictures? Of what?"

"Of you. With them. Owen Dixon and Randy Westing."

"But I haven't…what is this? Who are you?"

"I want to help…Mr. Parnell, please—"

But he'd hung up.

"That went well," Death said.

Casey leaned back against the wall. "And now he's probably going to call Bailey's dad, asking why some strange woman was calling him."

"Or not."

"You don't think he will?"

Death blew a chord on the harmonica, salvaged from the creek. "Not if he's into something shady. He won't want his friends to know."

"Unless Bailey's dad is involved somehow."

"Wow." Death lowered the harmonica. "You really do think the worst of people, don't you?"

"Not everybody." She looked up her notes and punched another number into her phone.

"Wainwright's."

"Davey?"

"Hey, I've been wanting to call you, but you aren't answering and…this is a different number."

"Yeah. Forget that other one. While you're at it, forget this one, too. Any word from Tom about that database?"

"Not yet. But I had somebody call this morning, ask where I sent the truck. It was a guy, and the number was blocked."

"Did you tell them where it went?"

"Sure. No reason not to. It's a huge junk yard, with lots of employees. These bozos will have a hard time pulling anything off there. And I warned the guys there about the possible interest in the truck. They'll be ready."

"Good." No reason for *more* people to get hurt. "What will they do if Westing shows up?"

"Stall him. They'll let him at the truck, but they'll make it take a long time. And they'll give me a call."

"Great work. Thanks. Will you let me know if Tom calls?"

"At this number?"

"It's the only one I have for now."

"And where is this number?"

"Good-bye, Davey." She hung up.

"He's going to find you, you know." Death blew in the harmonica. "One of these times."

"If he's the worst person to come calling, I can deal with that. Seems to me that's the least of our worries."

"Unless he and the others find you at the same time."

"You are a ray of sunshine, aren't you?"

"I try. So, what next?"

"I have Pat Parnell's address in Wichita."

"And no way to get there. Davey?"

"He's involved enough. Maybe Wendell today."

Death raised an eyebrow. "You trust him?"

"He covered for me." She flipped the phone open and dialed information. The operator put her through to the garage where Wendell worked.

"Blue Lake Gas," a man said. The bored one, Casey guessed.

"May I speak with Wendell Harmon, please?"

"Minute." The receiver crashed down—onto the counter, probably—and the man hollered Wendell's name.

A couple minutes later Wendell came on the line.

"Wendell, it's Casey."

"Hey! Where are you?"

Everyone was *so* concerned about that.

"Around. Any chance you could drive me to Wichita today?"

"Wichita?" He paused, and when he came back, his voice was muffled, like he was speaking behind his hand. "What do you need there?"

"Somebody I want to visit."

"I really wish I could, but we're slammed, so I can't get away. I could lend you my truck, though."

Casey stopped breathing for a few seconds. "I don't know if that's such a good idea."

"Aw, the truck looks worse than it is. It'll get you there."

"It's not the truck I'm worried about. I don't…my driver's license got stolen." Might as well go with the story she'd told the hospital clerk. Wendell didn't need to know her wallet was back in Ohio, waiting to incriminate her, if it hadn't already.

"I won't tell. Drive the speed limit, and you'll be fine."

Casey swallowed. The kids all had bikes. She could borrow one of them.

Death snorted. "You think a *bicycle's* gonna get you to Wichita?"

"I…don't think I can, Wendell. Thanks, though."

"Sorry. Come after work and I could probably take you. I'd have to call my wife, though. Tell her I won't be home for dinner."

"Forget it. I'll find another way."

"If you're sure."

"I'm sure. Thanks." She hung up and let her hands and head hang between her knees.

"You know," Death said, "one of these days you're going to have to face—"

"I know, okay? I *know*."

Death made a face and picked up the harmonica. "Geez, I'm just trying to be *helpful*."

Casey considered her options: Davey. Wait till after school and ask Bailey, who knew Parnell and would probably be getting hell for her part in all of this. Wait until after work and go with Wendell, adding his wife to the list of people who knew what was going on.

Or she could drive Wendell's truck.

She dialed Davey's number. He didn't answer, and the machine asked her to leave a message. She hung up. Sweat sprouted on her scalp and upper lip, and she went hot, and then cold. Could she do it? Could she get behind the wheel of a truck?

"Was Wendell's truck a stick?"

Death blew a discordant rush of air. "Nope. Automatic."

So she couldn't use that excuse.

"Come on, Casey," Death said. "I'll be with you every second."

"Oh, great. That helps *so* much."

The bag the kids had brought the food in was a backpack, and Casey stuffed her things inside it. She used the broken broom to sweep away her footprints, and made sure there was no sign she'd been there. She looked for cars, and headed down the lane.

In the past week she'd been in an accident, run from the cops, avoided Pegasus, made and lost friends, seen a couple of people die, and killed someone.

If she couldn't drive a truck, there was something wrong with her.

Chapter Eighteen

"Changed your mind?"

Casey caught Wendell outside on his lunch break and pulled him to the side of the building, where the other guys wouldn't see her. "If you're still offering."

"Sure. Here." He held out a keychain with more keys than Casey could imagine ever needing. "She's full up on gas, and ready to go." He grinned. "Figured you might be by."

"Thanks, Wendell."

"Anything else I can do?"

She peeked around his shoulder. "Don't tell the guys?"

"No reason they need to know. When will you be back?"

"When do you get off work?"

"Five-thirty."

"I'll be back by then."

"If not, it's no biggie. One of the guys can give me a ride home. One more thing." He pulled out his wallet and counted out twenty dollars. "Get yourself something to eat."

"Wendell—"

"Don't like seeing a woman look so hungry."

Casey took the money. "Thank you."

"You know where you're going, how to get to Wichita?"

"I think so."

He pointed up the road. "Catch the highway there; it'll take you right into the city. Got directions for once you're there?"

She had them. Terry's phone was equipped with the Internet and GPS.

"Okay, then, see you in a few hours."

"Thanks, Wendell."

He gathered up his lunch supplies and headed back inside.

Casey let the keys dangle by her side as she stared at the truck. Death stood beside her.

"I don't think I can," she said.

"First step," Death said. "Open the door."

Casey took a step, faltered, then took another.

"Come on. You can do it."

Casey tugged on the door handle, and the door swung open.

"Thank you." Death climbed into the cab and scooted across the seat. "Second step. Get in."

The sweat was back, and the hot flashes. Casey glanced toward the window of the gas station. Wendell was watching. She held her breath, and got in.

"Okay," Death said. "Shut the door."

She did.

"Keys in the ignition, turn them forward—"

"I know how to start the damn truck!"

Death sat back, hands up. "Sorry. Sorry. Just trying to be supportive."

Casey turned the key.

"Don't forget your seatbelt."

Casey growled, but buckled herself in and clenched her hands around the steering wheel.

"Take your time," Death said.

"I *am*."

"No need to be a speed demon."

"Will you shut *up*?"

Death sat back, whistling the theme from Knight Rider.

Casey eased her foot onto the gas pedal, turned the steering wheel…and stalled the truck.

Death stayed very still.

Casey wrenched the keys, started the truck, and floored it, screeching to a stop at the road. She blinked, completely disoriented.

"That way," Death said, pointing.

Casey swallowed, clenched her teeth, and pulled out.

Once they got within sight of the highway—it took twice as long as it should have, since she drove fifteen miles per hour under the speed limit—she was beginning to loosen up. She would be driving the opposite direction of the accident scene, so at least she wouldn't have to see it.

"So, this guy we're going to see," Death said. "You know he'll be home?"

"Nope."

"But we're going anyway."

"Yup."

"And if we have to wait?"

"Then we just do. Wendell said he can get a ride home."

"But then he'd have to explain to them and his wife why his truck was gone, and you want to avoid that, don't you?"

Casey eased to the right, merging onto the highway. The speed limit was sixty-five, but she didn't think she had that in her. She hovered in the right lane, going just above the minimum forty miles per hour. Her hands clenched the steering wheel, and she gritted her teeth so hard her head hurt.

"Try to relax," Death said. "You're making me all tense."

Terry's phone rang from where it sat in the middle of the seat.

"You know," Death said. "Statistics show that driving while talking on the phone is more dangerous than driving drunk."

Glad for the excuse to stop, Casey pulled to the shoulder of the road and flipped her hazards on. It was Davey calling.

"Hey," he said. "You know that database you wanted to see? Tom found someone who has it."

"Close by?"

"Next town over. Foraker."

The opposite direction of where she was headed. "Can you give me the guy's name and number?"

"I thought I'd just take you—"

"I'm on my way out of town, Davey. I'm not sure what my schedule is for the rest of the day."

He hesitated. "All right. It's actually a couple who runs the place. Matt and Nadine Williams. Deerfield Trucking. Foraker, like I said." He gave her the phone number.

"Thanks, Davey. And please thank Tom for me."

"Thank him yourself. He'd like to hear how this works for you."

Casey sighed. "Okay. I'll talk to you later."

She shut the phone and filled her cheeks with air.

"These folks sure want to be involved, don't they?" Death said. "Won't just leave you to your own devices."

"They're good people."

"And nosey."

"Not really. Interested."

She watched out the windshield, her hands limp in her lap.

Death gave a little cough. "So, are we going to continue on to Wichita, or are we taking a break here?"

Casey shook herself and shifted into drive. She swallowed.

"You got this far," Death said. "You can go a little farther."

Casey looked in the side mirror. Lots of traffic. Lots and lots of it. More cars and trucks than she ever imagined.

"It's clear," Death said.

Oh.

Slowly Casey eased back onto the highway, chugging along at minimum speed. Cars and trucks flew past her, the semis rattling both the pickup and her nerves.

"Prepare to exit freeway onto Route 254 in two miles." The GPS' female voice was soothing, as if it knew exactly where it was and who it was talking to.

"That's nice," Death said. "Very confident and calming. I think we should name her. Uma, maybe?"

"That's calming? *Kill Bill*?" Images of spurting blood and exposed brains filled Casey's mind.

"Okay. We'll name her Laura Ingalls Wilder. Is that better?"

Casey watched the road signs and tried to ignore Death's banter, not wanting to miss the turn and prolong this trip.

"*Prepare to exit freeway*," Laura Ingalls Wilder said. "*Route 254.*"

"Is this right?" Casey asked, panicked. "We're not in Wichita yet."

"Suburb," Death said. "Just outside city limits. Don't freak out."

The GPS dinged, and Casey turned off of the highway, her heart pumping. She followed the GPS' directions faithfully, if anxiously, and found her way to Pat Parnell's residential section. As Wendell had said, it was a new development outside the center city, with roads named after people. Patrick Road, Jennifer Street…Olivia Lane.

"*You have arrived at your destination*," Laura said.

Casey pulled into the driveway of the new house beside a semi, which sat without a trailer to the side of the garage. She hoped that meant Parnell was home.

Death stared at the house. "That's really something."

Casey had to agree. Obviously newly built, the two-story house sported a three-car garage, multiple dormers, and a spiral turret on the corner. The yard—half dirt—lay spotted with dead young trees, still tied to poles, and two raised flowerbeds, empty of all but weeds. The huge backyard held one of those wooden playground structures with two slides and a climbing wall, and Casey could just see the edge of a swimming pool.

Death gestured toward the front door. "Ready?"

Casey took a deep breath, centering herself, trying to forget what she'd just done. She hadn't driven a vehicle for almost a year and a half, and she was feeling it from her head to her toes. She rolled her neck forward, easing the tension, and tried to imagine a happier time.

That didn't work.

"Somebody's looking out the front window," Death said.

When Casey looked up, the face was gone. She took another deep breath, let it out, and opened the door.

The brick sidewalk led to a decorative front door, and the doorbell rang deep and loud. Nobody answered, so Casey knocked, and rang the doorbell again. While she waited she studied the barren flowerbeds, decorated only with a sign declaring the house "guarded by Ironman Security."

"Who is it?" The voice blared on an intercom, hidden behind a hanging plant by the door.

"My name is Casey Jones. I'm a friend of Bailey Rossford. May I please talk to you? Mr. Parnell?"

After another long minute, the door opened, and Casey tried to cover her surprise. The man in front of her was obviously the same man from Evan's photos, and from the picture at Bailey's house, but life had not been treating him well. His puffy, bloodshot eyes were sunken, his skin held a grayish tinge, and he'd lost probably thirty pounds. He winked his left eye, but Casey was sure he didn't mean to. His hands jerked, his knuckles cracked, and he glanced furtively over her shoulder. Casey looked back, but Death had disappeared. Even so, she wondered if Parnell felt Death's presence.

"May I come in?"

Parnell swallowed. "What's this about? You're not from the bank?"

"I'm definitely not from the bank."

His shoulders relaxed slightly. "And you're a friend of Bailey's? Danny, too?"

"Her dad? No, I don't know him."

He glanced behind her again, as if scoping the street, before stepping back. "Come in, then."

Casey tried not to react to the inside of the house. She supposed she should've recognized the empty flowerbeds and dead trees as clues, but what she saw here took her completely by surprise.

There was nothing there.

No furniture, no pictures on the wall, not even any curtains. The interior smelled like a mixture of new carpet and stale laundry—not exactly pleasant.

Casey gazed at the foyer's vaulted ceiling and chandelier and wondered if the upstairs was as unoccupied as the first floor. She couldn't hear any sounds. Not even air-conditioning.

"Come through here." Parnell led her through a hallway that went from front to back of the house and ended in the kitchen. There was furniture here—one card table and one battered folding chair. On the counter sat two photos—one of three children, and one of a high school football team. Parnell gestured to the chair. "Have a seat."

Casey chose to stand, looking out the sliding door into the back yard. The swimming pool she'd seen was empty, its bottom caked with leaves and dirt, and the swings on the swingset hung limp, water pooled in the plastic seats. A pole with empty bird-feeders tilted toward the ground, and a broken birdbath, its top cracked in two, crumbled beside it.

And Casey thought *her* life was depressing.

"What do you want?" Parnell stood beside her, shoulders sagging, no spark in his eyes.

Casey set her bag on the card table and pulled out the photo of him taking the package from Owen Dixon. "That's you."

He glanced at the photo, looked back out the sliding door, then slumped into the folding chair. "Where did you get that?"

"The trucker who was killed on Sunday had it."

"Evan. I knew he was up to something."

"You knew Evan?"

"Sure. He was one of the guys, you know? I mean, the ones you run into at truck stops or picking up a load. Another independent operator, like me. Nice guy." His voice cracked, and he swallowed, glancing toward the kitchen.

"Can I get you some water?" Casey didn't wait for an answer, but walked around the counter to the sink. She searched through several empty cupboards before finding a stack of plastic cups. She chose one, rinsed it out, and gave him a drink.

He sipped gingerly. "Last time I saw Evan, he was asking questions."

"About what?"

Parnell looked down at his drink. "Class A."

"The trucking company. You work for them?"

"Off and on. Whenever they call." He looked blankly at the equally blank wall.

"But don't you get called by other companies? As an independent operator you can work for any outfit you want, right? Isn't that how it works?"

"That's how it works."

"Places like Southwest Trucking? Tom Haab?"

He nodded. "Sure, I've driven for them. I like driving for them." His voice was wistful.

But he hadn't driven for Southwest for a couple years, Tom had said. "How often does Class A call you?"

Parnell gave a little laugh, devoid of humor. "Not as often as I need. Obviously."

"When was the last time?"

"A week ago. No, two weeks. Long enough."

"And what did you haul?"

He rubbed his forehead. "Electronics. Televisions, I think. I'm driving again this Friday."

Casey pushed the photo toward him on the table. "And what is Owen Dixon giving you in this photo?"

He bit his lip and looked away. "Nothing."

"I see."

He blinked rapidly. "Nothing that matters to *you*."

"Or to the cops?"

"Cops? You said you weren't—"

"I said I wasn't from the bank."

He stood up so quickly his chair banged backward onto the floor. "What do you want?"

She held out her hands. "Whoa. I'm not from the cops, either. Relax. I'm sorry."

His hands twitched more rapidly now. "I think you should go."

"How did you get started with Class A Trucking, Mr. Parnell?"

"Please go."

"Did they call you? Or did you call them?"

He stumbled around his chair and back down the hallway toward the front door. Casey put the photo back in her bag and followed. "Mr. Parnell? Did they call you?"

"They called me, okay? They called me and offered me a job. I took it. All right?" He swung the door open and stepped to the side. "Go now. *Please.*"

She hesitated, wanting to ask more about Owen Dixon and Randy Westing, and whoever it was that told them what to do—that boss Bruce Willoughby wouldn't name.

Parnell jerked his hand toward the door. "Go. *Please.*"

Casey walked past him, stopping in the doorway. "If you want to talk any more, please call me. Okay? You have my number on your phone."

His eyes widened, and he patted down his pockets. "My phone? On that phone?"

"Remember? I called you?"

He whimpered and ran back into the house, still searching his pockets. She heard a door opening, and Parnell talking to himself as he hunted. "What if they *find* it? What if they know she *called*?"

"Tragic case." Death sat on one of the flowerbed's raised brick borders, playing a violin. The melancholy tune hovered in the air, a perfect accompaniment for the depressing surroundings. Casey listened, waiting for Parnell's return, but when he didn't come back after several minutes she headed for her car, getting in without too much personal trauma.

Death stopped playing. "Did you happen to take a look at the photos in the kitchen?"

"Sure. His kids, and a football team. Is his son old enough for that?"

"Hardly. He's only six."

"So who was it?"

Death ran the bow across the strings. "Parnell."

Casey blinked. "He's got nothing in the entire house, but puts a photo of his high school football team on his counter?"

Death filled the passenger seat. "It's really very sad. Some men just can't mature past high school." The violin shrank to adjust to the interior of the car, but the tune was just as mournful.

"Let's go see what that database can tell us about our new friend, Pat Parnell," Casey said. She turned the key and backed away from Parnell's wasteland of a home.

Chapter Nineteen

The trip back wasn't as bad as the trip there, but that was probably because Casey was thinking more about Pat Parnell than she was about driving the trunk.

"I think you do better in that seat than this one," Death said, bowing a riff on the violin. "You're going a whole forty-*five* miles per hour this time. And you're not even sweating."

"*Prepare to exit freeway in two miles*," Laura Ingalls Wilder said.

Casey couldn't figure out exactly what had Pat Parnell so freaked out. He was afraid of cops, looked like hell, and about had a conniption when she mentioned her number being on his phone. She had to wonder—which came first? His deterioration or his job with Class A Trucking? He was obviously losing it—not only his health and sanity, but his home. How long could he keep that truck in the driveway? Unless it was paid off.

"How much would a truck like that cost?"

Death laid down the violin. "Don't know. A lot, I would think."

"So how can he afford it?"

"Seems to me he's keeping it for last."

A truck blew by them in the passing lane, and Casey's heart rate skyrocketed. "Why do they drive so *fast?*"

"Time is money, darling. Time is money." Death plucked the Dire Straits tune *Money for Nothing*.

"*Prepare to exit freeway onto Wickham Street,*" Laura said. "*After turning right, remain on current road.*"

Casey eased the truck onto the off ramp at the same time Terry's phone rang on the seat.

"Can you see who it is?"

Death squinted at the screen. "Your good friend Bailey. She wants to know '*whr r u?*' Want to reply?"

"No!" Casey snatched the phone off the seat and stuck it in the pocket on the side of the door. "She'll just have to wait to find out."

"Touchy, aren't you?"

A Wendy's restaurant sat just off the exit, and Casey went through the drive-thru, eating chili and a baked potato in the parking lot.

"Aren't you going to offer me any?" Death asked.

"No."

"Fine." Death pulled out the rubber band. Casey somehow refrained from retaliating with a wad of sour cream.

Casey followed Laura's directions to a large gray building with a huge sign out front. DEERFIELD TRUCKING. This outfit looked larger than Tom's Southwest, and the parking lot held at least fifteen cars.

"People," Casey said.

"They're just all over the place, aren't they?"

Casey mulled over her options for getting inside, and decided to try the hospital again. This time Bruce Willoughby answered his phone. He sounded exhausted.

"Hi, Bruce," Casey said. "You doped up too much, or do you remember me?"

"He says to meet him tonight. Behind the grocery store at the end of town."

"Who says?"

He hesitated. "Randy."

And all his homeboys? Probably. "What time?"

"He'll let you choose."

Casey laughed at Westing's attempt to make her feel like she had control of the situation. "Okay. Now."

Bruce hiccupped. "*Now?*"

"Sure. I want to talk to him, he wants to talk to me. Let's get it done."

"But I can't…he said…"

She knew he wouldn't go for it. "You don't know how to get in touch with him?"

"No. I don't."

Right. "I told you I wanted his number."

"I'm sorry, he told me not to—"

"Okay, okay. Tell him midnight." Might as well go with dramatic. "But no funny stuff. And I want to see just him. Not the whole crowd of them."

"Really? Midnight? I mean, good. That's good. I'll let him know." Casey could hear Bruce's relief. Randy had probably told him to get her to agree to his plan or else. Or else *what* she didn't know, but it wouldn't have been good.

"Thanks, Bruce. Hope you feel better soon." She hung up on his sputtering.

"Well," she said, "at least there won't be customers that time of night."

"Could be a few employees, though," Death said. "Stocking shelves and cleaning."

"We'll just have to avoid them. Just how I have to avoid the people here."

"You know he won't come alone," Death said.

"Of course not."

"And what would you have done if he'd agreed to meet you right now?"

"I knew he wouldn't. He needs time to get his men in position. Now be quiet." She dialed Deerfield's number, hoping Terry had unlimited calling, and a receptionist answered cheerfully.

"Hi," Casey said. "My name is Casey Jones, and—"

"One moment. Mrs. Williams is expecting your call." Her voice cut off, replaced by a Muzak version of a Nickelback song.

"Ms. Jones?" The voice was husky, like she'd had one—or a thousand—too many cigarettes.

"Yes. Mrs. Williams?"

"Nadine, honey."

"Um, Nadine, Tom Haab told me you have a trucker database I could take a look at."

"We do. When would you like to come in?"

"Actually, I'm sitting in your parking lot right now."

"Ah, yes, Tom said you aren't real big on people."

"Well, that's not exactly—"

"On *seeing* people. Should I say it that way? Anyway, I'll be out in a minute. Hang on, sweetie." She hung up.

The phone rang again and another text flashed onto the screen. Casey was ready to dismiss it as Bailey again, but saw it was Sheryl.

can u plz txt B? shes drvng me crzy

Casey sighed. For heaven's *sake*. She brought up Bailey's number and wrote:

I am fine.

She put the phone back in the door pocket and had to wait less than a minute before a short, stocky woman exited the building. Casey got out of the truck and waved. Nadine waved back, gesturing for Casey to join her on the sidewalk. "Now listen, honey," she said when Casey approached. "The only one inside the office is my receptionist, and she's more near-sighted than my granny, so you don't have to worry about her. Anybody else comes along you can duck behind a corner, all right? Come on, then."

Not having much of a choice in the matter, Casey followed her into the building. The receptionist's glasses were remarkably thick, but still Casey averted her face. They didn't see anyone else, and Nadine shut a thick office door behind them.

"Matt—my husband—might come in at some point, but you can trust him. Have a seat."

Casey sat in an old office chair, and Nadine scooted another one beside it and up to a computer monitor. "Now, Tom says you need to look up some people. Want to tell me any more about it, and why I should help you, other than the fact that I like Tom?"

How much should she tell her? "You know outside Blue Lake last Sunday? A trucker died?"

Nadine's face fell. "Evan Tague? Oh, that was so awful. How they could be so careless with that construction equipment –"

"It wasn't an accident. Someone put those machines in the road to stop Evan. But since the road was wet, and he didn't have enough time…" Casey shuddered. "He did his best."

Nadine eyed her. "And you know this how?"

"I was in the truck with him when it happened."

Nadine blinked, and looked Casey up and down. "And you're okay?"

"I know. It's crazy. But Evan got…I'm fine."

Nadine looked at the computer, and Casey could see she was trying to get her emotions under control. Nadine cleared her throat. "Evan drove for us different times. He was a good man. Matt was out at the crash site. He said even from where he was—" She swallowed. "Even where he was it looked like a bomb had gone off. He could see…could see blood on the windows." She fiddled with the computer's mouse. "You think some other truckers had something to do with…the accident?"

"A company called Class A Trucking."

"Class A? Never heard of them." She keyed something into the computer. "Hmm. There. Tells all about them. Founded eighteen months ago by two men. Owen Dixon and Randy Westing."

"No one else?"

Nadine glanced at her. "You're expecting a different name?"

Casey thought back to Bruce, relieved when she mentioned Randy as being her boss. "Yes, but I don't know who it is."

Nadine searched the screen some more, but ended up shaking her head. "Nobody else here that I can see."

"What about their business? Any problems?"

"Nope. Squeaky clean." She frowned. "Almost too squeaky clean. You mean to tell me nobody's made a mistake on paperwork or gotten a speeding ticket?" She wasn't convinced.

"How far back does it go? Their whole history?"

"No. Only a couple of weeks, so this actually isn't all that helpful. Now, you wanted to look at truckers, right? Tom could've helped you a little—there are Internet-based trucker databases, like truckersearch.com, that he could access, but to get the comprehensive list you have to have special circumstances. Matt's a part-time sheriff's deputy, so that's why we have it. I can check pretty much anything you want."

A *cop*? Davey hadn't bothered to tell her *that*. Another cold sweat broke out along her scalp. She was going to have to take a shower every half hour the way things were going.

"You okay?" Nadine's face creased with concern.

"Yeah. I mean…" She cleared her throat and tried to erase any guilt affecting her features. "That's legal? For you to check on the drivers?"

"Sure."

Casey had her doubts. "Okay, so how do we do this?"

"Give me a name."

"Pat Parnell." Might as well start with him.

Nadine punched it in, and Parnell's photo came onto the screen, with more information than Casey thought anybody should be able to get about a person. Yet another reason for her to stay as far out of the system as possible—anybody who knew her real name would know everything.

Parnell's likeness was from better times. He looked healthy, well-fed, and, if not supremely confident, at least comfortable with himself. The rest of the information was hard to read.

"So, what does it say about him?"

Nadine opened a new window and pulled up another database. "This is our own driver history. I thought his name sounded familiar. See, we used him a few years ago, even once early last year, but he's been out of our system completely since then." She flicked back to the official data. "Can't find him anywhere.

He might not be driving anymore. You think he had something to do with Evan's death?"

"Not directly. He probably didn't even know about it. How about Hank Nance?"

Nadine brought him up. "Same as Pat. Used to drive for us sometimes, now never. No traffic violations. Oh, here. Wanted for failure to pay child support."

"That's on there? Why?"

"Because he can't drive across state lines. He does, he's nabbed at weigh-in. Hasn't driven for anybody for almost two years."

"How about John Simones?"

Saying his name under her breath, Nadine put him into the computer. "He's still driving periodically. Nothing regular. But I don't see any outstanding warrants or indicators."

"Mick or Wendy Halveston?"

Nadine made a face. "Don't have to put them in. They won't be current in the database, because Mick can't drive. Everybody knows what happened two years ago. He can never drive again."

"Because he had an accident?"

"Because he had a physical problem that *caused* the accident. Seems he has some kind of heart condition. Whenever he sneezed or coughed, or even laughed, he'd pass out. That's what happened that day. He was talking on his phone, guy told him a joke, he laughed."

Casey closed her eyes. That entire family had died because Mick Halveston laughed at a joke. No. They died because he was driving when he should not have been. And talking on the phone while he should've been driving. "Mick was fine? And his wife?"

"Brand new cab. Airbags, the whole bit. They were both in the hospital for a while, but nothing permanent."

Like dying.

"Does Wendy drive?"

"Nope. Just liked to travel with Mick when she could. Guess they've had to find something else to do now. Maybe they've started a new brokerage." She grinned. "Who else?"

Casey was trying to put it together. Mick Halveston could never drive again. But she had pictures of him with his truck, and talking to Westing and Dixon. So if he was driving, it had to be under one of the names from the manifests.

"Casey?"

"Oh, sorry. One more. Sandy Greene."

Nadine put in the name, but came up blank. "You sure that name's right?"

Casey dug in her bag and pulled out her papers, paging through them. "Here it is. Sandy Greene. Driver for Class A Trucking."

Nadine re-typed the name, but again came up with nothing. She flipped to her own database, but he wasn't there, either. "Can't help you with that, hon. That's it?"

"How about on the manifests. Can you try these names?" She handed Nadine the stack, and Nadine typed in the first name. Bradley Hess. Lots of information—no picture.

"Looks like Hess has been driving exclusively for Class A Trucking," Nadine said. "Can't see any reason we wouldn't have used him. No traffic violations. No citations." She shrugged. "Model driver. Let's check out the others."

It was the same story with the rest of them. Each one showed records going back only two years, just about the time the other list of truckers had disappeared from the system, and each one had only a black and white box saying "no photo available." So Casey was right. Either Evan had stumbled onto a huge and unlikely coincidence, and these were all brand new drivers, or the other drivers had new names, and Evan had discovered them.

Casey looked down at her papers. What about Dixon and Westing? And the other thugs she had names for? She and Nadine went through them one by one, but none of them showed up in the system, except for Westing and Dixon, as owners of Class A Trucking.

"Can I get addresses and phone numbers for any of the truckers?"

"Sure." Nadine went back to each man and printed out his information. "You need me to contact any of them for you? Hmm. This is strange. All of these drivers—" she waved at the manifests—"they all have P.O. Boxes. No home addresses. Anyway, want me to call 'em?"

"No, thanks. I'll do it." Casey evened out the papers on the desk.

"So, what do you think?"

Casey sat back. "I don't know yet. It's all so…nothing's clear." Except that they were driving under fake names. But why? With the disappearing Class A logos and the fake IDs there was obviously something going on—but nothing she could put her finger on.

"So, is there anything I can tell Matt about Evan's death?"

"Not at this point. Not yet." Casey hesitated, then said, "Nadine…"

"What, sweetheart?"

"It's probably best if you don't tell anybody I was here. Or that you helped me look these guys up."

Nadine cocked her head. "And why is that?"

"You saw what happened to Evan."

"And you think it could happen to me, too?"

"I don't know. But I don't want you to take the chance."

Nadine looked at the computer for a few moments, then clicked out of the screen and deleted the site from her browser history. "You were never here."

"Thank you." Casey tried not to look too relieved. Besides wanting to protect Nadine, she also wanted to protect her own identity.

"But if you need anything more," Nadine said, "you have my number."

Casey stood. "Your receptionist still out there?"

"And still blind as a bat. But I'll check for others." She opened the door and peered into the lobby. "All clear. Can't promise about the parking lot, though."

Casey pulled the seed cap from her bag, where she'd stashed it for just such an occasion. "Thanks, Nadine. You've been great."

Nadine took a deep breath through her nose. "If someone's out there endangering truckers, I want them stopped. And if you can stop them…I'm all for that."

Casey averted her head from the sight-impaired receptionist, and ducked out to the parking lot.

Chapter Twenty

Casey was surprised to find the truck unoccupied when she got in, and wondered what kind of trouble Death was off causing. She looked at the empty seat across from her and wondered if she would be able to drive without the distraction of a passenger—even if that passenger was the Grim Reaper.

The dashboard clock said it was four-thirty, and Casey was determined to return Wendell's truck on time. She started the pick-up and pulled out of the parking lot, narrowly missing a car pulling in. The man at the wheel looked at her with surprise, pulling sharply to the right. Casey waved an apology and turned onto the street. Great way to not get noticed.

"*Make a legal U-turn,*" Laura Ingalls Wilder said from the door pocket.

Casey didn't need to go back to Deerfield Trucking, and she didn't need Laura harping at her for this trip, as she knew where she was going, so she shut off the application. From what she could see, Bailey had left her several more texts. Casey sighed. Having a teenager after you was worse than a pet dog. She firmly pressed the *Off* button and felt a weight lift from her shoulders.

It was almost five by the time Casey parked the truck at Blue Lake Gas and Go. Mr. Bored stood in the front door, thumbs hooked in his belt loops as he talked to a customer, whose back was to Casey. Mr. Bored tilted back into the shop, hollering, and Wendell came outside, wiping his hands on a rag. "How'd she do for you?"

"Perfect. It's been a long time since I've been behind a steering wheel. I was more worried about how I'd do for your truck. But no scratches." She smiled weakly, remembering the near miss in Deerfield's parking lot.

The customer talking at the office door turned to go, and Casey averted her face until she heard the car drive away.

"I'm sorry about him," Wendell said, meaning his boss. "He saw my truck was gone, and wondered what was happening."

"He'd seen me before. It's not a biggie." But the more people knew about her, the more nervous she became.

"So," Wendell said. "You get yourself something to eat?"

"I did. Thanks." She pulled out the change.

"No, no, you keep it. Get something later, when your lunch wears off."

"But—"

"Unless you want to come home with me for supper."

Casey groaned. A home-cooked meal. It was almost tempting enough… She stuffed the money back in her pocket. "Thanks, Wendell, I'd love to, but I'd better not."

"Figured that's what you'd say, but I thought I'd ask. You know my wife would be happy to feed you."

"I know. I appreciate it. And under normal circumstances…"

"But these are hardly normal. I understand. You need a ride somewhere? I'll be done here in a half hour."

Casey thought about where she should go next. Her meeting with Randy wasn't for seven hours, but she would be arriving a lot earlier. Until then? She needed to find a quiet place where she could make some calls to the truckers.

And maybe take a nap.

"I'm fine," she told Wendell. "Thanks again for the wheels."

"Anytime. Need the truck tomorrow?"

"Not that I know of."

"If you do, come on by. You can have it."

"Thanks, Wendell. I really appreciate it."

"I know. Have a good night."

Casey walked down the sidewalk to the first corner, and when she turned to look back, Wendell was watching her. She waved and disappeared down a side street.

The walk out to the shed felt familiar now, and very soon she saw the weathered wood. She began walking more briskly, but then halted. A harvester was kicking up dust in the field, shooting chaff out the rear as it gathered soybeans. So much for that location. At least for now.

Looking around, Casey turned back toward town, then ducked off to the south and found a still-standing cornfield. There were no tractors in sight, so she clambered through the rows until she could no longer see the road. It was a bit claustrophobic, but she only had to make room for one, as Death was still *in absentia*.

Not that she was complaining.

Casey got herself settled with her back against three stalks which grew together and pulled out the information she'd gotten from Nadine. Where should she begin?

At random, she picked Hank Nance, the driver who was wanted for failure to pay child support.

"Yo," he said, answering her call.

"Mr. Nance? My name is Casey Jones. I was wondering if I could talk to you about—"

The line hummed in her ear. She dialed again, wondering if Randy or Owen had warned him off, or if he thought she was someone who had hunted him down for the money he owed. This time he didn't answer, and she went straight through to voice mail. She left a brief message saying she wanted to talk with him about Class A Trucking, and that if he didn't call her back, she'd be in touch.

She tried Sandy Greene next.

"Listen, lady," he said. "I'm not going to talk to you, and you better not call me again, or you'll be sorry."

Lovely.

John Simones had a different attitude, but the message was the same. "I'm sorry," he said. "I really don't know what to tell you. I can't…please, don't call me anymore." And he hung up, too.

Casey sat back, letting her head fall against the corn, feeling the prickly stalk against her scalp. These people were scared. Scared to talk to her—to even answer their phones.

She only had one more number to call. Mick and Wendy Halveston. The couple in the photos. The driver who had killed an entire family when he'd overturned his truck. Casey hoped she'd be able to keep her feelings in check when she talked with them. She dialed. The phone rang until clicking into voice mail, and Casey sighed. Should she leave a message? No. It would just give them a chance to be warned of her call.

She let her hand fall against her shin, her arms wrapped around her knees. She'd pretty much just blown that whole angle.

The Bugs Bunny theme filled the air. The number displayed on the phone was the same one she'd just called.

"Hello?"

Silence.

"Hello? Is someone there?" Casey wondered if the call had been dropped.

"Um, hello?" A woman's voice, quiet and shaking. "This is… this is Wendy Halveston. Someone from this number just called?"

"Yes. Hi. My name is Casey Jones. I was wondering if I might talk to you about Class A Tr—"

"Not here," Wendy said.

"Okay, then where—"

"Tomorrow morning. The public library, in the reference section. Nine o'clock. I'll be waiting." She was gone.

Casey blinked, wondering what had just happened. These drivers were scared, and Wendy Halveston—she was scared, too. But something made her willing to talk.

Casey hoped she wouldn't change her mind by morning.

Chapter Twenty-one

Casey set the alarm on Terry's phone for a half hour and lay down to take a nap. She wanted to be sharp at the midnight meeting with Westing and whomever else he brought along. She awoke semi-refreshed, turned off the phone, and stood up to do some stretches.

"It's not even dark yet," Death said, strumming a guitar.

"I want plenty of time to get set up."

Death played a few more chords. "Set up for what?"

"You don't *really* think I'm going to just waltz in there expecting Randy to be alone and congenial?"

"Well, no."

"Good. You're not as dumb as you look."

Death made a hurt face. "But I try so hard."

"To be dumb or look smart?"

Death shrugged. "Either one."

Casey snorted and made her way through the cornstalks to the road.

"So what's the plan?" Death stayed one row in, while Casey walked on the pavement. The corn didn't even rustle. "What are we going to do?"

"*I* am going to check out *my* options."

"Are you going to beat them all up?" Death sounded hopeful.

"I don't plan on beating anyone up."

"Too bad."

Casey took a detour and found the grove of trees where she
and Death had rested after running from Davey's. The field
around it had been harvested, so there should be no one coming
anywhere near. She moved a largish rock, dug out a hollow
underneath it, and laid the bag with Evan's papers on the ground.
When she put the rock back and ran a stick over the dirt there
was no sign that it had ever been moved.

Satisfied, Casey looked for traffic and headed toward town.
The grocery store was easy to find, sitting all alone on the edge
of a residential neighborhood. Casey watched from behind a
Dumpster as customers walked in and out the front doors, lug-
ging bags or having their bags lugged by store employees.

"Nice little store," Death said. "Very hometown-y."

"It's probably owned by a local family. Definitely not a
chain." The lights in the parking lot had come on, triggered by
the fading evening light. "I don't see any of Randy and Owen's
guys. Either they're not here yet or they're in hiding."

"They're not that good."

"I agree. If they were here, I'd see them."

"Why do you do that?"

"Do what?"

"Speak like I'm not here. You said *you'd* see them. Not that
we'd see them."

"Am I hurting your feelings?"

"Yes."

Casey smiled. "Good."

Death turned away. Casey took the opportunity to slip across
the parking lot toward the back of the store. It would be darker
back there. Instead of lights on poles there were security floods on
the sides of the buildings. They weren't yet on, so Casey figured
they were either motion sensors, or were turned on and off from
a switch. A bread truck sat at the loading dock and two men
worked at unloading the pallets. Besides that, there were nine
cars—probably belonging to employees—and one semi trailer,
sitting without a cab. Casey waited until the bread truck was
empty, one man had signed a form, and the other had gotten

into the truck and driven off. When the store employee went back inside and the lot was still, Casey snuck over to the back of the trailer. It was open.

"Empty," Death said. "Wonder what was in it?"

"Nothing for quite a while." She swiped her finger on the trailer's bed and it came away dirty. "This lot's just a convenient place to leave something this big." She eyed it. "And I think it will be perfect."

"For what?"

In response, Casey walked to the front of the trailer and jumped up onto the hitch. Using the metals pieces meant for holding cables, she climbed up and perched on the roof.

"You're going to jump on them?" Death asked.

"Shh."

An employee came out the back door and leaned against the building, pulling out a cigarette.

"You know she can't hear me," Death said.

Casey hoped not.

Death wandered toward the woman, who had placed the cigarette between her lips and pulled out her lighter. She flicked on a flame and held it to the cigarette.

Death blew it out.

The woman flicked it once more, and once more Death extinguished it, giggling.

Again and again the woman tried, until she finally threw the lighter onto the parking lot and stormed into the building.

"You're cruel," Casey said.

"I would've thought you'd be glad of my intervention. Because of me she will live a few minutes longer, having not had that cigarette."

The door slapped open and the woman came back out, this time with a pack of matches. She struck the match. Death grinned, and blew out the flame.

The woman practically screamed with frustration, and lit one match after another, turning this way and that to avoid whatever draft she thought she was catching, until there was only one match left. With trembling fingers, she lit the match and held it up. Death leaned forward, lips pursed. The woman waited, then sucked in on her cigarette until the tip glowed orange. She crowed with triumph and exhaled happily.

Death put an arm around her shoulders. "Perhaps I'll be seeing you soon, sweetheart."

The woman shivered, looking around almost frantically.

Death blew on the cigarette, making the glowing end flare.

The woman dropped the cigarette and stared at it before crushing it under her heel and fleeing back into the building.

"Well," Casey said, "you've just ruined that woman's break time."

"Yeah. But it was fun."

Darkness was coming quickly now, and Casey took stock of the scene. The loading dock was bare except for two empty pallets, lying stacked one on the other. Another Dumpster sat along the far wall, and a picnic table was situated close to the back door on a patch of browning grass. On the one side of the property Casey could see homes, lights creating shadows on curtains, and on the other stood a line of trees. Directly behind the store was an open field of harvested soybeans. It would be dark where Casey sat on top of the trailer, the security lights not reaching her, and she could see every inch of the lot, except for the opposite side of the Dumpster. But she would know if anyone hid behind it, and no one would do that for at least another hour, until the daytime employees were gone.

Casey lay on her back, watching as the stars came out. It was a clear night, and the moon shone brightly, illuminating the parking lot without help from the security lights. The trailer was cold and hard against her back, and Casey longed for a soft, warm bed. She remembered the bed she'd slept on the week before, at Rose and Lillian's B and B, and she wondered what was going on in that little town. Eric's face swam before her, and images from that last night… Her shoulder throbbed, and she gritted her teeth.

"Not a good time to be thinking about that." Death lay beside her, also looking up at the sky. "Time instead to be clearing your mind for what lies ahead."

The sound of the back door reached her, and Casey quietly rolled over and peered over the edge of the trailer. Employees were filing out, aprons discarded, calling goodnight. Each went to a car and got in, the cigarette woman lighting up as soon as her door was shut. She peeled out of the parking lot first, and the others followed. Before they were all gone, two cars pulled in.

"Maintenance and stocking crew," Death said.

Soon all that were left were the two new cars and one of the original nine. A manager, probably, getting ready to close.

"I wonder what time it is," Casey said. She considered turning on Terry's phone to check, but decided it didn't really matter. The guys would be coming soon, to get ready for her.

Eventually the manager came out and drove away, leaving only the two cars. Randy and his men should be arriving momentarily.

They came more quietly than she expected, without a car. Owen Dixon, his blond hair shimmering in the moonlight, walked around the corner, scanning the area. Apparently satisfied, he waved, and several men followed, one of them Craig Mifflin, whom Casey had knocked out at Davey's scrapyard.

"Wow, they expect quite a battle from you," Death said. "*Five* of them. And Westing's not even here."

They weren't going to give her a fighting chance.

Owen pointed here and there, setting the men up where they wouldn't be seen. One behind the Dumpster, two between the cars, and one crouched behind the loading dock. Dixon walked toward the trailer and Casey held her breath. If he came up there, it would be all over. She pulled her head back to make it invisible from below and listened as hard as she could. A rock popped under Dixon's foot as he rounded the trailer, and Casey felt a slight shift as he stepped into the empty back. Casey put her hands flat on the roof, ready to jump up and fight if need be.

But Dixon didn't go any further. He'd just wanted to get up into the trailer so his feet wouldn't be visible from the ground. At least, that's what Casey would've done, if she had been him.

All six of them, seven if you counted Death, waited together for whatever would happen next.

Chapter Twenty-two

Casey was cold by the time Westing drove into the lot. She hadn't been able to move, for fear Dixon would hear, and dew had settled on her, chilling her to the bone. She hoped the guys were just as uncomfortable as she. At least they could huddle with their arms around themselves.

Headlights swung across the space, and the SUV stopped in the middle of the pavement. Westing got out of the Explorer and looked around. Casey watched from the darkness at the top of the trailer, confident she was invisible.

"She's not here," Dixon said from his hiding place, making Casey jump. "We've been here an hour, and there's no sign of her."

Westing crossed his arms and leaned against the hood of his car. "Good. Now shut up or she'll hear you."

So they all sat back and waited for Casey to show up.

Death giggled. "This would be funny if it weren't so stupid."

Casey glared at her companion. She wasn't laughing as her muscles cramped and she shivered against the metal.

Time ticked by. Nothing happened. Casey heard Dixon shifting now and then in the back, and could see three of the hiding men as they changed positions, trying to keep their feet from going to sleep as they squatted. Westing pushed off from the Explorer and marched forward, scanning both directions. He looked at his watch so many times it made Casey think of a little kid on a long car trip: Are we there yet? Are we there yet?

Dixon finally jumped down from his perch and walked into Casey's sightlines. "She ain't coming."

Westing spun around. "Get back there! She'll see you!"

"It's been almost an hour, man. She stood us up."

Westing turned in a circle, his arms rising, then falling. He let out a growl of frustration, slamming his hand onto the Explorer's hood. "*Damn* it!"

Dixon crossed his arms. "Yonkers is gonna be pissed."

"Don't…"—Westing held up a hand, pointing at Dixon—"… make it sound like this is my fault. We planned this out together. Yonk okayed it."

Yonkers? Casey knew that name. Why?

"Wasn't blaming you," Dixon said. "Just stating a fact."

Westing rubbed his forehead. "Why didn't she come?"

"Think one of the kids tipped her off?"

Casey tried not to react to the mention of the teenagers— assuming that is who Dixon meant. But who else would he mean? She wasn't in touch with any other children.

"The *kids* don't know. Just the one."

Casey closed her eyes. One was enough to screw them all. But *which* one?

"She got the phone last night," Westing said. "Where did she go?"

"Hey, Ballard!" Dixon barked the name toward the Dumpster. "Where did the woman go today?"

The man got up and walked out to Dixon. He was big, but not all of it was muscle. "Kid didn't tell us about the phone until this morning, so we don't got much. We found her up in McPherson—"

"Parnell," Dixon explained to Westing. "He's gone."

Oh, no. Poor Pat.

"Then she went out toward Hutchinson," Ballard said. "Figured she was paying a visit to Deerfield Trucking, but I don't know what she would've found there. By the time we got there she was long gone, and the girl at the desk didn't have any idea who we were talking about."

"And after that?" Westing was practically foaming at the mouth.

"We lost her for a while. She must've turned the phone off. But we caught the signal later and traced it to the middle of a cornfield. Don't know what she was doing out there, but we couldn't find any sign of her or the phone."

"And now?"

"She's nowhere."

Thank *God* she'd resisted the temptation to check the time. She didn't know how tightly they could pinpoint the signal, but she'd been that close to ruining everything.

"So what do we do?" Westing said. "Now that you've *lost* her?"

Ballard stepped back, gesturing to Dixon. "It's you guys' call. Whatever you want."

Westing turned on Dixon. "Well, Dix?"

Dixon shrugged. "Maybe she'll get back in touch with Bruce. We'll need to give him a message to pass on to her."

"And the kid?"

"Said she meets with them every night—maybe she's with them right now in the shed where she's been staying."

Casey breathed a quiet sigh of relief that the harvester had come to the field and she'd been forced to hide her bag elsewhere. But alongside the relief she fought a wave of sadness. Somebody in the little group of teens had given them all up. So much for solidarity.

"God, I hope we find her," Ballard said. "My wife's been seeing those ads for jewelry and won't let me forget our twentieth is coming up."

"Why do we care about your anniversary?" Dixon snapped.

"Yonk said we get this woman off our tail, payday will be coming soon."

Dixon snorted. "He's been saying that for the past six months."

"Shut it," Westing said. "Yonk's good for the money. He told us it would take a while. That we need to be patient."

"I'm *patient*," Dixon said. "I've been *patient* for a year and a half."

"So let's go," Westing said. "Catch this bitch before she has a chance to move again."

"And if she's not at the shed?"

Westing's face was grim. "Then she'll show up somewhere else. We'll get her."

The men climbed into Westing's Explorer—it had to be a tight fit, even with it being an SUV—and drove away, their lights disappearing into the darkness.

"Well, that was anticlimactic," Death said.

"You think? We just found out these guys are expecting a boatload of money."

"Big deal. Isn't everything about money? I mean, *yawn*."

"We also found out one of our kids is a rat."

"I bet I know who it is."

"With your Spidey-sense?"

"No, with my smart sense. You know Sheryl's hated you from the second she saw you."

"But she's annoyed with *all* grown-ups. Would she help these guys, rather than me?"

"They're badasses. She might like sticking it to you."

Sheryl was the one Casey *hoped* it was. Otherwise she'd done a crappy job reading them. Not that she'd tried all that hard. She'd let her exhaustion, lack of resources, and…let's face it… *loneliness* push her closer to the kids than she ever should've been. Besides, she liked all the others. Terry didn't care much for her, but he would do what was best for Sheryl—which was getting Casey out of town fast without involving their little group. Johnny was too dumb, and he hadn't been there when Casey had gotten the phone. Martin? Bailey? It hurt to think either of them would turn her over to the men. But whoever had done it, she couldn't let the rest get caught.

"Think the guys have a tracer on the phone now?"

"Probably."

"I'm going to have to risk it. There's no way I'll get out to the shed before the men."

Death considered, and nodded. "You don't really have a choice, if you want the kids out of there."

But *who* to call? She turned on the phone, muted the sound, and texted Bailey.

Dont tel thm its me Get out of shed now Wil b in tuch l8er

She sent the message. "Think she'll listen?"

"You know…" Death peered over her shoulder. "You're getting the hang of the texting thing. Better spelling."

Casey's phone buzzed.

Why? Whr r u?

Casey's fingers flew.

Just get out!!

"Speaking of getting out…" Death stood over her. "We should probably move on, now that you've turned on the phone."

Casey turned it off. "I wanted to make sure the men were gone before leaving."

Death disappeared, and was back in seconds. "They've split. Nowhere within a three-mile radius."

"You could look that fast?"

Death peered down at her disdainfully. "Are you forgetting who I am?"

Casey closed her eyes, and felt the weight of everything upon her. "No. I will never forget who you are."

"Come on," Death said. "Let's go. Do one of those flips where you arch your back and end up on your feet."

"How 'bout I get up slowly and painfully, like an old woman?"

"I guess that'll work."

She eased up, knees cracking, shoulder stinging. "Okay." She sighed. "Let's go find a traitor."

Chapter Twenty-three

Casey walked out to Bailey's house, arriving in a little over an hour. The night was dark and damp, and she shivered as she hid in the pine trees at the edge of the property. The men were nowhere in sight. Neither were any teenagers. Death had taken off a few miles ago, and Casey didn't miss the added chill.

Which window was Bailey's? She couldn't tell. It was practically impossible to see which window had black curtains, since they all were dark. She studied the house, trying to remember the lay-out, and finally decided on the second window on the east side. If she was wrong, well, she'd run like hell.

She gathered a handful of pinecones and situated herself under the window. She tossed one. Then another. The curtains swept aside, and Bailey's white face shone in the window. She glanced behind her, into the house, then turned back to Casey, a finger up. Her face disappeared and the curtains fell. Casey stepped back into the shadows, wondering how many kids were there.

Just one.

"Where were you?" Bailey demanded. "And what was the deal with the shed?"

Casey pulled her further from the house. "Somebody told."

The girl's face screwed up. "Told what?" She seemed genuinely confused.

Casey felt a tiny bit of weight ease from her shoulders at Bailey's apparent innocence. "One of your friends told…" How to explain? "…told the bad guys how to find me. They were coming to the shed. They're probably there right now."

"No. Nobody would give away the shed. That's crazy."

Casey held up the phone. "Someone also told them I had this. They've been tracking me all day."

Bailey's mouth dropped open. "So they know you're here? Right now?"

"No, the phone's off. But any time I had it on today they traced it, found out where I'd been, and went there."

And now Pat Parnell was *gone*, whatever Dixon meant by that. Had Casey gotten him in trouble by visiting? Gotten him *killed*? No, Death would have told her that.

"But why would someone tell?" Bailey said. "And *who* did?"

"I don't know. What do you think? Who would betray you all like that?"

Bailey was distressed. "*None* of them! They wouldn't…" She jabbed her finger at Casey. "You're just saying that. It didn't really happen. Why would you say that?"

"If you don't believe me, go out to the shed right now and look. The men might still be there."

Bailey jerked away, crossing her arms over her stomach. "I don't…" She shuddered. "What should we do?"

"Where are the others?"

"Home."

Casey really wanted to know which kid had told, but getting them back together tonight would be tricky. "We should sleep. I'll be in touch tomorrow. Okay? And listen…can we keep this just between you and me? Not tell the others until we figure out how to stop the leak?"

Bailey was silent for a few moments before shrugging. "All right."

"I need to see you all. Where would it work?"

Bailey hesitated, then swung around. "After school tomorrow, Johnny has a JV football game. We're all going."

Casey couldn't show up there. Too many people. "How about afterward?"

"Sometimes we get pizza in town. Sometimes we go to Newton, to the Denny's."

"And how would you get there?"

"One of us would drive everybody. It's about six miles."

Casey couldn't go that distance. "Can you make sure you go to the pizza place?"

"Yeah. They usually listen to me."

Casey had noticed. "Will you walk from the stadium?"

"It's right down the street, so yeah."

"What route will you take?"

Bailey's face scrunched up as she thought and she rubbed her face hard, smearing her eyeliner. "Up Adams to Main. It's simple."

"Any way you can go a different path, where there won't be many people?"

"I guess. I'd have to come up with an excuse."

"I have confidence in you. They'll do what you suggest."

Bailey paled even more in the illumination from the house's outside lights. "Okay. So I guess we'll go back behind the library, you know how you can see the stadium from there? There's a road that's more like an alley, and we can take that up toward the pizza place."

"What time?"

"Six?"

That should work. "Thanks, Bailey. I'll be keeping the phone off until then. No sense in leading them to us. Goodnight." She turned to go.

"Casey?"

She stopped.

"Why did you come to me? Why didn't you think I was the one who'd talked?"

"Because you're the real deal, Bailey. You care about the others, and about your group. You would never give away your hiding place."

Bailey frowned. "I care about you, too."

"Which only proves you're crazy. But thanks. I'll see you tomorrow. And remember…" She put a finger to her lips.

Bailey smiled brightly, her teeth shining. "You know me. I can keep a secret. Goodnight, Casey."

Casey smiled back, and slipped away into the night.

Chapter Twenty-four

The bed was huge. It was also soft, and warm, and there was someone else in it.

Casey sat up.

"Did I wake you?" Death stopped playing the Native American flute.

"No…no, I…" Casey sank back down to the grass in the little grove of trees. "What I wouldn't give for a mattress."

"And miss the wonders of nature? The fresh air, the blue sky—"

"—the pain in my backside."

Death looked hurt. "I certainly hope you are not referring to *me*."

"Hey, you said it." Casey crawled to the creek and splashed water on her face. "What time is it?"

Death squinted at the sun. "I would say…seven? Seven-thirty?"

Casey was meeting Wendy Halveston at nine. And she was *starving*. "I've still got a few dollars left. Suggestions on where I can go for food and not be noticed?"

"Honey, wherever you go, you're going to get noticed. It's like you haven't taken a shower in several days."

"I haven't."

"Well, then, no wonder you look that way."

Casey bit her tongue. Arguing wouldn't get her anywhere. "Too bad women don't still make pies and put them on the window sill to cool."

Death looked thoughtful.

"What?"

"Terry's parents own a bakery."

"So?"

"Think they throw out the things that don't sell, and that Terry doesn't take to the shed?"

"Oh, great. Now you want me to go Dumpster diving for stale bread?"

"It's not like it would ruin your clothes."

"No, but it might ruin my stomach."

Death played a quick tune on the flute. "You could go by the hospital again, grab some peanut butter and crackers."

Casey ignored this and stood up to do some stretching, careful not to break open the finally-healing scab on her shoulder.

Death groaned. "You're not going to exercise again, are you?"

"Don't have time." She stretched her arms to the sky, feeling the pull in her back. A mattress sure would be welcome. And she had no idea when she would ever sleep on one again.

"You should probably get a move on if you want to make your meeting on time," Death said.

"Yeah." She looked at the rock where the papers were hidden. "Think I should take that?"

"Be a little heavy."

"Not the rock, you moron, the bag of papers."

"Geez, I think you forgot your sense of humor back there in Ohio with the rest of your stuff."

"I think I'll leave the papers here. Wendy Halveston seems to want to talk. She doesn't need encouragement. And just in case I run into those guys…" She straightened suddenly. "Yonkers!"

"Gesundheit."

"No. The guys mentioned Yonkers last night."

"So?"

"Evan was talking about somebody named Yonkers…Willie Yonkers…right before the crash."

"And what did he say?"

She pushed on her eyes with the heels of her hands. "We were talking about kids, and families, and jobs…he said Willie Yonkers' family can't stand him, but that he has more money than he knows what to do with. Evan was jealous."

"And you think this is the same man?"

"How many people named Yonkers can travel in the same circles? It's got to be him." She glanced up at the sun. "If I hurry, I can…no, I can't."

"Can't what?"

"Use the library's computer. They won't let you without an ID."

"Bailey will probably have her laptop after school."

"Yeah, but I don't want to wait that long." She growled with frustration. Not having identification was more of a problem than she had ever realized.

"Well, you have to go anyway, or you're going to be late."

Death was right. Casey crept from her hiding place, leaving the bag, but taking her turned-off phone. Whenever she heard a vehicle she ducked into a field, if one was available, but each day there were fewer fields remaining unharvested. She just had to cross her fingers and hope the farmers on the tractors didn't wonder too much who she was and what she was doing, traveling along their quiet road.

She arrived in town about fifteen minutes early and tried to walk as unobtrusively as possible, going down Main Street instead of the residential sections, where a stranger would stand out. There weren't many people about, and when a car drove past she simply averted her head, looking toward shop fronts. The library parking lot, when she arrived, was mostly empty. Casey didn't see Westing's Explorer—not that she really thought it would be there, but it would be stupid not to look—and of course didn't know what kind of vehicle Wendy Halveston drove.

Casey stood in the shade of a tree for several minutes, waiting until the clock on the bank's sign across the street showed nine-o'clock. The library was a two-story building, the first floor actually a sort of basement, down the side of a hill, with the main entrance on the upper level, on Main Street. Casey avoided the front door and went inside on the lower floor, through a back door. The basement was cool and quiet, with dark conference rooms and a closed door declaring AV Equipment.

She came upon the open door of a staff room and would have snuck in for one of the bagels she saw on the counter if it hadn't been for the woman dunking a tea bag into a cup of steaming water. Stomach rumbling, Casey walked quickly past.

She took the stairs slowly, listening for other people, but saw no one until she reached the upper floor. The door opened into the children's section, and Casey moved quietly past a small play area, where a few mothers sat with toddlers, and found the reference section. Watching a few rows over from between stacks of books she could see only one person in the reference area. She hoped it was Wendy. She went over.

"Mrs. Halveston?"

The woman spun around.

"I'm Casey Jones."

"Where did you come from? I was watching." Wendy's hand fluttered toward the front desk, and then down. Casey recognized the older woman from the picture in the diner. She didn't look angry today, however. She looked worried.

"Shall we sit?" Casey indicated a table with chairs, which was surrounded by dictionaries, encyclopedias, and books on such varied topics as the greatest American plays and Civil War-era foods.

The woman sank into the closest chair and clasped her hands together on the table. Looking into her face, Casey thought the poor woman was getting even less sleep than she.

Mrs. Halveston looked furtively around the library, as if expecting someone else to come jumping out of the stacks. "Why did you call me?"

"I could ask the same of you," Casey said. "Why did you call *back*?"

Her mouth twitched. "I'm just...it's just..."

"I know about Class A Trucking."

Mrs. Halveston's eyes filled with tears. "Class A Trucking." It sounded like she wanted to spit. "What is it you know?"

"What do you *want* me to know?"

Mrs. Halveston reached into her purse and pulled out a wadded tissue, which she used to angrily wipe away tears. "It depends who you are, doesn't it? If you're with them, or if you're not."

"Class A?"

Mrs. Halveston waited, chin up, tissue clenched in her fingers.

"I'm certainly not with them, " Casey said. "In fact, I'm doing everything in my power to stay away from them. But...I would like to catch them at whatever they're doing and stop them."

Mrs. Halveston sniffled, and held the tissue against her eyes for a few moments. When she looked back up she said, "They drove him to it, you know."

Casey blinked. "Who? Drove him to what?"

"Patty." Mrs. Halveston closed her eyes. "Poor man. I never thought he'd do it."

Patty. "Pat Parnell. He *killed himself?*"

"Killed hims—No. Heavens, no. He just ran away. Left it all. Called Mick, said he was getting out, that he wasn't up for it anymore. Left his truck at the lot and took off. He's...he's completely broken."

Casey could've told her that.

"I'm not going to let them do that to Mick."

Mick. "Tell me what's going on, Mrs. Halveston. Please. I don't understand."

The woman gazed out the large window beside the table, which overlooked the back parking lot and the tops of several homes, but Casey didn't think she was seeing anything other than her own thoughts. Casey kept herself from pushing—the woman would tell her story in her own time.

"Mick had...an accident. With his truck." She glanced at Casey, and Casey nodded to show she knew of the crash that killed an entire family. "After that he couldn't get work anymore. He wasn't supposed to be driving with his condition, but driving truck is...it's what he *does*." She turned pleading eyes on Casey,

and Casey tried to remain expressionless. While she felt sorry
for Mick, she felt ten times sorrier for the family he'd killed
when he'd known he had a potentially fatal medical condition.

"He could only find odd jobs," Mrs. Halveston said. "I was
clerking at the grocery store, but that wasn't enough to pay the
bills. He felt responsible, and he tried to find something different, really he did, but nothing came up. Class A called him.
Said they were a new company and were willing to use him as
a driver, even with his…shortcomings."

Shortcomings that killed people. "So he took the job?"

"Yes." Mrs. Halveston's voice was a whisper now. "I tried to
get him to say no, but he wanted to drive. *Needed* to drive. So
I did what I could—I quit my job and said I was traveling with
him wherever he went to make sure he didn't…to make sure
he was okay."

So Class A Trucking hired a man who legally shouldn't drive.
Why? "How did they get around the legalities?" She asked, but
she already knew.

Mrs. Halveston hiccupped. "They gave him false identification. A new driver's license. Made his alter ego younger, healthier.
He was so much happier than he'd been in the years since the
accident. He was driving again, and everything was going great."

And everyone on the road was in danger of being crushed
when he fainted and his semi crashed. "What was his name on
his new license?"

"Simon. Simon Rale."

A match to one of the names in Evan's packet. Casey wondered which names fit the other drivers. What had Pat Parnell's
fake name been? Hank Nance's? And what was keeping them
legally off the road?

"So," she asked, "what happened? Why are you even talking
to me?"

Mrs. Halveston pierced her with her eyes. "Because things
didn't stay great. First it was just a gift we had to deliver to the
boss' nephew across state lines. It was wrapped up all pretty in
a bow. We didn't think twice about it—we were just happy to

help out, since Class A had helped us. We took it, and that was that…" She paused, looking down at the table.

"Until the next time," Casey said.

Mrs. Halveston wouldn't look up.

"And each time it got a little worse," Casey continued, "and soon you were transporting things you knew were wrong. What was it? Weapons? Drugs?"

"Oh, no!" She did look up at that. "We would never—"

"What were you hauling?"

"Nothing illegal. Just TVs, and frozen cauliflower, and… whatever they wanted."

"So the present to the nephew was just a test?"

Mrs. Halveston's lips pinched into a hard line. "I guess. To see if we'd do what they asked without question. We're not supposed to transport things, you know, other than what's listed on the manifest."

Just like they weren't supposed to drive with a false license.

"So…I don't understand. Why did they need to test you to see if you'd drive legitimate loads?"

Mrs. Halveston sighed heavily. "Because half the time they're *not* legitimate." Her shoulders slumped. "They're stolen goods."

"What?"

"It's a huge money-maker, apparently."

Crime often was. "How does it work?"

"A couple of ways. One is to simply show up at the warehouse with what looks like a real order. They load the merchandise onto your truck, and you leave. They don't even know they gave it to the wrong person."

"Don't they recognize drivers?"

"Oh, honey, do you realize how many drivers there are?"

Tom had told her. What had he said? One and a half million trucks on the road at any given time? Which meant there were many more drivers than that.

"Some suppliers might use only the same drivers from the same trucking companies, but these guys would know that. They go for the places that see different faces every day. Besides, the drivers are driving for Class A Trucking, too, so if they seem familiar…" She shrugged. "It makes sense."

"So Class A isn't doing the stealing?"

"Not technically. When we drive a legitimate load it's through Class A. When it's stolen…we're on our own as an independent driver."

So for Class A's real orders they would put the logo on their trucks. When they drove a bad shipment, they took it off. "What's the other way to steal loads, other than just showing up and taking it?"

"Paperwork."

"How so?"

Mrs. Halveston leaned her elbows on the table, her head sinking down. "It's all so complicated. But if I sell you a load of soup and I don't have soup, I'm going to have to get it from somewhere. I buy the soup from another place, get it, and then sell it to my customer at a mark-up."

"Not exactly stealing."

She gave a little laugh. "Not *exactly*. But my customer has no idea where I'm getting the soup, and the people selling me the soup don't know I'm selling it again for a profit. They could be selling directly to my customer, but I'm getting in the way."

"Sounds like regular business."

"It could be if it were up front, I guess. But the way it's done here, it's harming both the original seller and the customer through a dishonest business practice. I told you it was hard to explain."

But Casey did understand the term *stealing*. And she thought she knew what was going on with the drivers. "Class A hires drivers who can't drive elsewhere, then blackmails them into hauling stolen goods."

Mrs. Halveston's head sank even further.

"What did they have on Pat Parnell?"

"Oh, that poor man. He had a family, you know. A wife and children—I don't remember how many—and then had that unfortunate affair out in California. Every time he would drive out that way he would meet up with his lover, and…" She shrugged.

So Pat Parnell had lost his family over another woman. That was awful, surely, but Casey couldn't see how that could be used as blackmail anymore, since his wife obviously knew and had left him.

"The affair," Mrs. Halveston said quietly, "was with a man."

Oh. Casey remembered the notes in Evan's journal. *Carl Billings, SF.* The name of the other party, and, most likely, San Francisco, if he'd been heading out west, to California.

Mrs. Halveston continued. "His wife divorced him and took the children, and the company he'd been driving with—a conservative Christian outfit out of Bingham, said they couldn't have people like him driving for them, and fired him."

"But other companies wouldn't be that way. Why couldn't he go somewhere else?"

Mrs. Halveston shook her head sadly. "He and his wife had just built that house. When she divorced him, she left him with the house and all of the debt. He couldn't contest it—plus felt he didn't have a right to. Jobs would come in, but free-lancing full-time wasn't enough to satisfy all the lenders. Until Class A called him. I guess they knew him from somewhere. Told him they'd give him a better-paying job if he kept it quiet. The way he acted it was like they were his saviors. Now look where it got him."

Casey could picture it. A man sinking deeper and deeper, and suddenly a lifeline. He grabbed it, and it only got worse.

"It was all too much for him," Mrs. Halveston said. "What with losing his family, and his job, and then the bank called and said they would be foreclosing. He went to them to ask for help, but they turned him away."

"The bank?"

"No. Class A. He couldn't go drive for anyone else, because the guys had him over a barrel. If he left to drive for another company, they'd turn him in for something—believe me, they had plenty with all the jobs he did for them—and he'd lose everything for sure. Besides that, they hold his money. They say they're short on cash and they'll pay after his next job, or after the supplier pays the trucking bill. Half the time we don't see a paycheck for three or four months. But what are we to do? It's the same for the others. We all have something to lose."

"Hank Nance?"

Wendy nodded. "Turn him in for crossing state lines, and he'd owe all those months of child support."

Probably the months listed in Evan's notes. "And John Simones?"

"Paying his son's dues. Got charged with date rape at college, and John had to cough up the money for the legal fees. He took the job with Class A because it paid better, but now they have him on the wrong side of the law, since he's been driving stolen goods."

"But if Westing and Dixon turned any of these men in, wouldn't it just lead back to them?"

She snorted. "To whom? You can bet your life they don't have their real names on those false papers. Not like they have the drivers' names. Whether they're the drivers' fake names or the real ones, they have the truckers in their pockets."

Casey knew Wendy was right—she couldn't remember seeing any names on the manifests other than the truckers'. Dixon and Westing were listed as Class A's owners, but if that company was supposedly doing the legitimate work, they wouldn't be connected to the other. Besides, it would be their word against truckers who were breaking the law just by getting behind a wheel.

Westing and Dixon were taking a huge chance, though, with their names on the business. Their boss' name wasn't *anywhere*. "Mrs. Halveston, do you know the name Yonkers?"

"Like in New York?"

"No, like in a person. Is the name Willie Yonkers familiar?"

She shook her head. "Never heard of him."

Exactly what Casey thought. If Willie Yonkers was involved he kept it a secret from just about everyone.

"What are you going to do?" Mrs. Halveston's eyes were bright with tears and fear. "If they know I met with you they'll quit having Mick drive, and that would just kill him."

"I'm not going to tell them."

Mrs. Halveston scraped her chair back and stood. "I need to go."

"May I call you again?"

She licked her lips. "We're leaving this afternoon."

"On a job?"

"To Montana."

Great. All of those people in danger on the road. "Drive safely."

"Oh, we will."

Not seeming to hear the irony in the exchange, Mrs. Halveston peeked around the book stacks and scurried out of the library.

Chapter Twenty-five

The downstairs break room was empty when Casey walked past, so she went in and slathered two bagels with cream cheese, wrapping them in a napkin. She pulled a wrinkled dollar bill, left over from Wendell's cache, from her pocket and stuck it in the tin designated for coffee money. She wasn't yet so desperate she was ready to start stealing from libraries.

She stood just inside the library door. Where to go? She couldn't go back to the shed. The men had seen her at Davey's. She shouldn't bother Wendell again—even if he wasn't going to turn her in, one of his co-workers might begin to wonder what she was doing, hanging around.

"Tom Haab would probably let you use his computer," Death said.

Casey jumped. "You enjoy that, don't you? Scaring me?"

"Yeah. Sometimes."

"Um, may I help you?" A woman with a library nametag stood at the far end of the hall.

Casey turned partway, hiding her bagels. "I was just leaving. Thank you." She pushed out through the door and headed up the incline, away from the library and toward a side street. When she looked back, she could see the librarian watching her through the glass door.

Super.

"So how do we get to Southwest Trucking?" Casey tried to remember how Davey had driven. "It was a few miles west, wasn't it?"

"Kinda far to walk."

Death was right. And she'd been walking so much. For a moment she yearned for the old Schwinn she'd been riding back in Clymer just a few days ago. Old, but serviceable. And lots faster than walking. She sighed. "I guess I'd better get started."

At least she had the bagels to eat on the way, which instantly gave her more energy. She pulled the seed hat out of the bag and pulled it low on her forehead, shielding her eyes from the sun and her face from observers.

About a mile out of town she heard a vehicle coming. The field beside her was harvested, and there were no trees anywhere within hiding distance.

"Steady," Death said. "She's already seen you, so there's no point in freaking out now."

The car pulled up alongside Casey and slowed to a stop. The passenger window lowered and the woman at the steering wheel leaned out. "Give you a lift?"

The car was an older model that probably should have been traded in as a clunker long before. Despite the rust spots, however, the car was clean both inside and out. The woman wore jeans and a plain blue knit shirt, and her hair was pulled back in a messy bun. Her eyes sparkled with curiosity in her tired face.

"Too interested?" Casey mumbled to Death.

"I'm getting in." And suddenly the back seat was no longer empty.

"Thank you," Casey said to the woman. "I would appreciate it."

Once Casey was buckled in the woman glanced in the rearview mirror and continued on. "How far are you going?"

"Southwest Trucking. I'm not sure of the address, but it's a few miles out this way."

"Sure, I know them. In fact, it's where I'm going. Makes sense, I guess. There's not a whole lot else on this side of town."

"Do you work there?"

The woman's mouth tightened. "No. My husband's done a little driving for them in the past."

Casey kept herself from looking at Death. "And you live here in Blue Lake?"

"For now." She took a deep breath and let it out. "What about you? You're new to the area, I take it? Or just traveling through?" She glanced at Casey's clothes, taking extra time with the second pink shirt Casey had had to wear. Casey wished she had a jacket to pull around her.

"Yes, just…traveling through."

"And you know someone at Southwest?"

Casey did glance back at Death now. How much to tell?

Death shrugged and pulled out the bagpipe.

"Tom Haab," Casey said. "I'm going to see him."

"I know Tom. He started that company years ago, with his cousin, I think. Bob, my husband, grew up with them—I mean, he was a little older than Tom, but went to school with his older brother. They've done well for themselves. Bob says they're good at what they do. He recommends them all the time, but then, that would have helped him get jobs, too, when he was still driving."

Exactly what Tom had said was the best publicity—word of mouth.

"So do you know the other truckers?"

She shook her head. "Out of my circle. Bob didn't drive for Southwest often—he had a full-time job at Snyder's furniture, in Castleton? You don't know them? Well, they…he got laid off last month." Her mouth did that tightening thing again, pinching her lips together, making wrinkles in her face.

"I'm sorry."

The woman waved her hand. "No, I shouldn't be burdening you."

"It's okay. I just—I know a lot of people who recently lost their jobs. A whole plant shut down, and basically laid off the whole town with it. Really sad."

"That would be. But this wasn't the whole company. Just my husband."

Casey winced. "No seniority?"

"Oh, he had that. But he's also in the early stages of Parkinson's, which means he can get a little shaky. They decided he was a risk, didn't want to pay extra insurance on him, and—" she banged her hand on the steering wheel – "he was outta there. Nothing we could do."

This was sounding awfully familiar. "You didn't want to fight it?"

"Don't have the money, and apparently there's not a good enough guarantee we would win for lawyers to take the risk of getting paid on contingency. Bob can't even get another job. With that diagnosis he's certainly not going to be able to drive trucks—not that we would even put Tom in the position of making that decision."

"So what are you going to do?" Although Casey already knew the answer.

"What else could we do? We're moving back to my home, in Kansas City. My folks run a little hardware shop. They're barely making it, what with Walmart moving in, but they said they'll give Bob some work, let us move in with them until we get back on our feet. I sell jewelry—you know, I go to people's houses, have parties where we sell to their friends—but there's no way that can keep us going." She smiled sadly. "Our daughter is threatening to stay here. Wants to live with one of her friends. But I can't let her go, not yet." Her eyes filled with tears, and Casey pictured Sheryl's beautiful, angry face.

"I understand. You're doing the best thing you can for your whole family."

Sheryl's mom sniffled and reached for the tissue box in the back seat. Just when she was about to grab it she jerked away and fiddled with the knobs on the dashboard. When she'd made sure the air conditioning was off she reached back again, and Death scooted out of the way so she wouldn't come into contact. "Our son doesn't mind moving so much. He's not *happy* about it, but he's in sixth grade, he can still make friends easily. Sheryl—our daughter—she's a junior, and I hate pulling her out of school and putting her somewhere new, because your friends from high school, well, they're so important, aren't they? I mean, hopefully she'll go on to college or something, but it could be that these friends are the ones that will be with her forever. But the bills are already piling up, and we can't pay our mortgage, and what are we supposed to *do?*"

Casey didn't know how to respond. She knew how miserable Sheryl was, but her mother seemed just as miserable, and what does a teenager know about how much money it takes to keep her in clothes and food and shelter? Not enough.

Sheryl's mom pulled into the parking lot of Southwest and stopped the car. "I'm sorry." She blew her nose. "I didn't mean to go off on a tangent like that, tell you my whole life story."

"It's okay. It's the stranger thing—you know you won't see me again, so you can tell me whatever you want and it won't matter."

Sheryl's mom smiled. "You're right." She pulled down the visor and wiped smeared mascara from her face.

"You're not here to apply for a job, are you?" Casey asked.

"No. I wish. I asked Tom about it, and he said they don't have anything at all right now—and I would have taken anything to keep our family here. But what Tom did say was that he'd figure out a way to get our stuff to Kansas City. He told me to come out and talk to his assistant about scheduling a truck, so…here I am. The trucking connection will come in handy, after all. You ready?"

"Yes." They got out of the car. "Thank you so much for the ride."

"You're welcome. I hope…well, have a good trip, wherever you're going."

"And I hope things go well with your move, and your daughter, especially."

"Thanks. I need all the good vibes I can get. You going in?"

"I think I'll wait just a bit."

"Okay, then. Good-bye."

"Good-bye. And thank you."

Sheryl's mother straightened her shoulders and walked away, a picture of grace, sadness, and acceptance.

Chapter Twenty-six

"Poor woman," Death said. "Nice, too. How come her daughter can't be more like her?"

"We've caught Sheryl at a bad time. Who knows what she's like when she's not having to leave everything she loves?"

Death didn't look convinced.

"Are you coming?" Casey headed toward the back of the building, where Tom's truck sat. Casey knocked on his office door. Death had disappeared, but Casey could hear a banjo playing from the grove of trees in the next lot. She knocked again, and heard a voice drawing closer. The door opened on Tom Haab, a phone at his ear. He hesitated, then waved her in.

"Yes, yes, I'm here," he said into the phone. "But I'll call you back. I don't know, a little while. Okay." He flipped the phone shut and laid it on his desk. "So, what can I do for you?"

"If you're willing to help I'd appreciate it. But if you don't want me here, I'm gone."

"No, no, that's fine." He sat on his office chair and swiveled toward her, gesturing to another chair. "Dave seems to like you. Keeps asking if I've heard from you." He gave a quick smile. "Up till now I've had to disappoint him."

"I don't want to get him in any more trouble. Or you."

His eyebrows rose. "Am I in trouble?"

"I hope not. I'd like to keep it that way."

"So why are you here?"

"Because I need a computer, and yours was the only one I could think of."

"All right." He got up from his chair. "It's yours. I'm about ready to head out for lunch, anyway, so you can have the run of the office. I'll lock you in. No one will bother you." He went to the door and stuck his head out. "Kim, I'm going out, I'll be back after lunch."

Casey heard a woman's soft voice, but couldn't understand the words.

"One-o'clock?" Tom said. "I'll be back in plenty of time. Thanks." He shut the door and locked it. "Anything you need before I go? Oh, just a minute." He went back out the door, being careful to shut it behind him, then returned with a bag. "Here." He re-locked the door and dropped the bag on the desk. "Lunch."

Casey smiled. "Thank you. You can't imagine how grateful I am for that."

"You're welcome."

"One question before you go—do you know anyone named Willie Yonkers?"

He grinned. "What kind of name is that?"

"A rich one, apparently."

"Oh. No, I've never heard of him. If I had, I'd remember."

"Okay. Thanks."

"That's it? Nothing else? All right, then. See you in a while." He went out the back door, and Casey heard the bolt slide home.

She looked at the computer, but something didn't feel quite right. The room was too bright—too open. She closed all of the blinds, and turned out all of the lights except for a lamp sitting on Tom's desk. Much better. And now…

She had the computer and the entire office to herself. She could get all kinds of things done. She sat down…and opened the lunch bag. Egg salad sandwich. Chips. An apple. Two *home-made* chocolate chip cookies. And a can of Coke.

She was in heaven.

Keeping the food away from the keyboard, she typed in Willie Yonkers' name. Lots of hits, and they were all positive—working with a local Habitat for Humanity project, a celebration of his and his wife's 25th anniversary—mustn't have been a recent event, since Evan had said she'd left him—and his son Brad winning some big college debate. His daughter, Tara, was homecoming queen—wearing a dress Casey wouldn't let her own daughter be caught dead in, Willie had been appointed to the town council, and he had made a top ten list of "best small businesses in north-central Kansas." Business for what? Ah. Nothing even close to trucking. Flowers.

Flowers?

Not just a nursery. Fancy stuff. Orchids. Trees from South America. Even some special moss that was supposed to level off acidity in the soil. Things you couldn't get down at the local greenhouse. According to the testimonials Hollywood folks and television evangelists landscaped their properties with plants and trees from Yonkers' place, and there were several photos with NBA stars, politicians, and even one late night TV personality. In every one of the pictures, Yonkers stood smiling beside the famous customer, his expression smug, with a visible sense of entitlement. Casey hated him on sight.

Yonkers' expertise, naturally, led to one last article. Willie Yonkers' residence had a prestigious spot on the region's home and garden tour. Casey clicked on the images of his home to enlarge them. Inside shots of amazing interior design. Outside shots highlighting trees, flowerbeds, and fountains. Even one aerial photo. Wow. Quite the opposite of poor Pat Parnell's place. But then, Yonkers could afford the help of gardeners, housekeepers, and a whole slew of underlings Casey couldn't even imagine. Employees hired with the money Yonkers made by blackmailing people like Pat Parnell.

Yonkers obviously enjoyed his position in the community. He had his fingers into a little bit of everything, and somehow always came out on top, looking good. Where were the articles about his destroyed marriage, or the broken relationships with his children? Not newsworthy, apparently. Or else he'd paid to keep them out of the papers.

Casey drummed her fingers on the desk. Had Evan gotten too close? Did he know Yonkers was involved? She pushed her fingers against her temples, trying to remember exactly what she and Evan had talked about before... She shook herself away from the horrible images of the crash. What had he been saying?

Willie and Evan had spitting contests in first grade, Willie had more money than he knew what to do with, Willie's family hated him... But there had been no anger. Nothing to give even a hint that Evan had caught Yonkers in a criminal scheme. If anything, there was envy, and...*admiration.*

Casey closed her eyes and pictured Evan's information. She wished now she'd brought it with her. He'd matched the names to the photos—he probably knew some, if not most, of the drivers. Perhaps he'd seen some of them on the road—truckers run into each other at truck stops, diners, rest areas—especially if they frequent the roads in the same general area. Pat Parnell had even mentioned seeing Evan. Most likely Evan knew some of the drivers weren't supposed to be behind the wheel anymore and wondered what was happening. He'd found all their disqualifications. Knew they were driving illegally.

She thought about the manifests, all clipped together in a neat stack. Those papers—the physical papers themselves—were different. They, as compared to his notes and even the photos, were newly copied, all on the same pristine white paper. That's when she realized—Evan had just discovered the fake names. The copied papers hadn't had time to get bent and dirty and fingerprinted because they were brand new.

So why hadn't Evan told anyone? Why was the information still squirreled away in his truck?

And this time? I'm staying for a good long while. I've been working my tail off and I need a break.

Evan's words about home came back to her, as if he were sitting right there in the room. He'd *known* he finally had them cold, and he was going to turn them in. The problem was... someone else had known it, too.

Chapter Twenty-seven

"So you're not even going to stay till Tom gets back?" Death said. "Tell him how helpful his computer was? He is pretty cute."

"He's also pretty married. Besides, in case you've completely lost your mind. I'm not into guys at the moment." She'd been a little interested in Eric VanDiepenbos the week before, and look how that had turned out.

Oh, Reuben.

She went suddenly breathless and leaned against a tree, several feet from the Southwest parking lot.

"Yup, there he comes," Death said.

Tom pulled his pickup into his spot and went to his door, opening it with his key. A few seconds later he poked his head back out, looked around, then went back in.

"Too bad," Death said. "He seems like a nice guy."

"A nice *family* guy."

"Such a stickler for details."

"Yeah. Details that will keep me going to one place and not the other when I finally die."

Death gave an exasperated groan. "Are you still going on about that? Dying?"

"Until you give me what I want."

"Are you sure you still want that?"

Casey looked at Death, then at the ground, then at the blue sky peeking through the trees.

"What I thought," Death said. "Now, what's next on the agenda?"

Casey watched Death walk purposefully toward the road, and followed. As they picked their way through the trees she explained what she'd discovered.

"So Evan did tell somebody," Death said. "Somebody knew he'd found out what was going on."

"I don't think he found out all of it. He didn't seem to realize Willie Yonkers was involved. In fact, I think Willie Yonkers is the one he told."

"Why would he do that?"

"He respected him. Yonkers was on the town council, had a flourishing business, lots of money…heck, he was even a better spitter than Evan. Plus, he was from Evan's hometown. He liked him. He trusted him." A bitter taste filled Casey's mouth. It was so *hard* to know whom to trust.

"We need to go see Willie Yonkers," Death said.

"Yes," Casey said. "I'm afraid we do."

They got to the end of the wooded area and stopped.

"How do you propose we do that?" Death raised an eyebrow and stuck out a thumb, as if hitching a ride.

"I don't suppose Sheryl's mom is still here." She walked far enough along the road to see the Southwest parking lot. "Nope. I guess we could borrow Wendell's truck again, although I really hate to."

"After walking all the way back into town. Your feet have *got* to be hurting."

They were.

"How about Tom's truck? I'm sure he'd loan it to you."

Casey looked back toward the building. Should she involve him any more? But then, it was just a truck she was asking to borrow.

"Okay. We'll ask him."

"Good for you."

They made their way back through the trees and up to Tom's door. He didn't hide his surprise. "Back again?"

"Another favor."

"Shoot."

"May I borrow your truck?"

He regarded her for a few moments. "How long will you be gone?"

She calculated in her head. Forty minutes, Evan had said. With her driving it would be more like fifty. So, basically two hours of driving time, plus finding and talking to Willie Yonkers. "Three hours? Four?"

He glanced at his watch. "So you'll be back by five?"

"Yes." Her voice sounded more confident than she felt.

He held out the keys and dropped them into her hand. "Do I want to know where you're going?"

"No."

"Okay." He gave a little grin. "Try to bring her back in one piece. I assume you know how to drive?"

"Uh, yeah." If he only knew her history with vehicles.

She got in the truck, controlling her shaking hands, and was able to back out and leave without stalling, even with Tom watching.

"Score one for Casey Maldonado!" Death cheered when they were on the road. "Or, uh, Casey Jones! Whichever you are today!"

"Don't start counting too soon."

Death settled back and pulled out the harmonica. "So, where are we going?"

Casey groaned. "I have no idea. I just wanted to get out of the parking lot."

"Ooookaaay. Plans?"

"Well, we know he lives in Sedgwick. His business is called Exotic Blooms."

"Fancy. If not manly."

"I figure we get to Sedgwick, we can find the shop."

"And to get to Sedgwick?"

"Has to be west, because we were headed that way when we crashed. So we'll get on the highway and go that direction."

Death sighed. "If only Laura Ingalls Wilder could help us. Why do you even keep that phone with you if you're not going to use it?"

"Because there might come a time when I will."

"Whatever."

The highway turned out being easy to find, and within twenty miles they began to see signs for Sedgwick.

"Hmm," Death said. "You're smarter than you smell."

"*Look*, L'Ankou. The saying is you're smarter than you *look*."

"I know that. It's just that your smell these days has begun to overpower even your looks. And they ain't so great, either."

Casey flinched, and sniffed at her underarm. Was she really that bad? Or did Death just have an extra-sensitive nose?

The exit for Sedgwick loomed up on the right, and Casey took it. This area was a bit more populated than Blue Lake, which made her nervous, but nobody should recognize her here—except for Dixon, Westing, their guys, and perhaps even Yonkers himself. Yikes.

She took a road that led to less built-up land and pulled to the side of the road, where there was a deep ditch. She clambered down to the deepest part and scooped up some mud, using it to cover up most of the numbers on the pickup's license plate. She didn't want to take any chance of the guys seeing this truck and tracing it back to Tom. Not that she was planning on running into them, but she was now traveling on their turf.

She found a rag under the seat and wiped her hands.

"Muddy hands," Death said. "Perfect with your outfit."

"We *are* going to a nursery," Casey said.

Death laughed.

License plate obscured, Casey turned around and drove back toward town. "Think I can stop at a gas station?"

"One near the highway. They see so many people they'll have less of a chance of remembering you. Even in your present state."

"Will you stop already? I know I look—and smell—like crap, all right? It doesn't help to have you going on about it all the time."

"Sorry, sorry. Just trying to call it like it is."

"Well, quit."

Death was quiet the rest of the way back toward the highway.

Casey scoped out the Shell station, and was glad to see a pay phone and know she still had a quarter left over from Wendell's money. When the pumps were vacant she pulled up beside the stand. The phone book had been stolen, the metal cover dangling from its chain. This left her with a decision—use up the last of her money to call information, or go inside and risk being seen?

Since she had a full stomach, the decision seemed obvious. She ponied up the necessary change and called information, which put her through to Exotic Blooms.

The woman on the other end of the phone, who identified herself as "Ruby," was happy to give Casey directions from the highway, but laughed when Casey asked if Mr. Yonkers would be available to talk to her about some special orders. "Mr. Yonkers isn't involved in the day-to-day work as much as he used to be. But I'll be happy to help you with anything you need."

"The person who recommended your nursery suggested I speak directly to him."

A pause. "Well, I don't know why they would have said that. I've done the ordering here for the past couple of years. Who have you been talking to?"

Casey gave a little laugh, like she was embarrassed. "I don't want to get them in trouble. I'll be happy to come by and work with you. In fact, I'd rather do that."

Ruby sniffed. "That's fine. I'm here every day—that is, Monday through Saturday."

"I'll be by. Thank you. But, um, just to tell my friend I tried, do you have any idea where I might be able to find Mr. Yonkers? Or talk to him?"

Ruby's voice went just a bit chillier. "Mr. Yonkers doesn't spend much time here at all anymore. You'd have better luck catching him at home, or on his cell. You do have that number?"

"No, no, I don't."

Ruby hesitated. "I'm not supposed to hand it out. But if you want to leave your name and number I'll have him get back to you."

"Thank you, but I think I'll just tell my friend I tried and leave it at that. I'll be by soon to see if you can help me."

"And what is your name?"

"Good-bye, then," Casey said. "See you soon."

She got back in the truck, pleased she hadn't needed to go into the gas station, where she would most likely have been videotaped.

"We're not going to just dance right in, are we?" Death looked concerned.

"Of course not. We may not even *go* in. I just want to see what I can see."

"*Do you see what I see?*" Death sang from the familiar Christmas carol, and proceeded to play it on the electronic keyboard that appeared, which was so long it would have poked Casey, had it been solid. As it was, she shivered.

"Can you move that thing?"

"Oh, sorry." The keyboard shrank to the size of one a child would play.

"Exotic Blooms is on one side of a shopping center. The usual things—Old Navy, Lowe's, a Target, maybe. But there should be plenty of parking lot to hide in."

"Can we get close enough to actually see anything?"

"We'll try."

The nursery, when they found it, took up more than its share of the shopping area, with three enormous greenhouses, and rows of plants and trees out toward the road. Behind the greenhouses was a gravel parking lot large enough for the loading and unloading of merchandise, but it was empty, except for a wooden two-wheeled trailer, tilted with its hitch resting on the ground, and lots of nursery-type tools: buckets, hoses, mulch, and pallets of plants. Next to the lot was the back of the next store, with its own loading bays. A semi-trailer was backed up to one of them, and two men stood on the dock going over paperwork. Yonkers must not have had an actual loading bay like the big store, but there was plenty of room for a semi to maneuver in the lot.

Casey parked three rows from the front door and to the left, between an over-sized pickup and a Navigator, with a minivan to her back. Tom's truck was hidden unless someone would look at it straight on. From this vantage point she could see the entrance to the back lot, as well as anyone going into the store through the customer entrance. She recognized some familiar foliage sitting in rows to the side, and arranged on the sidewalk, but was astounded by the amount of things she couldn't name.

"It's a jungle in there," Death said. "Are you going in?"

"I don't know yet. I want to scope it out."

"Don't have a lot of time if you're going to get this truck back Tom by five."

"I know, but that doesn't mean I want to be stupid about it."

"Whatever." Death pulled out the rubber band and twanged it for a few beats before stopping. "You know, it's hard to get too scared of a guy who sells flowers."

"That's not all he's doing."

Death shrugged, and continued twanging.

At first Casey could concentrate. Only three people went through the front doors—two came out with purchases, and one went in. No trucks or vehicles of any kind drove into the parking lot. One woman strode back and forth across the store helping customers inside—Ruby?—and one young woman in low-slung jeans and a form-fitting shirt, with her hair piled on top of her head in a ponytail, slouched around the outside, flinging the hose this way and that, chomping gum so hard Casey was surprised her jaw didn't fall off. The girl turned toward Casey to water a row of waist-high plants with shiny, dark green leaves and bright red blooms, and Casey sucked in her breath. "What time is it?"

Death stopped twanging long enough to say, "Little after three."

"So that could be her."

"Who?"

"Yonkers' daughter. The one Evan wouldn't let his own daughter go near. What was her name? Tara."

Death looked at the girl, head tilted to one side. "Sulky, sexy, angry about something. Yeah, could easily be her."

Casey watched Tara Yonkers as she moved from plant to plant. Perhaps the daughter was the way in, but should she risk it? Let Willie's girl see her face?

Death began humming along with the rubber band, still playing that Christmas song, stretching the band to change its pitch. Casey tried to ignore the sound. She plugged her right ear with her finger. She held her hand up to the side of her face. She thought about how it would feel to punch Death in the solar plexus.

"Enough! All right! I'll go in! Just...*stop*!"

Death regarded her with wide, innocent eyes. "Are you talking to me?"

Casey jumped out of the truck, slammed the door, and stalked toward the store.

The girl looked up as Casey approached. "Help you find something?" It wasn't convincing. Tara Yonkers obviously didn't want to help anybody, and her being able to find something in the immense nursery was clearly a crap shoot.

"Your dad. I'd like to talk with him."

Tara snorted and pelted another plant with a stream of water. "Good luck. I haven't been able to get him to listen to me for years."

"So he's not here?"

"Look, lady, my dad adores this place, but you'd never know it. I'm here more than he is." She made a gagging sound.

"You don't like flowers?"

"I like flowers. But I like them when they're cut in a vase on the table. Not out here where it's roasting and dirty and smells like somebody's trash!"

The girl was right—it did smell. Nobody said flowers had to smell as pretty as they looked. Casey was glad if the stench covered up her own body odor.

"So where does your dad spend his time?"

Tara turned her hose toward another victim. "Why do you care?"

"Just figured it wasn't fair if he was in air-conditioning and you were out here…" She gestured to the lot.

Tara's lips puffed out, and she cocked a hip. "He hardly ever leaves home, can you believe it? Spends all day locked away in his precious office, eating popcorn and watching porn for all I know. It's not like he ever lets me in there."

Lovely father-daughter relationship. "So he never comes here?"

"Only at night, when he doesn't have to deal with the customers. Says he has all that *paperwork* to do. I think he just wants to check up on things, make sure the rest of us aren't messing it up, or stealing from him."

Or he comes to load and unload trailers in his back lot without employees there to witness it.

"Your house far from here?"

Tara turned toward Casey, letting the water run onto the ground. "Who are you? Why do you want to know?"

"Just…making conversation. But I'll go now. I have an appointment with Ruby."

The suspicions left Tara's eyes. "She's inside. Works her ass off for this place. She figures if she does well enough, makes herself *necessary*, Dad will pay her more. Or marry her." The girl shrugged. "Not that *I* care."

Of course not. "Well, thanks. I'll be going."

Tara didn't reply, but moved the hose so it was actually over a plant.

Casey glanced at the pickup as she walked toward the main greenhouse, and Death gave her a double thumbs-up.

The air that hit her was hot, humid, and smothering. Casey took a moment to get her breath as she studied the layout. Rows and rows of potted plants sat on tables that stretched from the front to the back of the building. Most were unfamiliar, but she did see some orchids, and something that resembled a rhododendron. On the floor at the front of each row a number had been painted onto the concrete, and overhead signs hung explaining the contents of each section. At the far end of the building several employees were unloading boxes of plants onto shelves. Their voices carried across the room, but Casey couldn't understand what they were saying. Casey walked toward the front door, where a woman, probably Ruby, stood at a counter with a customer, packing plants into a flat.

Casey didn't actually want to talk to Ruby, but she'd had to drop the name when Tara became too curious. Casey looked for another exit between her and the saleswoman—one that would take her out the front and to Tom's truck without contact. Nothing. She looked back at Tara and waited for the girl to turn so she could slip out the side.

Someone called from the end of the room, and Casey looked up to see one of the gardeners gesturing to her.

"I'm fine," Casey said, waving her hands.

But the gardener pointed to one of the others, who set down a box, clapped his gloves together, and started down the aisle toward Casey. Casey squinted at him. Did he look familiar? He was big, but his features—from this distance, at least—didn't look like any she'd seen in the past few days. That didn't mean he wasn't one of Dixon or Westing's guys.

Tara was still facing Casey's way, but Casey had been in the greenhouse long enough it would be feasible she'd had time to talk to Ruby. She stepped toward the door, but stopped.

A man had walked up to Tara, checking her out as he neared. He said something, and Tara looked up, immediately morphing from sulky watering girl to seductress. But that's not what bothered Casey the most. What bothered her was that the man was Owen Dixon.

Casey spun around. The gardener was halfway down the row now, getting close enough to see her face. She saw his, too—and she'd seen it before, at the crash site. She walked briskly toward the front counter. Ruby was just finishing up with her customer as Casey scooted past.

"Can I help you?" Ruby called after her, but Casey swung out through the front door, headed for the truck. She was thankful Tara wasn't the kind of worker to inquire if she'd found everything she needed—in fact, she'd probably forgotten her already.

"Hello?" The guy from the greenhouse was calling her. Apparently he hadn't recognized her, but was the kind of employee who hated seeing a customer leave without buying something.

Casey smiled and waved, trying to fend him off, but his call had alerted Dixon, and as Casey jumped into the pickup, she could see Dixon stiffen, like a dog on alert.

"Hey!" Dixon screamed. He sprinted across the lot, knocking plants aside and jumping over bushes. He was pulling something from his pants as he ran, and Casey ducked, waiting for the sound of bullets slamming into the truck. None came.

"He's on the phone!" Death said. "Get out of here!"

Casey slammed her foot on the accelerator and swerved around a little hybrid just backing out of a spot, blaring her horn as she went.

Death knelt backward on the seat. "He's still coming! And now the other guy, too!"

Casey swung out of the parking lot, narrowly missing a minivan, and yanked the truck into the left turn lane, where she screeched across an intersection in front of several cars.

"Yee-ha!" Death whooped.

Casey floored it, the truck screaming around two more corners, and headed away from the highway.

Death turned back around. "Where are you going?"

"They'll look for us on the highway. We've got to find another way." She reached across the seat and opened the glove compartment, dumping its contents.

"What are you doing? Watch out!"

Casey looked up in time to swerve around a slow-moving Volkswagen before resuming her hunt. "A map! I need a map!"

"There's something in the door pocket over here."

Casey unhooked her seat belt to give her the few extra inches she needed to pluck the folded paper from its slot. Keeping one eye on the road as it flew by, she shook the map open. "Look for another route. We need to get this truck back to Tom before they catch us and know he's involved."

Death scanned the roads. "There. If we can find Route 96 we can maneuver around back toward Southwest. But where is that?"

"Okay, we're going north. What's that road there?" She pointed to a road sign.

"Jackson."

"Is it on the map?"

"Too small."

They passed several more roads until they came to one large enough to be listed. "Okay," Death said. "Turn right here. Right! Here!"

Casey spun the wheel, knowing she needed to get her driving under control. She slowed. "Okay. How far on this?"

Death directed her until they found the road that would lead them back the way they needed to go. Not directly to Southwest, but at least in the vicinity.

Casey took several deep breaths and tried to slow her thumping heart. "So Dixon and one of the others are known to people at the nursery. They could be regular employees."

"And Dixon seems just a little too close to one of the kids."

"Tara."

"No." Death looked at her pointedly. "One of *your* kids. The teenagers."

"Right." The reminder settled on her like a weight. One of that close-knit bunch had turned her in. She was going to see them soon, and have to determine which one it was.

"But he does seem a little too familiar with Tara," Death said, shuddering. "He's her *father's* age, for heaven's sake."

Casey agreed. "Any sign of him?"

"Nope. I'm pretty sure you lost him. In a very adept piece of driving, I might add."

"It's called desperation." Her hands were shaking now, and she clenched the steering wheel. "We're lucky I didn't crash."

"Are we? I thought you would be happy for that. You could've run right into a telephone pole, taken yourself out for good."

Casey swallowed, her throat tight. "I could've."

"But you have something to finish here."

She looked out the side window.

"Why?" Death asked.

"Why what?"

"Why do you care so much about this? Why don't you just walk away? It's not like Yonkers stealing a few loads of this or that is going to change your life. It really doesn't seem like big time crime. It's not white slaves, or weapons, or even black market body parts. Now *that* would be interesting."

Casey was quiet for awhile. "Evan entrusted this to me. I feel responsible."

"There's got to be more than that."

There was. "Even if it's not drugs or something it's still destroying people's lives. Evan's. His family's. All those truckers'."

"But it's their own fault they're in this mess, isn't it? Having affairs, avoiding child support payments, not heeding medical problems."

"I know. But people are getting killed. And more will."

"And you might get yourself killed in the process. Bonus."

Casey didn't say anything after that, and Death pulled out the harmonica. Somehow "Amazing Grace" fit the mood.

Chapter Twenty-eight

Casey circled around Blue Lake on lonely roads, watching intently for other vehicles. The few she came across made her heart beat madly, but none turned out to be anything other than unfamiliar drivers. She made it back to Southwest a half hour ahead of schedule and used some leaves to wipe off the license plate.

Tom answered his door, keeping it partly closed. "I have people in here," he said quietly. "Figured you don't want them to see you."

"You figured right. I don't know how… Thank you so much for all you've done."

He took the keys, but kept his eyes on her face. "You okay? You look a little—"

"Just tired, that's all. I'm fine. And thank you. Thanks again."

He stepped outside, pulling the door almost closed behind him. "I asked around about a guy named Willie Yonkers."

Casey paled. "Tom, I wish you wouldn't—"

"I was discreet. Nadine, who you met yesterday, she hasn't heard of him, and neither has anybody in my office. The only one who said the name was familiar was a driver who said he thinks Yonkers is a guy from up in Sedgwick, has a flower place. He's taken some loads to and from there in the past, but not for a long time. He'd forgotten about him, actually, since he hadn't heard from him for so long. Said Yonkers probably uses another broker now. So if he has something to do with trucking it's merely as a customer."

She'd just let them go on thinking that, wouldn't she? "Great. Thanks so much, Tom. Now do me one last favor?"

"Sure." He said it, but looked a little weary.

"Forget I was ever here and that the name Willie Yonkers ever passed your lips. Okay?"

He frowned. "You serious?"

"Dead serious."

Death made an exasperated sound from beside the truck.

"So this is good-bye, then?" Tom said.

"I hope so."

"Oh." He hadn't expected that. "And I should tell Dave—"

"To forget about me, too. Please. It's for the best."

Tom didn't like it. "It's going to kill him, not knowing how things turn out."

"I think he'll survive that. Let's hope not finding out is the worst that happens."

Tom glanced behind Casey's shoulder, as if expecting to see someone there. "You're scaring me."

"Good. Keep yourself safe, okay?" She stepped back, turned, and walked into the woods.

"Very dramatic," Death said, and played Taps on a bugle.

Casey trudged through the trees, toward the road. "I have to get a move-on. It's time to meet the kids."

"And have you thought about how you're going to handle that?"

"Actually, I have. I think the guilty party will give it up."

Death laughed. "You think she's just going to volunteer the information? In front of her friends?"

"Or *he*. We don't know it's Sheryl. But I think whoever it is is going to be very surprised to see me, thinking the men will have gotten to me by now."

Death didn't seem convinced. "And this is all if you can get there in time. At this pace, you're going to be late."

"You know, I didn't get my exercise in today." Casey began running, thankful she had had a good lunch to sustain her. She wished she could have some of the pizza the kids were going to order, but she couldn't get greedy.

By pushing herself, Casey was able to get to town with twenty minutes to spare. Students and parents were flooding from the stadium to their cars and downtown, so she assumed the game was over and the other kids would wait for Johnny before heading to the restaurant. Keeping her head down and wishing it were dark, Casey merged into the crowd and made her way toward the library and the alley behind it.

"Hey! Wait!"

Casey stiffened. Two teenage boys, laughing, ran past her, knocking her sideways into a young mother with a stroller. Casey made her apologies and watched as the boys caught up with the girls they were chasing. Would she ever be free of worry that someone would find her? Cops or Pegasus or her family? Or Yonkers and his men?

Angling away from the stream of people, Casey walked through the library parking lot and down the alley. The backs of the buildings had signs with the names of the businesses, and Casey stopped at Luciano's Pizzeria. A Dumpster sat at the side, and Casey slipped into the shadows behind it. From her vantage point she could see only a short stretch of the alley coming up toward the restaurant, and nothing in the other direction, both of which made her uncomfortable. The rest of the little area behind the restaurant—room for two parked cars, plus the Dumpster—was full-up.

"Anyone coming?"

Death perched on top of the Dumpster, playing an African drum with a steady beat. "Nope. Hope Bailey can convince the others to come this way." *Thump. Thump.*

"I'm not worried about her. What about the other direction?"

"Nada. Well, some woman's emptying out her trunk, donating things to the little thrift store, but she looks like she's about eighty. " *Thump. Thump.* "I don't think she's a threat."

"Can you stop with the drum? I can't hear footsteps if you're doing that."

"You just aren't a music lover, are you?"

"*Shh.*" Voices were coming down the alley. Young, loud voices.

Casey made out Sheryl's words first. "It's creepy back here. I don't know why we can't just go in the front, like normal people."

"We've never come this way before." Johnny. "How do we even know which place is the right one?"

"Signs, Johnny, see?" Martin. "They tell you which store it is."

"Oh. Never noticed that."

"We'll miss the crowd this way," Bailey said. "Someone said we ought to try it."

"Who said that?" Sheryl again. Pouty.

"I did." Casey stepped out from behind the Dumpster.

Sheryl shrieked and grabbed onto Terry's arm. Terry had been startled, too, but mostly looked pleased that Sheryl was touching him. Martin laughed out loud. Bailey surveyed her friends with narrowed eyes.

And Johnny looked terrified.

"What are you d-doing here?" His head whipped back and forth, as if he expected to see someone else—someone he didn't necessarily want to see.

Oh, Johnny. Casey met Death's eyes, and Death shrugged helplessly.

"We can't meet at the shed anymore."

"Why not?" Martin sounded surprised.

"Somebody else knows I've been staying there, and it would be better if they didn't find me. Or you."

"Who knows?" Martin asked. "Who told them?"

"Also," Casey said, ignoring his questions, "I wanted to return this to Terry." Casey held the phone out. "Seems I can't use it anymore."

"It's dead?" Terry took it and pushed the power button. "I just charged it before I gave it to you."

"No, it's not dead. But I have a feeling I was supposed to be."

"*No,*" Johnny breathed. "No, they said—"

Bailey's mouth dropped open. "Johnny?"

"What is it?" Sheryl said. "What's going on?"

Casey was going to try to keep things calm and ask Johnny to explain, but Bailey stepped up and punched him in the arm. "How *could* you?"

"Whoa, whoa." Martin grabbed Bailey around the waist, barely avoiding the fist she re-aimed at Johnny. "What's going on here? What did Johnny do?"

Tears overflowed Bailey's eyes, and she shoved away from Martin, stalking several feet away.

Casey gave a grim smile. "You want to explain to them, Johnny? And tell us just how much danger we're all in?"

"We're not…I mean they're not…" He stopped, looking miserable.

"Johnny," Martin said. "*What did you do?*"

Johnny stepped back so he was against the brick wall of the building and sank to the ground, his head in his hands.

"Johnny, come on!" Terry stepped closer, his phone in his fist, as if he were going to throw it as his friend.

"Guys, stop." Sheryl pushed past them both and hunkered down beside Johnny. Her expression was surprisingly gentle. "Johnny, what happened? It's okay. You can tell us."

Johnny raised his head and wiped his nose on his sleeve. "I didn't mean to…I just wanted…"

Sheryl put a hand on his knee. "It's okay, honey. Tell us."

Bailey had come back to the circle, but stood apart from the others, her arms crossed tightly over her stomach. She stared at the ground, but Casey knew she was listening to every word.

"My dad," Johnny said. "He was talking about this lady that ran away from the hospital. I mean, the other doctor was talking about her. About you." He glanced up at Casey, and then quickly away. "He said this other doc was checking you out and you took off. The doctor was worried about you—that you were hurt—and then he thought he saw you back at the hospital, but you didn't stop. I told Dad he didn't have to worry, because you were fine."

Casey closed her eyes and gave a small, humorless laugh. Poor Johnny. He just wasn't too bright.

"Johnny, you *idiot*!" Terry said. "Can you not keep a secret for two seconds?"

"Terry!" Sheryl's voice was sharp. "He didn't do it on purpose. It slipped out."

"Maybe. But what did you do *next*?"

Johnny sniffed. "I didn't do anything. My dad about jumped down my throat asking what I meant and where I'd seen you, and…and he threatened to ground me for two months if I didn't tell him. *Two months*!" He looked up at his friends. "I wouldn't be able to see you guys forever! All I would be able to do would be go to school and football." He shuddered. "Can't you see? I had to tell him! Because what if…" He glanced at Casey. "What if it was true, what Sheryl said that first night? That she's bad?"

Bailey growled. "What did you tell him, Johnny?"

He swallowed. "That I'd seen her. That she was hiding out in your shed and we were helping her."

Bailey's nostrils flared, but it was Martin who said bleakly, "You gave up our place, John. We can never go there again."

"Of course you can," Sheryl snapped. "It's not like this is going to go on forever. She'll leave, and we'll go back to doing what we always do. Or, you guys will, since I'll be in freaking Timbuktu."

"But they *know*," Terry said. "They know about the shed."

"Just my dad," Johnny said. "He's the only one."

Casey clicked her tongue. "Really, Johnny? Is he really the only one?"

Silence hung in the air.

"Who else, Johnny?" Bailey's voice was flat.

"Well…" He looked at his hands. "Dad made me tell Dr. Shinnob, who wanted to know all about how you were looking. He said he wasn't going to come after you, because it was your choice and all whether you came in. But then…" He stopped.

"Johnny," Bailey said.

"Dad made me go to the cops."

"The *cops?*" Casey said, her voice louder than she'd intended.

"Yeah. He said you were wanted for questioning, so I needed to tell them what I knew."

"When was this?"

"Yesterday morning."

"After I got those reports," Martin said.

"And you told them what, exactly?" Casey asked. "It's important."

He chewed his lip. "Well, where you were staying, like I said. That's really all I knew."

It could've been worse. But how had Dixon and Westing found out about the *phone?*

"Oh," Johnny said. "I forgot. A cop came up to me at school, said you weren't at the shed. He wondered where else you could be. I said I didn't know, but he should just try—" he looked at Bailey, fear in his eyes "—that he should just try calling you, because you were...you were using Terry's phone."

"Ahhh!" Bailey threw her hands up and grabbed at her hair. "Johnny, you are such a—" She stopped herself and stood still, her eyes squeezed shut.

"It was a cop, Bailey! What was I supposed to do?"

"You were supposed to keep your trap shut to begin with!"

"Bailey." Casey shut the girl up with a look. "Johnny, I need you to think hard now, okay? What did that cop look like? The one who came to your school?"

"I don't know. Shorter than me. Blond hair. Old."

"Old?"

"I mean, like your age. He had super green eyes."

Owen Dixon. How had he tracked down Johnny *and* known about the shed? Probably the same way Casey herself had found out what the police were thinking—they'd gotten police reports. Or someone in the police had talked to them. Could Yonkers have that pull? Absolutely. He was on the town council in Sedgwick, and would have access to the police there. They would tell him whatever they could. He might have expressed interest in what was happening, and when this news came down the wire they contacted him. Or else he'd just asked.

Casey looked at the haggard group of kids. They were angry, sad, disappointed…and in danger.

"Okay, guys, listen," she said. "You can't go out to the shed again—"

"Never?" Terry wailed.

"—until this is taken care of. Until I am gone and the men are, too."

"What men?" Bailey frowned.

"The ones who are after me. One of whom talked to Johnny at school yesterday."

"One of—" Johnny paled. "You mean he wasn't a cop?"

"No, Johnny, he wasn't."

Johnny moaned. "He wasn't wearing a uniform. He said he was undercover, trying to help you without scaring you off."

"I'm sure he was very convincing."

"I'm sorry." He sniffed again, and Sheryl patted his arm.

"I don't blame you," Casey said. "I'm the one who got you all involved. I just want to get you *un*involved until it's over."

"Oh," said a voice from behind her. "I think it's already over."

Chapter Twenty-nine

"*Run!*" Death said.

Randy Westing stood smiling in the middle of the alley. Flanking him were Owen Dixon and Craig Mifflin, the man she'd knocked out first at Davey's. Neither of them looked quite so pleasant. Behind them, expressions neutral, were the other two large men Casey had seen behind the grocery store.

Casey swiveled, shoving Bailey behind her, along with the other teenagers.

"You think you can save them all?" Westing asked pleasantly.

"You don't want them. You want me."

"Oh, I don't know," Westing said. "They probably know enough to help us. Especially the one."

"Hey, there, *Johnny*," Dixon sneered.

Johnny moaned. "The *cop*."

Dixon jerked his chin up. "Thanks for the tip about the phone. Led us right to her when she turned it on here a few minutes ago."

Casey carefully didn't look at Terry.

"*Run!*" Death said again.

But Casey wasn't about to leave the kids in the hands of the men. Not that she had much of a chance of escaping, anyway. Behind her were two cars, a Dumpster, and a U of brick walls. The five men were spread across the alley, and even if she should get past one, the other four would be close behind. The only chance she really had would be the door to the pizza place.

"Bailey," she said. "Take everybody into the restaurant."

"But—"

"*Go.*"

"I'm not leaving you."

Casey ground her teeth. "Martin?"

"Right. Come on, everybody." He gently pushed Sheryl and Terry toward the building.

Johnny stood, stepping up beside Casey, his body tensed. "It's my fault. I'm staying."

He was a large presence, which was nice, but he'd only be a liability in a fight. Casey would have to spend all of her time either protecting him or worrying about him.

"Johnny." Casey spoke without taking her eyes off of Westing. "The best thing you can do for me is to take Bailey and go inside. *Please.*"

"I told you," Bailey said. "I'm not—"

Johnny picked Bailey up and swung her over his shoulder, trying to avoid her flailing arms and legs.

"Johnny! Put me down! I'm staying! She needs us."

Westing laughed out loud. "She doesn't need you, sweetheart. She needs something else. Like an army."

Casey did have something else. Death leapt from the Dumpster. "I'll do what I can."

The back door of the restaurant slapped shut, and Casey was relieved to know the kids were inside, out of danger. "You realize they'll call the cops."

"Probably already have. That's why we'll make this quick."

Death moved between Westing and Dixon, arms outspread to go through their chests. Both men shuddered, but kept their eyes on Casey. Death couldn't take someone before his time, and Casey couldn't depend on mere distractions to get her through this. She took a deep breath through her nose and readied herself for what was to come.

"So where's Evan's stuff?" Dixon growled.

"Easy now." Westing's voice was silky smooth. "She'll tell us."

And sign her death warrant. "It's in a safe place."

"I'm sure it is. Not on you, I'm afraid?"

"Not even close."

"You had it with you when you went to see Bruce at the hospital."

"I wanted his reaction. How is he, by the way? Will he ever walk again?"

Westing nodded. "Modern medicine, you know. But thanks for caring. It's not like it's the first knee injury he's ever had. He'll be fine. I suppose someone else knows where Evan's information is?" He kept smiling, his pose casual. The other men, however, were ready, even with Death running fingers up and down their spines.

"The kids don't know. They've never even seen it."

Dixon frowned. "Of course she'd say that."

"I think it's the truth," Westing said, amused. "The Cross kid didn't know anything when he thought you were a cop. You *did* ask him about it, didn't you?"

"Of course I did."

Casey went cold, thinking how easily Dixon could have harmed Johnny.

Death stood beside Dixon, an arm around his shoulders. Dixon shivered, glancing around him.

"Boys," Westing said. "I think we need to persuade this lady here to help us."

Mifflin didn't wait for the others, but came for Casey quickly and ferociously, head down, fists up. Casey dropped onto her right leg and lifted her left, flexing her foot. Mifflin ran right into it, expelling all the air from his diaphragm in a gush and bending over, hands on his gut. Casey planted her left leg and brought her right leg up around and down, axe-kicking him with her heel between the shoulder blades. Mifflin went slack, doing a face plant on the ground. He was out.

Casey turned to run for the restaurant door, but Dixon had already gone around to the back of her, cutting her off. She darted behind the second car, which gave her about four feet to move between the brick wall and the little Focus. Dixon grabbed for her neck with both hands. Casey grabbed his right hand, bent his elbow down into an arm lock, and smacked his face against the trunk of the car.

One of the other men climbed onto the trunk and kicked at her head. She ducked and grabbed his planted leg, pulling it toward her. He fell backward onto the car, half on, half off the trunk, his elbow cracking against the back window.

Dixon, blood running from his nose, reached over the guy's leg and grabbed Casey around the shoulders, spinning her and knocking her face against the brick wall, bear hugging her from the back, trapping her arms. Dizzily, she kicked back at his shin, but her foot glanced off his leg. Dixon spun her around, kneeing her in the stomach. When she bent over, he pummeled her in the face with both fists.

Other hands were grabbing for her now, yanking her from behind the car. Dixon continued to hit her.

"Dix, stop it. You're done." Casey thought it was Westing's voice, but everything had gone fuzzy, and her vision doubled as she looked at the faces.

She stumbled, but was yanked upright, Dixon's fist connecting once more, an uppercut to her stomach.

"Dixon! Bring her to the car."

Someone grabbed under her arms while another picked up her feet. They carried her down the alley and tossed her into the back seat of a waiting car.

"Have a nice ride," Dixon said, and punched her in the face.

Her lights went out.

Chapter Thirty

Casey hurt all over. Her head pounded, and her ribs throbbed, maybe not broken, but bruised, for sure. Her eyes, when she opened them, didn't open far, and even when they did she couldn't see anything in the dark. She tried to raise a hand to feel her face, and to remove the gag from her mouth, but her arms were tied behind her, roped in with her feet. Her cheek lay against a dirt floor, and her nostrils were filled with the tangy scent of peat moss and vegetation.

She closed her eyes, trying to remember what had happened. The last she could picture was the sight of Death's anxious eyes in the unfamiliar back seat, just before she blacked out. She didn't want to think about what had caused her to do that.

Voices mumbled in the background. Angry, low. Men. She had no idea what time it was, or whether anyone even knew she was gone. The kids. She took a sharp breath, gasping at the shot of pain it sent through her body. Were the kids all right? Where had they…the pizza place. They'd gone inside. Had they *stayed* inside? God, please let them have stayed inside.

"The kids are fine. Freaked out, but otherwise okay." Death sat against a bag of fertilizer, hands clasped tightly at bended knees. "You, on the other hand…I thought you looked bad *yesterday*."

Casey groaned.

"Martin called the cops as soon as he and the first two got inside. Told them there was a bad fight out back of the restaurant, and men with guns. He probably should have just told them to get there fast, because with his warning they weren't about to come without back-up, and they took forever getting there. By the time they arrived you were long gone. The teenagers were a mess, all trying to talk at the same time, and the cops weren't sure who or what to believe."

Death leaned over and placed both hands on Casey's ribs. For once it felt good—like an ice pack. Casey moaned, and Death shushed her gently. "It'll be okay. You'll be okay. Although I had to say I wasn't sure if you were about to get your wish and go with me to the other side."

Casey's eyes blinked open. Had she really been that close? That close, only to come back here, to this pain, and this place?

"Sorry, hon," Death said. "You have to hold on a little longer."

Casey looked past Death's face toward the ceiling. Her eyes were adjusting enough she could see foliage above Death's head. Unfamiliar foliage. She let her eyes close again. Yonkers' greenhouse. That's where she was.

"Drove right here," Death said. "Like Yonkers was expecting you to be delivered. Haven't seen the man yet, but from the sound of their conversation he's coming soon, and they're not happy. You still haven't given them what they want."

A surprise, since Casey couldn't remember what she'd given them. As long as she hadn't given them the kids. The kids…her eyes opened. Were the kids okay?

"The kids are fine." Death smoothed her hair with a chilly hand. "I told you that a minute ago. They're all with their parents. Safe and sound."

Casey relaxed, wincing as her ribs moved.

"Uh-oh," Death said. "Here he comes."

An overhead door opened and a vehicle drove into the building, its headlights illuminating the jungle standing over Casey. She was surrounded by plants and trees—hidden from the sight of anyone who might stumble in unawares. The overhead door slid shut, and the car turned off. "Where is she?" The voice was loud, echoing in Casey's head.

"Over here."

Casey looked up at Death, who crouched over her protectively. "Don't worry, sweetheart. I won't leave you."

Casey tried to take comfort in the cold cushion at her back.

"So. This is our troublemaker." The man squatted, studying her face. "Looks like she ran into a little trouble herself."

Casey blinked up at him. Yonkers. She recognized him from the photo in the paper. He was clean-shaven, with a receding hairline, and seemed to be wearing a *suit*. This was the man everyone was talking about? The guy they were so loyal to? He looked like…like a *dentist*.

"Seems you know a little bit more than is good for you, don't you?" Yonkers studied her, as if confused. "But I don't know you. Should I? I usually know people who come around, or I've at least seen them before." He looked at her some more. "Of course, it's hard to tell with your face being all…" He wrinkled his nose. "Dix!" He stood and Dixon appeared at his elbow, also looking down at Casey. His nose was swollen, and already the skin around his eyes was turning black and blue. "Bring her into my office. We're expecting a delivery tonight and I don't think it's necessary to show off our little problem here."

"Sure thing."

Yonkers patted his hands together, as if shedding them of dirt, and walked back the way he'd come.

"Miff!" Dixon said. "Help me move this."

Mifflin was chewing gum when he got there, his mouth open, like an ugly horse. Casey closed her eyes and braced herself, turning her face toward Death's chill.

"Hang in there," Death whispered. "It's going to be—"

"*Aaah.*" Casey groaned beneath the gag as the men gripped her, one under each arm.

Dixon laughed. "Little bit of your own there, girl. Can't say any of us feel too bad about it."

Mifflin grunted. "Not sorry at all."

Casey's head hung as they dragged her, bound feet scraping the ground, toward the far end of the room. They took her through a doorway, banging her against the doorjamb, and held her up.

"Put her there."

They dumped her onto a reclining lawn chair and she fell off, smashing her nose on the floor.

"On the *chair*," Yonkers said. "Untie those things if you have to."

"But Yonk, if we let her loose her she could—"

"Look at her, Craig. Do you really think she's in any shape to escape?"

"It's not escape I'm worried about."

Yonkers snorted. "I didn't realize you were such a little girl, Mifflin. Especially when surrounded by your team. Now *untie* her."

Mifflin was anything but gentle as he worked at the knots. He finally got so frustrated he sawed through them with a knife, managing to knick Casey several times as he did it. Finally, he and Dixon grabbed her and threw her onto the chair.

Casey pressed the side of her face into the weave of the seat. *L'Ankou. Please. Take me away.*

"Not now, dearheart. It's not your time." Death ran cold fingers through her hair.

"Now," Yonkers said. "Miss…Jones, was it? I suppose that's as good a name as any at this point. Miss Jones, I understand you were in the truck with our unfortunate friend Evan a few days ago."

Casey breathed around the gag in her mouth. *Evan? Who was Evan again?*

"The trucker," Death whispered. "Evan Tague."

Right.

"Dix," Yonkers said. "Take that thing off her face."

Dixon untied the knot on the gag, yanking out some of her hair in the process, and unwound the fabric from her face. She stretched her mouth open and shut, easing the pain.

"How was it you were in Evan's truck, Miss Jones? Had you planned to meet somewhere?" He waited, and when she didn't answer asked, "Just how deep were you into this with him?"

She swallowed, her mouth dry from breathing through it, and tried to speak. Her voice wouldn't come.

"A drink, Mifflin. Do I have to tell you everything?"

Mifflin left the room and came back with a glass of water, probably straight from the hose. He poured it on her face, some of it actually making it into her mouth. She tried again. "Hitched. Ride."

"Oh, I see. You hitched a ride. From where?"

Where had she been? She thought she shouldn't tell him. Somehow it didn't seem… "O…hio."

"Ah, yes, Ohio. Lovely state. We do lots of business with people in Ohio. And you just happened to be traipsing along in Ohio when Evan drove up with his wealth of stolen information, is that right?"

Was she supposed to answer?

"Answer him." Dixon kicked the chair, jarring her so that she could hardly catch her breath from the pain shooting through her ribs.

"Dix, give her some time. She can't think straight, since you guys got so carried away. There, has she fainted now?" Casey's eyes opened to slits, and she saw Yonkers sitting behind a desk, his hands folded on top. A large window, blinds down, framed him as he watched her. "Oh, you're awake. Good." He came around to the front of the desk, pulling an upright lawn chair a few feet from her. He sat and leaned over, his face inches from hers. "When did you and Evan join forces?"

What day of the week had it been? How long ago? "S-Sun… day."

"Ah, Sunday. Just hours before his little accident. Such a shame. A shame things worked out the way they did—for both of you. You know, we really didn't want Evan to die." He tilted his head, looking into her eyes. Was that sorrow she saw there?

She blinked as he went fuzzy around the edges.

"Miss Jones?" He patted her cheek roughly. "Miss Jones?" He sat up, sighing loudly. "Well, congratulations, guys, you've done her in so hard she's no good to us at all."

"Can we get rid of her, then?" Mifflin sounded all too eager.

Casey strained to keep her eyes open—she wasn't about to let him kill her with her eyes closed.

"No you can't get *rid* of her, you idiot. We need her. We need what she has. And unless you know where it is…"

"You know I don't."

"That's what I thought."

Casey's eyes drifted shut as she held on to the understanding that Mifflin wouldn't be killing her just that moment.

"The kids," Dixon said. "The teenagers."

Casey kept her eyes shut, but her heart beat faster.

"What about them?" Casey heard Yonkers get up and move behind his desk.

"Don't you think they know where it is?"

"The Cross kid told us to look at the shed. We did. It wasn't there."

"But—"

"He thought you were a cop, Dix, remember? He would have told you. Look, haven't we been over this?"

A phone rang, and Dixon answered. After a brief conversation his phone slapped shut. "He's here."

"Good. Let's get him in and out. No reason to keep him while we've got other…complications."

"You got it. This is Sandy Greene, though. He was pretty pissed she called him. He probably wouldn't mind getting a few punches in."

He and Mifflin both laughed, and shuffled toward the door. Casey listened as hard as she could when they'd gone. Only one person breathing.

"Yonkers," Death whispered. "He's the only one left. Can you move?"

She certainly couldn't take Yonkers out, if that's what Death was wondering. Yonkers had been right to tell his men not to worry.

"Just try to do something," Death said. "Move a finger. A toe. He's not watching."

She managed to move both. When she'd done that, she concentrated on her hand. Her left wrist seemed to be the one part of her that didn't hurt.

"Well, that's a plus," Death said. "How about an ankle?"

The left one seemed okay. In fact, from what she could tell she didn't have any broken bones except for maybe some ribs. She'd had broken ribs before, and what she was feeling was very familiar. There was no telling what kind of internal bleeding she was suffering—she vaguely remembered getting hit numerous times in her abdomen.

"Yonk?" Westing's voice jerked Casey back into the room, and she held as still as she could. "Want to see this? Sandy got some extras, and I'm not sure what you want done with them."

Yonkers growled. "How many times do I have to tell these guys? No extras—just what's on the paperwork."

"I know."

"There's a reason these people can't drive legit anymore. Too stupid."

Yonkers' footsteps followed Westing's, and the door slammed shut. Casey's impulse was to relax, but she knew this could be her only chance to get free. Or, if not free, to at least arm herself. Biting her lip, she eased into a sitting position, sliding her legs off the chair, her feet on the floor. Her vision swam.

"Steady," Death said. "I can't catch you, you know."

Casey took as deep a breath as she could and looked at the top of Yonkers' desk. Papers. A clock. Picture frames. Not much within reach. She stretched as far as she could and snagged a pencil. Not newly sharpened, but when you were thrusting lead into someone, it didn't need to be.

"Coming back!" Death hissed.

Footsteps and angry voices were heading their way.

Casey slid the pencil up her shirt and lay back on the chair just as the door opened.

"But they were just sitting there!" a man said. "A whole pallet of Wiis. Don't tell me you can't unload those."

"Of course I can," Yonkers said. "And I can come up with paperwork for them, too. But what if you would have been stopped? What if someone had found those in your load? You don't have the authorization for them."

"I hid them way in the front, no one would've checked in— Hey, who's that?"

Casey knew he was talking about her. She held down her fear. Dixon had wanted to let Greene have a crack at her. Would Yonkers allow it? She thought about the pencil hidden in her shirt and wondered how much damage she could do with it before the rest of the guys stopped her.

"That," Yonkers said, "is someone who *crossed* me."

The statement hung in the air.

"I'm sorry, sir," Greene finally said. "It won't happen again. You have my word."

"And your word is *so* good. Get out of here. And keep your hands off things that aren't on the orders."

"Yes, sir. I'm sorry, sir."

"*Go.*"

Footsteps shuffled, and left.

"Tell me why we hired him, again?" Yonkers, sounding irritated.

"Friend of Dix's," Westing said. "Got into trouble for hitting his wife and needed to go underground. Wasn't a driver, but Dix said the man could learn, and he's been doing okay."

"Until tonight. If he does it again we'll have to cut him loose."

"I'll warn him."

Westing left, and Casey allowed her eyes to open a crack. Yonkers sat behind his desk, shaking his head. All this time she'd been thinking of him as some mysterious, evil man behind a vast trucking conspiracy. Looking at him now, in his suit, surrounded by greenery, it was hard to think of him as being behind anything more evil than killing plants. It was his buddies she had to worry about. They were the loose cannons.

Yonkers closed his eyes and clenched a pen in his hand for several moments before standing suddenly and walking around the desk. Casey closed her eyes and concentrated on being limp.

Yonkers sat in the other lawn chair—Casey could hear it creak—and she felt his breath as he leaned toward her. He grabbed her face in his hand and turned it this way and that before tossing it back toward the chair. "Westing!"

Casey hoped he didn't see her jump.

"Yeah?"

"I'm going home. She'll probably wake up in a while. If she does, find out what she knows...*without* killing her. We don't need any more bodies."

"Sure thing. What if she dies anyway?"

Yonkers paused. "You were supposed to keep Dix from—I *told* you I needed her alive. Preferably able to *talk*."

"You know how Dix gets. He was always that way, even in high school."

"I know. But this time...we can't *do* this kind of thing. It's going to get out. Talk to him, will you?"

"Okay, Yonk."

"And if something happens...I don't know. Cover her with mulch and we'll figure something out."

Yonkers left, but Casey could feel Westing still with her in the room. He came close, and she concentrated on relaxing, as if she were unconscious.

He poked her with the toe of his shoe. "I don't know who you are, lady, but I'm telling you—you give us what we want, or you'll be sorry. So will those precious kids you found. Dix and Mifflin get a little crazy when they get mad. And when they want their *money*." He gave her another little shove with his foot, then left the room, closing the door solidly behind him.

Chapter Thirty-one

After Sandy Greene's truck drove away, it was quiet. Too quiet. Where had all of the men gone? Casey couldn't imagine they'd left. In fact, Yonkers had told Westing to stay. Casey yearned for some more water, but Mifflin hadn't left any extra. She worked her mouth, trying to summon up a little saliva, but there was nothing.

What had she been in the process of doing?

Escaping. Right. She looked around the room. There was no way she was leaving through the door. Even as quiet as they were, she knew the men had to be just outside, waiting for her.

It would have to be the window. She took a deep breath, biting her lips together so she wouldn't cry out, and once again eased herself into a sitting position. She looked around. Death had deserted her. She was completely alone. Gripping the side of the chair, she gradually placed her weight on her feet and pushed herself up from the chair. Her head filled with white noise and she fell forward against the desk, knocking several pens to the floor. She perched there, waiting for running footsteps. No one came.

Once her head cleared she could feel every injury her body had suffered. Her ribs ached with a vengeance, and her head felt as if it were being squashed between two rocks, but at least her joints were moving, and she was starting to get used to the taste of the blood in her mouth from where Dixon has smashed her face against the bricks. Keeping her hands on the desk for support she worked her way around it, toward the window. By the time she reached the other side, she was exhausted, and leaned heavily on the desk. The white noise was coming again.

She eased down into Yonkers' chair and let her eyes roam across the room. There was nothing much of interest. The wall was filled with photos of Yonkers with celebrities and their purchases—some of the same pictures she'd seen on the Internet. A few plants sat around in the corners, and draped over the tops of file cabinets. The desk had photos, too, and she studied them blankly. His daughter Tara's senior picture. His son's graduation. A football team. She laid her head on her arms, waiting for the dizziness to pass. When it did, she raised her head. A *football* team?

She picked up the picture and looked at it more closely. It was the same photo she'd seen on Pat Parnell's counter, in a place of honor, along with the shots of his kids. As her eyes focused on the individuals, something connected in her foggy brain. There was Yonkers, in the middle, holding the football. Surrounding him were other familiar faces: Westing, Dixon, Parnell. All of the men she'd dealt with during the past week. She laughed to herself. Evan had given her the clue long ago, when he'd referred to this group as The Team. This was no masterminded gang. No global conspiracy. This was a high school football squad gone bad. And Yonkers was the quarterback.

She looked down at the papers she'd been resting her head on. Smears of her own blood covered up what was printed there—numbers and words. What exactly did they say? She squinted, trying to make them clear. When she succeeded, she saw these were unpaid orders for plants and flowers—seemingly legitimate invoices for Exotic Blooms. No other papers were on the desk, but there were several drawers, two of them large enough for file folders. She pulled one drawer out, the effort causing sweat to pop out on her scalp. There was nothing but information about Exotic Blooms. Shipment after shipment of plants, flowers, seeds, bulbs, trees…all of which would have to pass rigorous tests before being transported from another country, or even across state lines. The Department of Agriculture wasn't about to let foreign flora bring disease which could wipe out the region's own crops or plants. So these loads would have to be Class A's legitimate shipments. The paperwork the authorities would actually see.

Casey pushed a key on the computer keyboard, and the monitor came to life. You'd think with all Yonkers had to hide he'd be a little more careful. She blinked hard, trying to stop the dizziness. Her vision cleared and she looked at the screen, clicking on all the different folders. Again, all about Exotic Blooms, but this time everything she saw pointed to one thing: Exotic Blooms was going under. All of those celebrity customers? Gone. All she could find for the past year and a half were piddley orders from locals. She found a couple invoices dealing with importing a few exotic palm trees to south Florida, but the star athletes, the TV personalities, the politicians—all had apparently decided that expensive flowers were something they could do without. Or should at least be *seen* to be doing without.

Yonkers had just about lost his shirt.

So was that what the trucking thing was all about? Had he slapped together this slate of bad drivers and aging football players to make a few extra bucks and save his business? That's not what she'd heard the night before. Owen Dixon, at least, was expecting a huge payoff sometime soon. It looked like he was going to receive a huge disappointment, instead. Casey wondered how hotheaded Dix would deal with *that*.

There was nothing on the computer about Class A trucking. No truckers, or false IDs, or fake manifests. So if the information wasn't there tying Willie Yonkers and his buddies to the death of Evan Tague, where would it be? What had Yonkers' daughter said? Tara? *He hardly ever leaves home, can you believe it? Spends all day locked away in his precious office, eating popcorn and watching porn for all I know. It's not like he ever lets me in there.*

So that's where the information would be, if it existed. And no one would ever find it if Casey died in this smelly greenhouse. No one would find her stash underneath that rock out in the grove of trees. No one would believe Evan Tague died because he trusted the wrong man. And no one would know they had to protect the little band of teenagers who had offered her shelter.

Casey had already spent too long sitting at the desk. Westing would be coming to check on her any minute. At least he had orders not to kill her—not that it would stop Dixon or Mifflin, if he left her alone with them.

Spinning the chair toward the window, Casey reached the string at the end of the blinds and pulled. When it was all the way up, she grabbed the windowsill, pulled herself up, and almost fell down when she looked out the window.

Someone else was looking in.

It was a familiar face—black and white, pale skin with dark hair. Bailey? The girl's eyes went wide, and she jerked back, falling against Johnny, who stood behind her. He set her aside and placed his hands on the window, pushing upward. It didn't budge.

He was mouthing something to Casey. She wavered where she stood and tried to read his lips. What was he saying? He was pointing at the middle of the window and gesturing with his hand. Up? Under?

And then there was another face, but it didn't belong. Older. Grayer. Concerned. He was saying something, too. The same thing. Above? Allowed?

Unlock. They wanted her to unlock something. The window. Casey found the metal clasp in the center of the pane and twisted it. Johnny was doing something outside. Taking something off. A screen. And then Davey Wainwright—how could it be that he was there with the kids?—was pushing the large window to the side, reaching in, grabbing her.

Casey groaned, and Davey froze. She listened. Was someone coming?

"Mr. Wainwright, we have to get her out." Johnny again, whispering.

Then they were lifting her out, holding her under the arms, easing their hands under her legs. There were more of them, not just Bailey and Johnny and Davey, but others, looking down at her, eyes wide, and scared.

"Come on, over here, this way. Somebody put that screen back. Close the window." Who was that? Someone else talking quietly, so quietly Casey almost couldn't hear it.

Around the old wooden trailer they carried her, lit only by the lights from the front parking lot. Faces anxious, jaws clenched as they hurried next door, through the loading dock for the big box store, toward Old Navy, to a covered pickup truck, onto the bed, under a cap, where blankets lined the floor, and people lined the sides of the truck.

The tailgate squealed as someone pulled it up, and Davey knocked gently on the truck's back window. They started to move. Casey looked up into another kid's face. What was her name? The girl held a cool cloth to Casey's swollen face.

"We've got you, Casey. We've got you now. Everything's okay."

Casey did her best to believe her.

Chapter Thirty-two

"I think she's waking up."

Casey blinked up into Bailey's face. Bailey's bloodshot eyes were ringed black with smeared mascara and eyeliner, and her hair stuck up in all directions. "Casey, it's me. Bailey. We got you out. You're okay."

Okay was a relative term. She knew she was okay in that she was alive—for the moment. The fact that she hadn't died of internal bleeding yet gave her hope that she wasn't going to. But she knew they all *weren't* okay in that Yonkers and the rest of those men would be hunting them down. If that band of dangerous dimwits could find her.

"Who got me out?" Casey managed to say.

"The five of us. Well, and a couple more people. Davey and Wendell."

The two men stood so she could she them. "But how…?"

"My phone." Terry stood at her feet. "It was Sheryl's idea. We looked at everybody you'd called, or who'd called you. We found Mr. Wainwright, and he called Mr. Harmon."

"What about…cops?"

Everyone shuffled their feet and looked around at each other. "You didn't seem real keen on cops," Davey said. "The kids called them to the pizza shop, but then the men took you away, and when it came down to finding you, we figured we'd do it ourselves without involving police. Thought you'd want it that way."

Casey gave a little laugh. She'd risked all of their lives, and here they were, risking their lives again. For *her*. "But how did you find me? I didn't tell any of you where I was going."

Davey frowned. "Wish you would've. But I called Tom. He said you'd been asking about somebody named Willie Yonkers, so we looked him up. Figured you might be with him. We checked his house first, but it was completely dark. Went to his business next. We just got lucky."

She was the one who'd gotten lucky. But the kids… "He didn't see you at his house?"

"No." Wendell. "We staked it out from down the road."

"And Terry and Sheryl went for a walk past it." Bailey smiled. "They look the most normal of any of us."

"Hey!" Martin said.

"The house was totally dark," Sheryl said. "Kinda creepy, like nobody lives there."

"His office," Casey said. "The information is there."

"What information?" Davey sounded exasperated. "You won't tell anybody *what* information!"

"About the trucks."

"The trucks. You mean *the* truck? The one Evan died in? Or *trucks* as in the ones you were asking Tom about?"

"Those. Tom's."

"Class A Trucking?"

"No. That's legit. For the flower place."

"Class A is legit?" Davey sounded surprised.

"But he uses them. The truckers. They do other jobs. Makes it look like they're from other companies. Falsifies paperwork."

"But for what?"

"Stealing loads and reselling them. He thinks he's going to make enough money to save his business. The rest of the guys think they're making money to get rich." Casey was tired of talking up at faces and tried to sit up. Martin and Bailey rushed to help, pulling her arms, and Sheryl shoved something soft behind her back. When the waves of pain passed, Casey asked, "Where are we?"

Davey grinned. "Work."

Casey looked around. Of course. The trailer at his scrap yard. "But they *know* about this place."

Bailey frowned. "Where else could we go? They've been to the shed, my parents are home…"

Casey closed her eyes and let her head fall forward. "I need… painkillers."

Sheryl rifled around in her purse and thrust two pills under Casey's face, along with a glass of water. "Tylenol with codeine. I took them when I got my wisdom teeth out."

"I told them you need a doctor." Johnny spoke from behind everyone else, and he shoved through to see her. "You don't look…well, you look bad. My dad could…it's my fault." He ducked his head.

Casey declined the pills, taking two Extra-Strength Tylenol Davey found in his first aid kit, instead. "I'll make you a deal, Johnny."

He looked up.

"You stop blaming yourself. That's the first thing."

His mouth twitched.

"The second is that if we can get Yonkers…if we know you all are safe…I'll go see your dad."

His lips tightened. "We could just take you there."

"You could *try*."

His mouth fell open slightly, and his eyebrows rose. "You mean you would fight us—"

"I'm going to get you safe, Johnny. Whatever it takes."

Bailey pushed Johnny to the side to get in-between him and Casey. "She's not going to fight us, Johnny. Don't be an idiot."

His face clouded.

"Oh, good *grief*," Bailey said. "I didn't mean it. It's just the way we talk to each other. Friends do that."

He looked at her, clearly not sure what to believe.

Martin punched his shoulder. "Come on, man. Lighten up. She called me a moron just yesterday."

Sheryl grunted. "And she called me a—"

"We need to get out of here," Casey said. "Before they show up."

"And go where?" Bailey seemed relieved to change the subject.

Casey clenched her jaw. "To get Yonkers, where else?"

"I don't know…" She heard the doubt in Bailey's voice.

"Give me a minute," Casey said. " A few minutes. Okay?"

Gradually the pain medication went into effect, morphing the shooting pains into dull aches, but Casey's head felt like it was wrapped in a huge transparent cotton ball. Her hearing was still off, and everything moved just a bit in slow motion. Bailey and Sheryl gently swabbed her face with cool cloths and alcohol—a can of beer they'd found in the back of the office fridge. The beer stung like everything, and stank, but at least it cleaned out the wounds. Casey held an ice pack over her eye and the left side of her face, and tried to stay present in the room.

Wendell didn't like any part of the plan, vague as it was. "You really shouldn't be going anywhere, least of all to confront a criminal. Look at you."

"I'd rather not. Look at myself, I mean. As for going anywhere—I'm not sending you folks out to do my dirty work."

"But why is it yours?" Martin got up from where he'd been sitting on the edge of Davey's desk. "This isn't really your problem, is it?"

"Told you so." Death was back, leaning against the doorway. "You always get into messes that aren't your problem."

"I've made it my problem," Casey said. "And dragged you all into it. I need to end it—to bring Willie Yonkers and his guys into the open. Otherwise we're all in danger. They're not criminal geniuses, but they're greedy. That's what makes them dangerous."

"Yonkers doesn't know me," Wendell said. "I'm the only one, right?"

"He doesn't know us, either," Bailey said.

"But his buddies do." Casey looked at each of the teenagers. "They've seen every one of your faces."

"So what do we do?" Terry had been quiet until now. "We can't exactly go marching into his house and steal his papers."

"Why not?" Bailey asked. "*He's* certainly not playing by the rules."

"Terry's right," Casey said. "If we take things out of his office, they might not hold up in court."

"Who cares about court?"

"I do. And you should. It's how he's going to get stopped and put away. And it's how these truckers will get taken off the road for good, where they can't hurt anyone any more."

"So," Terry said again, "what's the *plan*?"

"We have to get the cops into his house."

They all stared at her.

"*You* want to call the *cops*?" Martin said.

"No. You do."

He jerked backward. "I do?"

"Aren't you the one who's got a girl inside the police department?"

His ears went red. "She gave me those reports. I don't think I can get her to do anything else."

"*Martin*." Bailey tweaked his arm. "She is so in love with you she'll do anything."

"Ow! She's not—she doesn't work for them, you know. Her *mom* does."

"But she knows all the cops and can steal you reports and stuff without getting caught."

"She doesn't have to take anything this time," Casey said. "She just has to make a phone call. Think she'd do it?"

"A phone call?" Martin shrugged. "Probably."

Bailey rolled her eyes. "Of course she would."

"Davey," Casey said, "do you think Tom would help us a little more, too?"

"Wouldn't know why not. He was bummed you left him with no explanation."

"Well, he should soon be happy then, because he's about to understand it all."

Chapter Thirty-three

"I still don't like it," Wendell grumbled. They were driving in his truck back toward Sedgwick, and the road seemed to be made of potholes.

Casey gritted her teeth, trying to hold her torso still. They'd propped her up with pillows to ease the bouncing, but so far it hadn't helped a whole lot.

"I don't like it, either," Casey said, "but it's the only way to keep those kids away, at least for a while."

"For a few minutes there I thought we were going to have to tie them up and lock them in Davey's garage."

Casey gave a little laugh, but it hurt too much to continue. The kids and Davey were still back in Blue Lake, following up on various items, each—except for Terry—armed with a cell phone.

"*Prepare to turn right in two miles onto Peachtree Lane,*" Laura Ingalls Wilder said. She was also part of the plan.

"Almost there," Wendell said. "You sure you're up for this?"

"I have to be." The painkiller was still in effect, dulling her senses, but she had more in her pocket, ready to take if the pain got to be too much to bear.

Wendell had the radio tuned to a country station to soothe his nerves, he said, and Death played along on a lap guitar from the space behind the seat. Casey was fighting sleep now, and the music wasn't helping. She assumed Wendell would wake her if she fell asleep, but she was afraid her head would then be even fuzzier.

"*Prepare to turn right in point five miles onto Peachtree Lane,*" Laura said.

The road came up, the street sign bright in Wendell's headlights, and they turned.

"*Destination on the left in point-four miles,*" Laura said.

Wendell cut the headlights and drove slowly past several homes on over-sized lots.

"*You have reached your destination.*"

Wendell drifted to the curb and cut the engine. "Wow. Talk about money."

"Except he's losing his," Casey said. "He's got a spot on the town council, his daughter's homecoming queen, his son attends an excellent college, he's one of the region's top businessmen—he has to keep up appearances or he'll lose all respectability. Or he thinks he will." She looked at all the visible windows. "I don't see any movement or light, do you?"

"Nothing. Do you think he knows you escaped?"

"I'm betting he doesn't. The guys wouldn't want to tell him. He's still the star quarterback, and they'd be embarrassed to tell him they screwed up—*again.*" She looked at the dark yard. "Okay. He's alone here. The other guys are too obvious to be here and us not know it." She picked up Terry's phone. "Think they're still tracking this?"

"Did they see you give it back to Terry?"

"Don't know. Maybe I'll give them a call."

"Wait a minute." Wendell opened his door.

"Where are you going? Wendell, don't."

He put a finger to his lips and quietly closed the door before walking across the street to Yonkers' house and disappearing into the shadows.

Casey glanced behind her, where Death had stopped playing. "Could you go with him?"

"I can't do anything for him."

"Just keep an eye out."

"Your word is my command. Hold this." Death tossed the guitar at Casey. It landed in her lap and disintegrated, sending pins of ice through her legs.

Several minutes later, Wendell and Death were back. "Nobody out there," Wendell said, "and no movement in the house, or lights in the back half."

Death shrugged. "All clear."

Casey frowned at Wendell. "What if they had been waiting? Do you want to end up like this?" She gestured at her face. "Or what if you tripped an alarm and security shows up?"

"Somebody had to do it. Anyway, he's definitely alone, and I stayed well away from windows and anything else that could've triggered anything." He smiled at her. "Relax. Time for the show."

Casey punched the number for Exotic Blooms into Terry's phone. It rang several times before someone picked up. "Hello?"

"Westing," Casey said. "Nice to hear your voice."

"You... Where are you?"

"My phone's on. Why don't you see if you can figure it out? But just in case you can't...think about who I need to talk to, and who you definitely don't want me talking to. Be kind of embarrassing for me to show up on his doorstep unescorted, wouldn't it?"

"What? You're at—"

"See you soon, Randy."

She hung up.

Wendell grinned. "You got your stuff?"

She clutched the bag with Evan's information. "I've got it." She dialed Sheryl's and Bailey's numbers, texting *r u rdy*. Bailey texted back almost immediately. *Check*. Sheryl's text said simply, *Yes*. Casey tucked the phone in her pocket and carefully climbed out her door. Wendell met her at the front of the truck. She shook her head. "You're staying here."

He smiled some more. "No. I'm not."

Casey glared at him. She could have taken him out so he couldn't follow, but what would be the point? The whole idea was for no one else to get hurt, and it would be rather pointless if she did it herself. "Come on, then."

He held out his arm and she grabbed it, realizing she might as well take help when it was offered.

"It's just like a wedding," Death said from the other side of her. "Except instead of a bride you're a beat-up Uma Thurman." Death gasped. "Just like in the *movie*."

"Will you *stop*?"

Wendell hesitated. "Stop what?"

Casey took a deep breath. "Nothing. It's the…it's my head."

The sidewalk to the house was lined with some kind of sweet-smelling blooming bush, the flowers closed up for the night. The moon and the stars were out, and the air lay heavy and entirely still.

Yonkers' doorbell was a simple *ding-dong*, and Casey wondered if it was loud enough to wake him, should he actually be sleeping. Yonkers didn't respond, so Casey rang the doorbell again. When there were still no footsteps, Casey banged on the door.

The door cracked open and Yonkers stood there in a bath-robe, a gun held out in front of him, through the opening of the door. "Don't try anything," he said, his voice shaking. "The guys are right behind you."

Right.

Casey shoved Wendell to the side and grabbed the doorknob, yanking it closed on Yonkers' wrist. Yonkers screamed, and the gun dropped onto the front stoop. Casey pushed the door back open, hitting Yonkers' toes, and he screamed again. Casey stepped into the house, grabbed Yonkers' arm, and twisted it behind him.

Wendell picked up the gun and followed, closing the door.

"I want to see your office, Willie," Casey said. "Which way do we go?"

He groaned, holding his wrist against his stomach.

"Wendell," Casey said, holding out her bag. "Want to scout around?"

Wendell took the bag and jogged away, the gun still in his hand.

Death leaned over to look in Yonkers' face. "Pathetic little worm."

Casey agreed.

Wendell soon returned, the bag gone. "In the back on this floor. Door's open."

"Great. Nice of you to welcome us this way, Willie." Casey steered him toward the back of the house and into his office. Tara, Yonkers' daughter, had guessed popcorn and porn, but she was way off.

Yonkers' walls were filled with maps, driving schedules, truck routes, and all kinds of things Casey didn't understand. Evan had said Willie Yonkers sat behind his desk telling other people what to do. That could be the case, but it looked like deciding what to tell those people was a full-time job. Just not a lucrative enough one to accomplish what it was set up for.

"Exotic Blooms is dying," she said.

Yonkers moaned, holding his toes, which were most likely broken from being slammed by the door.

Death took a look at the toes and made a face. "Nasty."

Casey dropped Yonkers into a chair and spun around to the front of it. "Your real business is going bankrupt, isn't it, Mr. Yonkers?"

He whimpered. "I don't have to tell you—"

"I think you'd *better* tell me. And tell me fast." She leaned over and whispered, "We don't have a lot of time."

He glared up at her. "I set off the alarm. And called my guys."

"Did you?" Casey sat on the arm of a chair across from him. "I can believe you called the guys, but somehow I don't think you want law enforcement coming across all this." She gestured at the walls.

His mouth opened and closed several times, like an ugly fish in a bathrobe.

"So tell me," Casey said. "How did you get the idea for the trucking scam? The trucks at your store going in and out?"

"I said I'm not telling—"

"Come on, Yonkers." Wendell sidled up to the chair, the gun visible at his side. Casey hoped he knew what he was doing with it. "At least give us a hint."

Yonkers saw the gun and licked his lips. "An order came in wrong one day. We got a whole load of crockpots and toasters instead of plants. We laughed it off, but it stayed with me. If that sort of thing could happen by accident, then—"

"—it certainly could happen by design," Casey said. "Of course. And the drivers? How did you find this dismal crew?"

Yonkers snorted. "It wasn't hard. Nance had dropped off lots of loads at Exotic Blooms before falling behind on child support. Once I got him on board, he knew a guy, who knew another guy… Pat was on our team and needed a job after—" He shuddered. "It's like anything. One scumbag leads to another."

"And you don't count yourself among them?"

His face went red. "I am not…I am a *businessman*. I don't do…*those* things."

"Oh, I see. You leave the messy stuff for the others. That's exactly what Evan told me. That you sit behind your desk and tell everyone else what to do. That you could make things happen."

"He said that?" Yonkers blinked. "I thought he trusted me."

"Oh, he did. Why else would he have told you about the theft and illegal driving ring he'd discovered?"

"He didn't—" But Yonkers' face gave him away.

"Evan was getting too close, wasn't he? He'd found your guys, and Class A Trucking, and the thefts. It was only a matter of time until he realized you were behind it and you certainly couldn't have that. It would make you *look* bad."

"I didn't…he didn't…"

"So you killed him."

"No. I didn't."

Casey grabbed Yonkers' bathrobe and pulled him closer. "Evan's daughters no longer have a father. That's because he's *dead*. Because you *killed* him."

"But we…the guys didn't mean to. They just wanted to stop him where he couldn't get away. It was supposed to be an acci—"

"Yonk?" A voice called out from the hallway.

Casey tilted her head at Wendell and he drifted back, behind the open door.

Owen Dixon came in first, scowling when he saw Casey.

Westing was next. "Dixon, get her."

"Nope." Wendell stepped out from behind the door, gun out.

Dixon reached for his belt, turning toward Wendell, and Casey sprang off the chair, grabbing Dixon's arm and pulling it straight out behind him, in an arm lock. "You should've learned the first time, at the accident site, Dix. *Never turn your back on me.*"

He growled and tried to grab her with his other hand, but it was fruitless.

"But you…" Westing faltered. "You were a mess. There's no way you could have escaped."

"She did." Wendell grinned, but Casey could see his anxiety in the whiteness of his knuckles and the brightness of his eyes.

"What are you going to do?" Westing stood still, hands out as Wendell held the gun on him.

"I'm going to listen to the story," Casey said. "While we wait for the others."

"I love stories," Death said, clapping.

"Others?" Yonkers sounded hopeful. "Are the rest of the guys coming?"

From the expression on Westing's face, it didn't look like it.

"You know," Casey said. "Cops, ambulances. They tend to react when someone calls, saying a woman is being attacked."

"Attacked?" Westing said. "You?"

Casey shrugged. "Delayed reaction. This face didn't come from walking into a door. First, though, I think Mr. Yonkers has something he needs to tell you and Dixon."

"I do?" Yonkers' eyes widened.

Westing looked at Yonkers. "He does?"

"Sure. You know, *Yonk*, about how you created this trucking scheme to save your business. How it's not making as much profit as you'd hoped. How you're still going bankrupt, and you don't have one penny to give your *guys* for their hard work and patience."

"It's not true," Yonkers sputtered. "She's just trying to pit us against each other."

"I don't have to. Randy, you have your phone?"

"Yeah."

"The other guys still at the nursery?"

He nodded.

"Give them a call. Have them go into Yonkers' office and check the numbers on the computer. The files are easy to find."

Westing took out his phone, but hesitated.

"Randy," Yonkers pleaded. "You've got to trust me."

"I *have* trusted you." He dialed the number.

Dixon struggled again to break free, but Casey held him fast. It was almost boring, how easy it was.

"Randy, don't," Yonkers said.

"Miff," Westing said into the phone. He gave instructions on where to go and what to look for. They all waited, Dixon breathing heavily, Yonkers white as the papers Mifflin would be seeing on the desk.

Westing slowly looked over at Yonkers, his eyes hard. "I see. That's very interesting. No, I'm not sure what it means, but I'm going to find out here in a minute." He quietly closed his phone, staring at Yonkers.

"What is it?" Dixon said. "What did he say?"

Yonkers looked at the ground, not making a sound.

"Sounds like your patience might not pay off, after all, Dix."

Dixon let out a growl and tried to yank away from Casey. She held him tight.

"Ah, perfect timing." Casey cocked her head. "Here comes the cavalry."

The sirens were distant, but on their way. It sounded like more than just a couple.

Casey glanced at Death, who was blowing into Westing's ear, making him jerk around, like a bug was bothering him. What if her plan hadn't worked? What if the cops coming up the road were the wrong ones? What if the kids insisted on showing up and got hurt? What if the gun in Wendell's hand went off? What if, what if, what if… This was why she preferred doing things on her own, when she didn't have her own posse who insisted on being involved.

She glanced at the desk, where Wendell had dumped the contents of Evan's bag. "Interesting paperwork there on your desk, Mr. Yonkers. You might want to have a look at it before the cops arrive."

Yonkers jumped up from the chair and limped around his desk. All of the remaining blood drained from his face. "Where did you get these? All of this? This is…this is…" He looked up at her. "This is Evan's information."

Dixon growled again, and Westing closed his eyes, muttering something under his breath.

Yonkers shuffled through the papers, growing more and more frantic. "This is…but a lot of this…"

The sirens grew louder and stopped outside. Yonkers began shoving the papers into his top drawer.

"Police!" The front door banged open, and footsteps sounded in the front hallway. Just as they approached the door Wendell tossed the gun to Westing and crouched on the floor, hands in front of his face. Westing caught the gun automatically in his right hand.

Casey let go of Dixon and fell at his feet, arms over her head. "Stop him! Please! Stop him!"

"What?" Dixon stood over her, hands out.

Cops streamed into the room, weapons drawn, pointed at the three men who stood. "Hands up!" the lead yelled. "Now!"

Dixon's mouth dropped open, "But—"

"Now, mister!" One of the cops held a gun on Dixon, while another disarmed Westing.

"Is this the information?" The lead cop stood at the desk, his gun on Yonkers.

Yonkers looked at him, his eyes wide. "But you aren't Sedgwick police. Where's Chief Swinton? Where's…"

"Over here!" the cop said to his team. "Start documenting this paperwork."

"No!" Yonkers screamed. "She planted it! She brought it in here!"

The cop, who *just happened* to be married to Tom's friend Nadine Williams, from Deerfield Trucking, glanced at Casey. "I don't think she's in a condition to be planting anything, sir. And these things on the walls? She planted those, too? Just how long did you give her in here before your men began beating the crap out of her?"

"No!" Yonkers said. "It wasn't like that!"

"Yeah, well, you can tell us the whole story once we get to Blue Lake."

"Blue Lake? Why Blue Lake?"

Matt Williams glared at him. "Because that's where this is going to end. Right where you and your men killed Evan Tague."

Yonkers' eyes rolled back in his head, and he fell, only just getting caught by Williams and another cop. "Get him out of here," Williams said.

Dixon and Westing were already being hustled out, and a man knelt over Casey. "Ms. Jones?"

She blinked up at him. "Dr. Cross?"

He smiled grimly. "Seems you and my son have been getting to know each other."

Casey sighed, letting her eyes close.

"Let's get you taken care of, shall we?"

With the doctor's and Wendell's help, Casey stood, wincing at the pull on her ribcage.

Death *tsked*. "And here I thought you were in bad shape *last* week."

"It's good cops can't tell cleaned up wounds from fresh ones," Johnny's father said. "At least not at first glance, when they're rushing in to save the damsel in distress."

Wendell snorted. "Some damsel."

Casey would have elbowed him, had she the strength.

An ambulance sat in Yonkers' drive, and the men steered her toward it.

"The kids?" Casey asked. "Are they all right? They're safe?"

Without a word Dr. Cross opened the back door of the ambulance and he and Wendell lifted her in, although there wasn't much room, seeing as it was entirely filled with smiling teenagers.

Chapter Thirty-four

"They're squealing like little girls," Death said. "Or little boys, depending on your point of view."

"Glad to hear it." Casey sat on the edge of the hospital bed in the private room, now empty of doctors, nurses, orderlies, and teenagers. The cops had been kept at bay so long they'd finally given up and gone home, saying they would return in the morning. Only Death remained.

"Yeah, they're ratting each other out right and left. They're especially fingering Yonkers. Guess the whole image of him as the quarterback has gotten tarnished after all this time—and after the loss of the money they thought they were getting. But none of them will be able to outrun Evan's death. They're toast for that."

Casey eased off the mattress and exhaled through her teeth. The narcotics had helped a lot, but couldn't take away all the pain. At least she knew she wasn't dying from a perforated colon or some other internal damage. She'd kept up her part of the bargain with Johnny and had allowed his dad—along with the ever-thorough Dr. Shinnob—to run tests and poke her and look so deep in her eyes she thought they could probably see China. They'd returned with a diagnosis she could live with—beat up but healing.

Casey hoped Johnny would keep up his end of the bargain and forgive himself. It would help if the other kids would forgive him, first.

"The drivers are getting hauled in as we speak," Death said. "Except for Parnell, who's apparently disappeared from the face of the earth. I could find him, if you want."

Casey shook her head, then regretted it, her head spinning. "No. Let him go. He's suffered enough. Is my shirt in that little closet?"

"You mean your darling pink one?"

"Yes. The pink one. The only one I have."

"I'm not sure which is better. That shirt or your hospital gown. Why don't you wear the scrubs? The kids left them, along with your make-up."

The kids. She wished…

"You can't stay here," Death said. "You know that."

She shuffled to the closet and pulled out the scrubs. Still clean. And much more comfortable than jeans would be while she healed. She pulled on the pants, tying them loosely around her waist, and painfully pulled the top over her head, dropping the gown onto the floor.

"Wow," Death said, "you *must* be feeling like crap. You didn't ask me to avert my innocent eyes from your nakedness."

Casey stuffed her jeans and the awful pink shirt into the backpack, along with whatever she could scrounge up from the room—soap, tissues, the toothbrush they gave her.

It was the middle of the night. Way past the time she should have left. She spent too long putting on her shoes, then eased the bag over her shoulder.

Death waited at the door. "Time to hit the road?"

"Let's go."

Dr. Cross had put her at the far end of the quiet hall, right by the stairs. He knew she wouldn't be staying—that was part of her separate deal with him. She'd given him her lawyer's address, where he would send her invoice for treatment, and had guaranteed he'd be paid. He hadn't argued. Casey figured he would just be glad to see her go and leave his son in peace.

The stairs weren't exactly fun, and by the time she'd reached the ground floor she was ready to rest. She sat on the bottom step to catch her breath.

"You can go back up and crawl in bed," Death said.

"Don't tempt me."

"Oh, I have much better things to tempt you with, my dear."

"Who are you now, Clark Gable?"

Death preened.

Casey grabbed the railing and hauled herself up. "According to the train schedule, there's one that stops in the next town at two to load boxcars. We need to get a move on."

"You're serious. You think you're going to be able to get there in your condition."

"It's the only condition I've got, and I'm not about to step into another truck."

"How about another car?"

Casey jerked her head up, and almost fell. "Bailey?"

The girl stood inside the door. "I knew you were going to do this. I knew you wouldn't stick around till morning, when we could say a proper good-bye. I just wasn't expecting to find you blabbering to yourself at the bottom of a dark, empty stairway."

Casey sagged against the railing. "Bailey, I—"

"That's fine. I'm sure it's the drugs." She rolled her eyes to show just how convinced she was. "Come on." She grabbed Casey's bag and held the door open.

Bailey's car was just outside, and she helped Casey into the front seat. Casey looked around. "What? No others?" Death was the only occupant of the back seat, and held a little drawstring music box, which was playing Brahms' Lullaby.

"I'm doing this on my own."

"How come?"

Bailey eased the car from the curb and maneuvered her way out of the parking lot. "They've had enough of the fun."

"This is fun?"

Bailey kept her eyes on the road. "It has been for me. I mean, not the part where you got beat up and stuff, and definitely not when Johnny gave our hiding place away, but..." She twitched the way people do when they're trying not to cry.

Casey rested her head on the seat back. "So they didn't want to come?"

Bailey shrugged. "I didn't tell them I was coming."

Ah.

Bailey glanced over. "So where am I taking you?"

"The train station in Newton."

"They don't have one."

"Not an actual passenger one. A loading dock."

Bailey shook her head. "You're half dead and you're going to go traveling around the country like a hobo?"

"I am a hobo."

"No, you're not."

Casey didn't have the energy to argue.

After several minutes, Bailey gave a little laugh. "Did you see how Sheryl was hanging onto Terry at the hospital tonight?"

"Yeah. I don't think he had any idea what the rest of us were even talking about."

Bailey giggled. "No clue."

"You weren't hanging onto Martin."

Bailey's face glowed red in the light from the dashboard. "I'm not the sort to go hanging on boys."

"No, I wouldn't think so."

"Besides, now he feels like he owes that dumb girl from the police department for connecting them with Matt Williams."

Casey winced. "Sorry."

"He'll get over it."

"And Johnny?"

"I *don't* like Johnny."

"No, I mean will he get over it? Over everything that's happened?"

"If we decide not to kill him. Just kidding," she said quickly. "He'll be fine. Now maybe his dad will ease up on him. And I'll try to stop calling him an idiot."

"That might help."

Silence again.

"I'm going to ask my folks if we can start meeting at my house. We've got that huge rec room, and nobody ever uses it."

"Good plan. Although it will probably have to be at normal hours."

"Well, we'll see about that." She grinned.

They arrived in Newton and drove around for a while before finding the factory with the loading dock. The train had already arrived, and open cars were being filled with boxes of goods. Bailey killed her headlights and drifted into a corner of the large parking lot.

Casey had a sudden thought and searched through her bag. She pulled out Evan's family photo. "Do me a favor?"

"Another one?"

"Send this to Evan Tague's family. Tell them it was the last thing he saw. Please."

Bailey chewed on her lip, then took the photo, smoothing it out with her finger. "So, this is it? We help you take out the bad guys, and you leave us?"

Casey reached over and wrapped a hand around Bailey's wrist. "You've been a great friend. I just...I can't be that kind of friend for you right now."

Bailey turned and looked at her, her face wrinkled with distress. "But why? What are you running from?"

Casey glanced at the back seat. The music box was quiet now, and Death waited in silence.

"I don't know, Bailey. Sometimes it feels like I'm running from everything." She smiled sadly. "Someday, when I've outrun it, I'll get in touch."

"You promise?"

Casey gave the girl's wrist a squeeze. "I promise."

Bailey looked at her some more, as if deciding something. "Well, okay, then." She undid her seatbelt and got out of the car.

Casey got out, too, easing the backpack over her shoulder. "Bailey, what—"

Bailey opened the trunk and heaved out an old black duffel bag. "Here. Open it when you're on the road. Or on the train. It should hold you over for a while."

"Oh, Bailey, you've done so much."

"Stop, or you'll make me cry."

Casey grabbed her and hugged her hard. Bailey hugged her in return, and Casey's breath caught at the pain. But it was worth it.

Finally, they let go of each other and Casey stepped back. She picked up the bag, turned around, and walked toward the train.

Neither she nor Death looked back.

To receive a free catalog of Poisoned Pen Press titles, please contact us in one of the following ways:

Phone: 1-800-421-3976
Facsimile: 1-480-949-1707
Email: info@poisonedpenpress.com
Website: www.poisonedpenpress.com

Poisoned Pen Press
6962 E. First Ave. Ste. 103
Scottsdale, AZ 85251